LOOSE *Ends*

Magnolia Series: Book One

Taylor Dawn

COPYRIGHT 2016 TAYLOR DAWN

Attribution — You must attribute the work in the manner specified by the author or licensor (but not in any way that suggests that they endorse you or your use of the work).

Noncommercial — You may not use this work for commercial purposes.

No Derivative Works — You may not alter, transform, or build upon this work.

Inquiries about additional permissions
should be directed to: taylor@taylordawn-author.com

Cover Design by ZH Designs
Edited by Wendy Garfinkle

This is a work of fiction. Names, characters, places, brands, media, and incidents are either the product of the author's imagination or are used fictitiously. Any resemblance to similarly named places or to persons living or deceased is unintentional.

ISBN: 13 – 978-1523720231, 10 - 1523720239

Acknowledgements

Of course I have to thank a few people for their amazing work and help on Loose Ends.

Thank you to my editor, Wendy Garfinkle for yet again showing me that I haven't fully grasped the concept of where commas need to go.

Thank you to my cover designer, Zee Hayat, you brought my vision to life and I love it.

To Stephanie Stacker, thank you for helping me out by formatting my smutty creation.

To my dear author friend A.M. Willard. Thank you for being there for me through the exhausting task of writing yet another book. I will always be your bitch and yes, you can play with my feet anytime you want.

To another author friend, Brandy Jellum. You rock for keeping me on track and listening to be complain about life in general.

Last, but of course not least…My amazing group of loyal fans and readers! You guys are the glue that holds this all together. I love you guys so much. You are the ones I do this for and I hope you all enjoy Loose Ends as much as I did.

Peace, Love and Pages

Taylor Dawn

Loose Ends is dedicated to the dreamers of the world…

Prologue

"**I HAVE TO GET OUT** of here," Ava chanted to herself as she stuffed as many articles of clothing into her bags as she could manage. There wasn't time for her keen organizational skills that would normally be incorporated in something like this. It was do or die time. If she didn't get the hell out of her apartment in the next fifteen minutes, she wasn't sure she'd *ever* be able to leave.

Yanking shirts from their neatly hung spots in the small closet nearby, she shoved them into the duffle bag with the rest of the already crumpled clothing. Wrinkles were the *least* of her worries at this point. Darting into the bathroom Ava scooped what she could of her toiletries into the bag in her hand, trying to ignore the constant buzz of her phone in the other room. There wasn't a snowball's chance in hell she was answering that damn thing. In fact, the phone wasn't going with her on this trip. It would be just one more way *they* could track and find her.

She couldn't afford that kind of thoughtless mistake. Once she finally left, she'd be a ghost. The only people who would be able to find her would be the government—with all of their satellites and NSA bullshit—but she was going to try her best to fly under their radar, too.

After taking what she could from the bathroom Ava went back to the bags of clothing, zipped them up, and headed for the door. Instinct alone caused her to peer through the peephole to make damn sure someone wasn't waiting on the other side. Letting out a resigned sigh, she finally swung the familiar door open and looked back one last time at her cramped Chicago apartment. Being forced to leave something you loved—even if it *was* tiny—was a kick to the gut. It was someplace she'd felt safe, a place that'd been her sanctuary from the outside world. But in the course of the past few hours, it'd become the worst kind of prison. One she couldn't bear to be in for even a few seconds longer. She tossed her bags into the dimly lit hallway and pulled the door closed behind her. Bothering to lock it was a waste of time. They'd get in there no matter how many locks were in place. Might as well save the landlord some repair money.

The door clicked into place, signifying the finality of her decision. It wasn't really a choice, though—more of a preservation thing. It was this or stay here and be a victim of what was coming. And that was *not* an option.

Ava hefted the bags on her arms and ran down the steps of the apartment building. Her feet protested the jaunt but it was either wear the pink plaid pumps or leave them behind. There just wasn't room in her bags for them. Since they happened to be her favorite pair of heels, she couldn't bear the thought of leaving them behind. Soon she busted through the outer entryway of the building and was on the sidewalk, looking both ways to make sure no one was trying to follow her. By her calculations she had about four minutes to get the hell out of Dodge, so she scurried along until the familiar shade of a yellow cab came whizzing in her direction. Ava dropped a bag to free a hand and threw it in the air to flag him down. He practically screeched to a halt. She wasted no time tossing her bags into the car and climbing among the cracked greyish vinyl.

"Where to?" the driver gruffly bit out.

"The bus station, please. And if you make it snappy, there's an extra hundred in it for you." She looked out the back window with paranoia. There still wasn't anyone she recognized but that wouldn't last long. They had people everywhere. Soon her once-sacred home would be turned upside down.

"I think I can make that happen. Hang on." He laughed and slammed on the gas pedal of the car.

Ava's spine jolted into the back of the seat but she wasn't complaining. It was better than staying on the street waiting for them to find her.

When the driver buzzed in front of the bus station she hopped out quickly and threw him a wad of cash — including his extra hundred bucks. She snatched up her belongings and hurried inside to buy a ticket. Ava didn't have a destination in mind. All she knew was that she had to get out of Chicago. Away from the danger that would surely be on her ass if she didn't leave now. As she walked through the sliding glass doors, the entire place was abuzz with people. She didn't want to be seen. She wanted invisibility if at all possible. At least this was a public place. If they had people here, maybe the number of travelers around would deter them from doing something stupid and getting caught red-handed. She continued to walk to the ticket counter while ducking her head and not making eye contact with anyone nearby. As she neared the counter, she pulled her wallet from her purse and glanced at the board behind the attendant on duty. It boasted the destinations to which the busses ran, but which one should she take?

"Can I help you?" he kindly asked, clearly seeing the indecision on her face.

"I just need a ticket please." She didn't look him in the eyes.

"A ticket to where?"

Shit. "Um, I'm not quite sure." Ava began to fidget.

"Well, if you want a ticket, you have to know where you're going, Miss." He chuckled.

"Uh, where would you recommend?" She wasn't sure why the hell she'd even ask him that, but there it was.

He let out a belly laugh behind the protection of the full-body sneeze guard. "Honey, I'm not a travel agent." He leaned to the side and looked behind her which put her entire body on edge. "Now, if you'll be so kind, I need to sell tickets to people who actually *know* where they're going."

Ava turned slightly and saw a petite elderly woman behind her. "Oh." She stepped out of line and motioned for the other woman to take the vacated spot. "Go ahead, I'm so sorry."

She once again glanced around at her surroundings, trying to get a bearing on what she was actually doing. This wasn't something she'd ever dreamed she'd have to do. Her life had an order, a purpose…so she thought. Now everything came down to making a decision about what would keep her safe. What would distance her from the people who would harm her? She tilted her head back and checked the board behind the man once more as he finished up with the geriatric woman.

As her eyes raked over the list of destinations several times, one location stood out. Stepping back up to the counter after the elderly woman had gotten her ticket squared away, Ava inhaled a deep breath. The man behind the glass glared at her expectantly, drumming his chubby fingers on the counter beside the computer keyboard. Ava raised her chin with a hint of confidence—one she really wasn't feeling at the moment—and spoke, "One ticket to Biloxi, Mississippi, please."

Chapter One

Two years later

"JUST A LITTLE OFF THE TOP?" Ava glanced in the mirror at Jack Thompson. He'd been stepping into the small one-chair salon since she'd planted her new roots in Biloxi, Mississippi. Every week like clockwork, Jack would plop his alcohol-soaked ass in the styling chair so Ava could take the extra quarter of an inch of hair off his mostly bald head. Jack was one of those men who constantly ogled her chest, but she wasn't one to complain—the guy was a fantastic tipper.

"You know the drill, Ava." He smiled.

"I think you only come in here to see me, Jack. You don't really need a haircut this week," Ava joked while spreading the styling cape over his body, snapping it around his sweat soaked neck.

"You caught me." He began to laugh but was interrupted by his own coughing fit. "Don't tell anyone." He finally recovered and patted his heaving chest.

"You have my word." She made a "cross my heart" motion and reached for the electric clippers hanging from a hook on the wall. Every time she flipped the switch on the cutting tool it was like a sound of home. A comforting racket that told her this was who she was, and where she was supposed to be.

Watching the small chunks of hair fall across the cutting cape as she worked, Ava whipped the clippers across Jack's head until he was completely bald once more. "Alright, you're good to go." She brushed some talcum powder across his neck and unsnapped the cape, its familiar *whooshing* sound another comfort in her small business.

"Much better." He rubbed a hand across his scalp and grinned. "Not sure how I managed until you got here."

"What can I say, I'm a miracle worker." Ava shrugged. She jerked her head around when a snort sounded behind her. Ready with a retort to whomever was rudely interrupting her and her client, she stopped at the sight of what could only be described as "man candy" standing in the doorway.

His entire body was backlit with a glow from the beaming sun filtering through the plate glass door. Her eyes raked over his physique, her mouth drying up like a Miniature Mohave Dessert with each dose of eye-fucking she managed to shell out. *Holy shit balls. Who let the sexy beast out of his cage?* Her dry mouth dropped open while she continued to stand there gawking at the artwork of a man in the doorway. Under a dark blue sleeveless t-shirt sat broad muscled shoulders and biceps that were clearly made for hard work. *I have some hard work he could do,* she internally mused. A flat stomach led into lean hips that were tucked into an extremely dirty and worn pair of blue jeans. Scuffed-up cowboy boots were on his feet with the jean bottoms tucked into each one. *Okay, yuck. That's not cool, at all.* She decided to move her gaze back to his face. *Holy Christ on a cracker!* She didn't think they even made men like him anymore. *Whew!* His jawline held at least a days' worth of scruff but under that un-refinement was a gorgeous bone structure that was the right amount of masculine and perfection. Bits of curled-up light brown hair peeked out from underneath his filthy camouflaged ball cap and when he lifted his head just a tiny bit, she could see a set of glittering blue eyes. Every single feature on this man was nothing shy of gorgeous. The pants tucked into the boots she could deal with if it meant being able to mentally screw him for as long as he stood there.

"Are you gonna stand there and ogle the shit outta me all day, or can a man get a haircut?" He had a knowing smile on his face.

"Uh, yeah sure." Ava nervously gestured to the styling chair.

"Here ya go, young lady. I'll see ya next week." Jack cut in and laid the payment for his haircut on the counter beside the silver hair dryer.

"Thank you, Jack. Same time next week." Ava gave him a pat on the back like she did every single week.

Once Jack was through the door, the air in the salon became somewhat uncomfortable. She was all alone with the tall drink of water but somehow she was parched beyond belief.

"Where do you want me?" he asked.

She had several places she *wanted* him, but none appropriate to say out loud. "Right here." She spun the chair around in invitation.

Ava had never had an issue with nervousness when doing her job. Each client was money in her pocket and she'd been trained by the best. But for some strange reason, this guy was causing her hands to tremble. Her only savior would be her knack for conversation; *that* was one thing she knew how to do. *Talk.* "So, how do you want me to do you?" *Shit!* "I mean…do it. How do you want me to do your hair?" She felt the flame of embarrassment crawl up her face.

The chuckle that escaped his sexy lips resonated around her causing a shudder to rack her overheated body. Trying to keep busy she draped the cutting cloth over him and began to fasten it around his neck. *Oh, God, his scent.* He was putting off an aroma that was a combination of expensive cologne and fresh Mississippi soil. Thoughts of leaning down and trailing her tongue across the smooth expanse of his neck crossed her mind. *No, I can't do that.* She mentally slapped her wrist with a ruler.

"Just clean it up a bit. I've got a date tonight," he said. The thought that some other woman would get the pleasure of his company sent jealousy and disappointment coursing through her veins. What was she supposed to say to that?

"Congrats." The dumbest thing possible flew out of her nervy lips.

"Yeah, thanks. I guess." He raised his eyebrows.

"No, I didn't mean it like "oh you're so hideous that you couldn't possibly procure a date'." Ava tried to explain.

"What the hell does "procure" mean?"

"To obtain…you know, to get a date?"

"Gotcha. Well, I appreciate you thinking I'm *not* a dog."

"Thanks." She ducked her head in awkwardness. "I'm Ava by the way." She decided to introduce herself to lead the conversation away from its current territory.

"Luke. Luke Daughtry." He did the same.

"Nice to meet you, Luke." And it *was* nice to meet him. Even his name was sexy as hell. How could such perfection be wrapped up in even more perfection? Was this a dream? Was she going to wake up and find that this whole day never even happened? Wouldn't *that* be an epic disappointment?

"Let's get you looking great for your date, shall we?" Ava steadied her nerves and began her routine. She was damn good at what she did. This wasn't the time to get all tongue-tied crazy over a hot guy in her chair. It was time to put her skills to work and make Luke look good for his lucky date. Damn the bitch, whoever she was.

"I'm all yours." He looked in the mirror and gave a sweet half smile. If only his words were true and he *was* all hers.

Grabbing her spray bottle of water she began to mist the liquid over the gleaming strands of Luke's hair. She raked her fingers through the shaggy mop to distribute the water and cop a feel of his silky strands. Once he was prepped enough, she picked up her shears. "Here we go."

Normally Ava was extremely chatty when doing her job, but with Luke she couldn't find the right words to say. Everything she thought of sounded ridiculous, even to her. The silence was killing her. "I haven't seen you around. Are you new in town?" she asked as she snipped off the curled ends of his hair.

"I'm originally from here. Just moved back a few months ago."

"Oh."

"My grandma passed and left me her house and property in the will. I figured I'd come back, fix it all up and sell it for a nice profit," he added.

"Where were you before here?" She relaxed a bit as the conversation progressed.

"You sure do ask a lot of questions." He shot her a slightly annoyed look in the mirror.

"I'm sorry. I didn't mean to pry."

"You're one of those nosy hair dresser types aren't you? You like to get in everyone's business and spread gossip around town like a busybody."

Whoa, what's his problem? She took a step away from the chair and fought the urge to stab him in the neck with the two blades of German steel in her hand. No, she wasn't one of those types. If anything she was far from it. The fact that Luke thought she was something she wasn't made her see red. "Look, I don't give a damn about you. I was attempting to make polite conversation because that's what I do to keep *you* from thinking I'm a stuck-up asshole. But clearly you're the asshole here."

"Could you put those scissors down? I don't feel like getting impaled today." He smirked.

"They. Are. Shears," she corrected.

"Oh, excuse me. Could you put your pruning shears down, please?" He spun himself around in the chair and gave a look that she felt straight to her toes. "I'm not trying to be a dick," he stated. "I just hate people digging around in my personal shit."

"Fine." She stepped back toward him and his yummy man smell intensified.

"Everything okay?" He raised an eyebrow.

"Just dandy. Do you want me to finish your hair?" Ava held up the comb and shears.

"Only if you promise not to slice and dice me."

"I promise." Grabbing the back of the chair, she spun it around until it was facing the mirror once more.

"Some women are ugly when they're pissed, but not you. You're kinda cute when someone ruffles your feathers."

Was that some sort of compliment? "Thanks," she mumbled. Silenced surrounded her once again as she finished up his haircut. Being around Luke was half torture and half pleasure. She needed him out of her shop before she either tackled him to the floor and fucked him six ways to Sunday, or slammed his head in the shampoo bowl and drowned him. The first option was for sure the best one, but number two was looking mighty tempting as well.

Her fingers couldn't unsnap the buttons to the cape fast enough when she finished with him. Whipping the cloth from his body she turned to hang it on its hook on the wall.

"How much do I owe ya?" He pulled his wallet from his back pocket and began riffling through some bills.

"No charge."

"Is it free haircut day and I didn't know?" Luke's attempt at a joke did nothing to lighten Ava's mood.

"No. I just figured since I called you an asshole I wouldn't charge you. Again, I apologize."

"Sweetheart, if that's the worst thing you ever call me, we'll be just fine. Here." He held out a fifty dollar bill.

"I don't have change for that." She flashed an apologetic smile.

"Keep the change." He tossed it on the counter beside a stack of tips.

"That's a $40 tip!" Her voice cracked as the words left her mouth.

"Glad to see you have math skills." He snickered.

"I can't take that big of a tip, it wouldn't be right."

"Jesus. Okay, how about this, you keep it and maybe one night you can buy me a drink?" Luke began to bargain.

"Are you *sure*?" Ava looked at the money and back to Luke and his magnificent eyes.

"*More* than sure."

"Okay. Deal." She extended her hand for him to shake.

Luke did the same and when his calloused fingers and palm roughed over her smoother skin, it caused a ripple effect of awareness throughout her entire body. Her hand jerked out of his almost on its own accord, her palm now feeling like it'd been singed in three thousand degree flames.

"See ya round, Ava." Luke threw his ball cap on his head and issued a wink in her direction.

"Bye," she whispered as he exited the shop.

Watching him walk out the door was painful in a way. Yeah, he was rough around the edges in the personality department, but underneath he seemed like a nice enough guy. Everyone had flaws, right? Ava grabbed the broom and began sweeping up the small piles of Luke's freshly cut hair. She sighed as she looked up into the mirror stationed on the wall. "Why can't my life be normal with someone like him?" She voiced the question aloud to the empty room. "Why do I have to be on the run from criminals like this?"

Chapter Two

LUKE LEFT THE SMALL SALON and headed for his pickup truck. It was instinct to glance at his surroundings but nothing had seemed out of sorts in this town since he'd moved here. Using the story of a dead grandmother's estate was working for his cover, but he knew the real reason for him being in Biloxi would eventually come to light. And after meeting that reason today, he wasn't sure he wanted this job at all. Either way, he had a phone call to make.

He reached for the burner phone in the console of his truck and dialed the one number that was saved.

Holding it up to his ear, Luke listened as it began to ring on the other end.

"Yeah," a familiar gruff voice answered.

"Found her," Luke affirmed.

"Where the fuck is she?" The guy on the other end seemed equal parts relieved and pissed.

"What do you want with her?" Luke suddenly became curious what someone like his employer would want with a gorgeous blonde like Ava. Besides the obvious of course.

"Look, you son-of-a-bitch, I pay you to find people and do your goddamned job. Not to ask me fucking questions." It sounded like the guy took a drag off his cigarette through the line. Luke then heard him exhale the smoke and let out a slight cough. "I'll ask you again, where the fuck is she?"

There was really only one reason someone would hire him. They wanted someone dead. His best guess was that these people didn't just want Ava found like they'd originally said, they wanted her to disappear. But why? Luke made a split-second decision. "She's in Phoenix." His voice was steady as he lied.

"Don't be lying to me."

"What reason would I have to lie? You paid me half a mil to find this chick." Luke laughed.

"Fair enough."

"So, what now?" he asked, but knew the answer.

"I want you to keep tabs on her for a few weeks. Document where she goes, who she's with and when she wipes her fucking ass. Report back to me a few times a week."

"My job isn't to play detective, my job is to…"

"Your job is to do what I tell you to. So fucking do it!" The guy screamed into the phone and abruptly hung up.

Luke lifted the console and tossed the phone back inside. He sat back in the truck seat and wiped his hands over his face. If they didn't want her dead, then that meant she was of some importance to them alive. So what secret was Ava hiding that made her so damn valuable? Seemed he was going to be hanging around Biloxi for a while to find out what secrets Ava held.

"Over here!" Ava heard her friend Brandi shout as she walked through the doors of Bo's Beer Bonanza. It wasn't the trendiest of bars, but it was local and quaint. It was a survival tactic to stay away from chain restaurants and bars that had security cameras. Being seen on camera somewhere could've resulted in her past catching up with her quicker than she wanted it to. It was bound to happen eventually, but by taking simple measures like trying to *not* be captured on film, it might draw things out just a bit more.

Brandi was sitting at a pub table near the bar so Ava went over and took a seat in an empty chair. "Hey." Picking up the laminated menu she scanned the list of drinks even though she already knew what she wanted. She slid the sticky menu across the small table and let out a hefty sigh.

"You look wiped. Busy day?" Brandi patted her arm and gave a look of sympathy.

"It was steady but not swamped."

"How you stand on your feet all day and throw hair around is beyond me."

"I love doing hair. It's all I've ever known since I graduated high school."

"Yeah, but why on earth did you move from California to the south to do hair?"

Ever since Ava moved to Mississippi, Brandi was full of questions. Truth was, she didn't move from California. It was actually Chicago. But telling everyone her real story wasn't an option. She hated lying, but it was another necessary piece of her puzzle. Her life had been amazing in Chi Town. A top stylist at the Paul Mitchell Academy, a clientele that any stylist would die for and a rent-controlled apartment. What more could you ask for in life? Ava's move to Mississippi wasn't really a fall from grace though, it was an *OMG I tripped over grace and landed right in a steaming pile of shit.*

"Just wanted a change of scenery." She gave another bullshit answer to the person who'd become her best friend in Biloxi.

"You're out of your mind. I know I tell you that every time I see you, but I'm just gonna say it again." She smiled.

"And I *love* your honesty." Glancing around the semi-crowded bar, Ava tried to spot a waitress. "Where's the damn wait staff tonight? I need a drink."

Brandi began to wave her arms in the air to get someone's attention. "Here comes Jeannie."

"Hey, girls. What can I get ya?" Jennie was a buxom redhead who had the assets all the men went for. Huge knockers. She also sported a perky ass, *and* legs that were sixteen miles long. How one human being could have so many checkmarks in the positive column was beyond Ava. Some people got the short end of the stick when it came to looks and others were given the whole damn orchard.

"I'll have an apple martini and keep them coming please," Ava placed her order while trying not to think what it would be like to own a set of twins like Jeannie had.

"Do you want another beer, Brandi?" Jeannie asked.

"Sure thing, sugar." Brandi winked at Jeannie.

The sexpot waitress sauntered off and Ava gawked at Brandi. "What is *wrong* with you?"

"What? I was only being friendly."

"Sugar? Really? Why don't you ask her to sit on your lap while you're at it?" Ava shook her head. She'd bet money that Brandi was already halfway to a good buzz.

"You know I only go for the toad stools, *not* the lily pads," Brandi hooted.

"Here ya go, ladies." Jeannie was back in record time, setting the drinks on flimsy paper napkins. Was it too much to ask for paper coasters? Ava shouldn't have expected more than that, though, after all, the bathroom stalls were constructed of particle board and latched closed with coat hangers. *High class.*

Taking a sip from the edge of her martini glass, Ava cringed a bit as the alcohol slipped past her tongue and down her throat. One thing about it, Bo's sure gave you your money's worth when you ordered a drink. Two martinis and Ava could very well be on the floor singing the alphabet in a Russian accent.

"So, how's the new digs coming along?" Brandi pulled Ava from her thoughts of her drink's potency.

"Good, I guess. I have a ton of painting that needs done but other than that I think I'll like it."

"I'm jealous. I wish I would've found a steal like that on the beach." She was referring to the two-bedroom beach home Ava had found. Only, it *wasn't* a steal. "Thirty-five thousand for something in that location is crazy." One more thing Ava hadn't told the truth about. She really paid two hundred grand but no one needed to know *that* piece of information.

"I guess I got lucky." She raised her glass and took another sip of the burning drink. No one knew her, not personally anyway. They didn't know where she came from or what she was really doing in Biloxi. The truth was, she was running. Two years so far and her past hadn't come back to bite her in the ass, yet. For now she was staying. It seemed to be safe and pretty much low-key. Perfect for someone trying to flee from a dangerous former life.

"I can come help you paint if you want," Brandi offered.

"Oh, I think I can handle it."

"Well, if you change your mind, let me know."

Ava scanned the bar once more. It was habit. She wanted to know who was there, what they were up to and more importantly, how to make her exit quickly if the need arose. She did one full pass and then back again. Once the room scan was complete she looked down at her now empty drink. Sensing someone behind her, Ava's head shot up, her entire body on full alert. She was ready to run if need be.

"Evening, ladies." A man came around and sat a drink on the table in front of her.

"Luke Daughtry," Ava said and rolled her eyes.

"Thought you could use a new drink." He pointed to the low tumbler of dark amber liquid on the table.

"I thought I was supposed to buy *you* a drink?" she pointed out, looking around him. "Aren't you supposed to be on a date?"

"Got stood up." He shrugged, causing his manly shoulders to strain the fabric of his short-sleeved plaid shirt. Not the most stylish of clothing, but somehow Luke made it look sexy.

"That's a bummer." She frowned even though she was secretly glad he'd ended up not going on a date.

"Just wasn't meant to be, I guess. Mind if I hang with you ladies tonight?" He pointed to the empty stool at the table.

"Uh, sure," she agreed.

"Might as well drink that." He pushed the glass closer and the scent of it mixed with Luke was beyond intoxicating.

"What is it, anyway?" She held it up, studying the tumbler like it was a beaker filled with flesh-devouring acid.

"Whiskey." His mouth quirked up on one side as he flashed her a semi-cheeky grin.

She slid it back to him. "No, thanks. I don't do hard stuff."

"I'm sure that chick drink you've been sipping has hard shit in it."

"Yes, but it's mixed with other stuff."

"Come on, just give it a try." He shoved the glass back in her direction.

"Are you trying to get me drunk, Luke?" Why did it feel so damn good to say his name? It rolled off her tongue and sweetened the palate like a spoonful of sherbet during the dog days of summer.

"Maybe." He flashed a sly grin.

That partial smile did it for her; she grabbed the glass and tipped it back. The pungent alcohol hit every taste bud full force as it became a struggle to swallow the wretched liquid. After it went down *with* a fight, she began sputtering and coughing. "That," *Cough*. "Was," *Cough*. "Awful," *Cough*.

"It'll put hair on your chest." He laughed hysterically while Brandi only sat in shock.

"I don't think females are supposed to have a hairy chest." Ava held her hand to her chest trying to keep the fiery liquid from coming back to make an encore appearance.

"Yeah, you're right. I don't have much on mine, either. Guess I need to drink more whiskey." Luke winked.

Damn that wink of his.

Brandi finally piped up. "Let's see it." Ava looked over to see a twinkle in her eyes. Brandi was all about the guys. If there was a hot one in the room, he was most certainly on her radar. Or her Guy-Dar as Brandi liked to call it.

Clearly Luke didn't mind a challenge either. He grabbed the hem of his button-down shirt and lifted it up. "Here ya go."

Oh, holy hell. Not only was the guy packing guns that would put a shooting range to shame, he was ripped with a stomach that could be a brail treasure map to the goods below. Hell, there was even an arrow in the form of a *V* pointing directly where she knew *X* marked the spot. Ava's cheeks warmed and she turned her head away. Every woman in the place was peering toward the action at their table. This wasn't good. She didn't need this sort of attention.

"Yeah, not much hair there." Brandi giggled.

"Okay, He-man. I think you've displayed your manliness enough for one night." Ava motioned for Luke to pull his shirt back down.

He did just that, leaned closer to her and whispered in her ear, "I think you liked it though."

She turned her head to look at him and it just so happened that their faces were mere inches apart.

What would it be like to kiss someone like him? To move the rest of the way in, put my lips on his and go for it? she thought.

"You haven't the slightest idea about what I like." Ava decided to do the smart thing and pull away.

"You're probably right. But I could take you out maybe get to know you a little better," he offered.

"Luke, I'm sure you're a super nice southern guy and all, but I'm not looking for a relationship."

"I didn't say I wanted to marry you. I just want to take you out. Have a little fun."

"I think I'll leave you two alone." Brandi grabbed her drink and fled the table.

"Lovely," Ava huffed.

"Scared to be alone with me?" Luke asked in a teasing tone.

"I'm not scared of much."

"I doubt that."

Yeah, she was attracted to Luke with his southern drawl, his slightly forward behavior and his earthy/manly scent. But starting anything with a man wasn't a good idea. She needed to keep her focus on her business and staying safe for the time being. It wasn't even a guarantee that she'd be around a week from now. Ava decided it was time to put him in his place.

"Here's the deal. I don't date guys who refuse to tell me about themselves. You seem to fall in that category. So if you think pouring whiskey down my throat will get me to have a romp in the sheets with you…you're *wrong*."

"Fair enough." He stood and began to walk away.

Damn it. Hurting his feelings wasn't on the agenda. She only wanted him to back off a little. Ava threw some bills on the table to pay for her drinks and tossed her purse strap over her shoulder. She followed Luke out the door and tried to catch up as he stomped through the gravel parking lot ahead of her.

"Luke, wait." She jogged up next to him but he kept walking. "I'm sorry." Ava stopped, out of breath.

"Hey, no big deal. You made it clear you have zero interest in me. So it was nice meeting you, Ava." He walked over to a jacked-up Chevy pickup truck.

"I never said I *wasn't* interested in you!" she yelled while throwing her hands in the air.

He turned around and looked at her with a serious expression. "Do you think I'm sexy?" He did a little hip wiggle.

"Are you joking right now?"

"Do you want to kiss me?"

"Now you're just being ridiculous."

"Have a good night, Ava." He did that cutesy wink thing again and climbed inside the truck.

Oh, hell no. No one walked away from her like that. She'd show him. She ran forward and went to the passenger side of the truck. After flinging open the door she hopped in the cab with him.

"What the hell do you think you're doing in my truck?"

"This." She scooted over to him and grabbed the back of his head. Her lips crushed to his as she waited for him to relax. When he did, their mouths melded together like they'd been kissing each other their entire lives. *Wow.* Ava felt the kiss all the way to her freaking DNA. Time seemed to halt as they became tangled in the kiss together. Unfortunately it ended abruptly when Luke pulled away with a look of shock on his face.

"Jesus, woman." His breathing was uneven and he grabbed his chest.

"Goodnight, Luke." Ava gave a little wave and climbed down from the truck. She didn't look back when she began walking to the doors of the bar. That'd show him.

What in the hell just happened? Luke sat in the idling truck in the parking lot of Bo's. His body was still zinging with the feeling of his lips pressed against Ava's. Son-of-a-bitch. This wasn't good. He'd only wanted to spark her interest enough that he could keep tabs on her for the next few weeks. He'd never had the intention of doing anything beyond a fake friendship with her. Sure he flirted in the bar. But that was a way to open a line of communication with her. Now the only talking he wanted to do was with his body, on hers, for hours upon end.

"Fuck!" He smashed his palm on top of the steering wheel. Not only did he have the complication of being extremely attracted to someone he was being paid to watch— and in the end murder— he now had a raging hard-on that probably wouldn't go down with an ice bath. "Fuck me," he cursed again.

Chapter Three

MONDAY MORNING CAME and Ava dragged her sorry ass into the salon just a little before eight a.m. That was the bad thing about owning your own business and being the only one working there. You had to be there constantly to be able to make money. Not that she didn't want to work, she did. It was all she really kept from her former life. It was the only thing that kept her grounded and made her feel just a fraction safer in her chaotic life. And of course there was the money. She needed to have some sort of income. Dipping into the stash of money she'd brought with her wasn't a good idea. Eventually it would come back and kick her in the ass. No, using more of that money wasn't going to happen. She'd already used a huge chunk of it to pay for her home. She wasn't going to be stupid and blow every cent. They would want their money back eventually. At least this way she would still have some left to hand over when the time came.

"Good morning, sunshine!" Brandi breezed through the salon door as soon as Ava flipped the sign around to OPEN.

"Don't you have a job to get to?" Ava groaned. It was sickening how cheerful Brandi was in the mornings. That type of behavior shouldn't be allowed until one was filled with at least 15 cups of coffee.

"Not until noon." She plopped down on the small sofa in the waiting area.

"You suck."

"Only on days that end in Y." She smirked.

"Gross. I don't need to know about your sucking skills."

"I have great sucking *and* blowing skills, I'll have you know." Brandi giggled.

"Ignoring you," Ava called as she went to the back of the shop to finish turning on the lights.

"I've been thinking about your painting situation for the new house," Brandi called.

"And?"

"I have the name of a company that would do it. They could come in and have it done in no time. That way you wouldn't have to kill yourself trying to get it all done and be here, too."

"No, thanks. I'd honestly rather do it myself."

"Fine, be that way." She stuck out her tongue and put down the out-of-date Cosmo mag she'd been flipping through. "So, what was with the hottie Friday night?"

"Nothing." Ava shrugged nonchalantly.

"Oh, come on. I saw the way he was looking at you. He wants you…baaaad."

"He does not. Luke is just another pain in the ass redneck looking for a piece of ass."

"And the problem with that *is*?"

"I don't want to be someone's booty call, Brandi." Ava plopped down in the styling chair.

"Didn't sound like you wanted a relationship, either."

"Maybe I don't *know* what I want."

"I think you want Luke and you're too afraid to admit it." She waggled her eyebrows.

"It's so damn complicated."

"Complicated is what people say when they're being a pussy about life. Grow a pair and figure out what you want. No one's going to do it for you."

"I'm not a pussy!" She grabbed a comb and launched it across the room, nearly pelting Brandi in the head with the toothed plastic.

"Uh, yes, you are. Look at you. You're gorgeous. I would give my left tit to look like you. *And* you have a great personality. Jeez, Ava, you're the complete package."

Ava swiveled the chair around and glanced in the mirror. She didn't really look at her reflection much. Even when she was standing behind the styling chair she avoided the mirror as much as possible. Her appearance had drastically changed when she left Chicago. Her normally light brown hair was changed to a golden blonde, her soft blue eyes were masked by contacts that turned them a rich amber and her face, well, she didn't change anything about it but she had a pair of glasses she'd throw on if she felt like someone recognized her. But as far as feeling beautiful, she didn't. She felt invisible, which was the one thing she was going for. Anonymity was key when running for your life.

"I think you should give Luke a chance," Brandi added while Ava was still looking herself over in the mirror.

"I don't know." All she could think was how things might turn out if who she was running from found her here in Mississippi. Luke could get hurt. "I'll think about it." She stood and went to the back of the salon to grab a stack of clean towels for the day.

"You'd better think fast because he's on his way in here, now."

"What!" Ava shouted as the white pieces of fabric flew from her hands and landed in a heap on the floor. "Dammit!" she yelled.

"Is Ava here?" Luke's voice rang through the shop and caused Ava's skin to prickle.

"Yeah, she's in the back getting naked for you."

"Brandi!" Ava reprimanded. She scooped up the pile of towels and carried them to the front of the shop.

"Bummer, she's still got her clothes on." Luke smiled brightly.

"Don't you have someplace to be?" She pinned Brandi with a stare hoping she'd get the hint that she needed to go.

"Yup, sure do. Catch y'all on the flip side." She jumped from her seat and darted through the door.

"Sorry about her. She's an odd duck." Tucking her hair behind her ears in a nervous gesture Ava began to work on folding the towels again. To her surprise, Luke joined in. "What are you doing?"

He stopped halfway through folding and raised his eyebrows. "I'd say brain surgery, but you'd know I was lying."

"You don't have to help me," she said politely.

"I know I don't have to. I want to." He flashed a toothy smile that had her thinking back to the kiss they'd shared in his truck just a couple days ago. He must've had the same idea. His eyes dropped to her lips but quickly went lower to her chest.

"Uh, up here." Snapping her fingers she got his gaze to return to her face. "What can I do for you today?"

"Right. I'm here because I wanted to ask you out. On a date," he added.

"You came by on a Monday morning to ask me out?" She eyed him suspiciously.

"Yup." He rocked back on his heels. "And I wanted to know if you do, uh…"

"Do what?" she prodded.

"Waxing," he whispered.

"Waxing?"

"Yeah, you know where you put the hot wax on and then rip it off with a sheet of paper or whatever." He wouldn't make eye contact.

"Yeah, I do waxing."

"I need something taken care of," he said sheepishly.

Ava's eyes became wide and she sucked in a sharp breath. "Oh. I don't do *that* sort of waxing. Uh…just…uh…"

What? No! Oh, God! I don't want *that* waxed!" He jumped back and grabbed the crotch of his jeans. "Holy hell, are you crazy?"

"Me crazy? You're the one asking for hot wax poured on you," she defended.

"I was hoping you could take care of this." He stepped forward and pointed to the area between his eyes. There were a few stray hairs there, but hardly enough to qualify as a uni-brow.

"Oh. Yes, I can take care of that."

"Do men really have their junk waxed?" He looked mortified.

"Some do." She shrugged. "Come back to the shampoo bowl, I'll take care of your *issue*."

"Is this gonna hurt?" He sat in the shampoo chair and leaned his head back into the bowl.

"Hurts like hell." She began to spread the wax on his skin. He flinched at the warmth suddenly touching the delicate area between his eyes.

"I think you're gonna enjoy this *way* too much." Luke closed his eyes, waiting for her to yank the cloth strip off of his face.

"It's payback for the whiskey incident." *Yank*. And off the strip went. And with it, the six or so errant hairs that used to reside between Luke's eyebrows.

"Holy shit!" He shot straight out of the chair and began to rub in between his eyes. "Damn, that smarts."

"Quit being a baby. Man up." She shoved at his shoulder to force him to lie back down. Once he was relaxed again she began to rub lotion on the freshly waxed area.

"Ahhhh, you can do that all day." He smiled.

"Fat chance, buddy. I have better things to do than rub lotion on your face." She laughed.

"It puts the lotion on its skin," Luke did his best *Silence of the Lambs* impression.

"Don't quit your day job," she joked. "What *is* your day job anyway?" Ava stood to throw the used waxing materials in a nearby trash bin.

"I'm an independent contractor," he stood, still rubbing his face.

"Like building things?"

"I do more tearing down than building, but I'd like to get more into construction."

"There're some amazing homes here in the south. You'd probably make a killing restoring some of them," she mentioned happily.

"Let me get done with my first building project and I'll see how that goes."

Ava dropped the subject; it was none of her business what Luke did with his days. She needed to worry about herself. She finished cleaning up her mess in the shampoo area and went to the front of the salon. She took a seat in her chair to have a short break before her first client of the day showed up in thirty minutes.

"So, what're your thoughts on the *date* situation?" Luke asked while rubbing his waxed face.

"Can I get back to you on that?" She turned away, not wanting to answer him. Yes, she wanted to go on a date with him, but her inner voice was screaming at a high pitched wail 'D-A-N-G-E-R!'

"No," he shot back.

"You're not much of a southern gentleman are you?"

"Do you want me to be?" he teased.

"I want you to be…*you*."

"This *is* me. So go on a date with me." Now he sounded like he might be begging a bit.

"On one condition." She spun around in the chair.

"This doesn't sound good…"

"Just listen would you?"

"Well?"

"I don't want to go to any chain restaurants. And I don't want to go to Bo's."

"That puts a bit of a limit on things." He scratched his head.

"I'm sure you'll figure it out. You look like quite the resourceful guy." She looked him up and down wondering just how resourceful he *could* be.

Luke looked as if he were in deep thought. "Got it. I'll pick you up here Friday after you close." He rubbed his hands together.

"Where're we going?"

"It's a surprise." He gave a cat-that-ate-the-canary grin.

"At least tell me what kind of clothing I need to wear. Casual? Semi-formal?"

"Comfortable. I've got this covered."

"Okay, fine. I'll see you Friday."

"Have a good week, Ava." He went to the door and pushed it open. "Oh and by the way…I had to take care of myself when I got home Friday night. That kiss was sweeter than all the sweet tea in the south." He winked and was gone.

Ava sat in her chair, her face blooming with color.

Did he really just say that? *Holy Moses*. The image of Luke Daughtry "taking care" of himself was for some reason a welcome image in the drought that was her brain.

Chapter Four

THIS WASN'T HOW THE PLAN was supposed to go but for reasons unbeknownst to him, Luke couldn't help but flirt with Ava when he was around her. She was the kind of woman who shined brighter than any other around her. She was special. Those facts didn't take away the fact that she was also a paycheck. Money in his pocket if he did this job the way he was supposed to. Time to make another call.

"Daughtry here," he said as soon as the line cleared on the other end.

"Did you get a location on her?" the other man asked.

"Biloxi, Mississippi."

"Strange choice." The man laughed.

"What now?" Luke asked.

"Just keep an eye on things for a bit and check in periodically."

"Will do." He hung up.

If this shit got any more complicated he'd need an archeologist to dig through and sort it all out.

"I knew you'd give in eventually." Brandi giggled.

"Piss off and paint that wall like you're supposed to be doing."

"Hey! Be nice or I'll leave."

"I told you not to come over anyway. So you won't hurt my feelings," Ava bit out.

"You're not getting rid of me. I needed something to do. It was either barge in on you or take Nana to bingo. You're kind of saving me tonight."

"Glad I could be of help. Now stop dripping paint on the floor and put it on the walls."

"Aye, aye, captain."

Lucky would've been an understatement when thinking about finding a friend like Brandi. Sure she was a bit of a pain in the ass, but she was always there to lend a hand. And she'd been the friendliest to Ava when she was just a stranger in town. In the beginning Brandi was the typical nosy townsfolk. But as time went on she stopped digging. She respected the privacy Ava wanted and they didn't argue too much about it. It wasn't like she found pleasure in deceiving Brandi; she had no other choice. Anyone who knew what'd happened in Chicago would've possibly given up her location. She couldn't risk that. Opening a business in town wasn't the smartest way to stay anonymous of course, but there were ways around being publicized. The local newspaper constantly wanted to do an interview for their business section but Ava found reasons and excuses to say no. She didn't do any sort of advertising for the salon and her business license was under the alias she'd created. To the people here, she was Ava Greenwood. No one knew her real name, and it would stay that way. To her *Avalyn Woods* was long forgotten.

"You look zoned out," Brandi observed.

"My mind is going crazy lately."

"Do tell?"

"Not happening." She snickered and turned back to paint a new wall.

"Always so private. I swear one of these days I'll crack open that nut of yours."

"I don't want you anywhere near my nut."

"Speaking of nuts...*please* tell me more about Luke."

"No way! You're so damn nosy."

"Come on. Indulge me. I need a fantasy to keep me going. I've hit a dry spell that can only be the equivalent of a mouth full of saltine crackers."

"That's TMI. And Luke, well, he seems nice enough. He's kind of private like me I guess."

"What's with you people? Don't you know you're supposed to post every little detail about your lives on Facebook and tweet out shit on Twitter? Get with it."

"I like my life the way it is. Hassle-free."

"You sound like an old person."

"And you sound like someone who's going to get choked with that drop cloth if you're not careful."

"Point taken. I gotta pee anyway; where's the bathroom?"

"All the way at the end of the hall. I have to get something out of the garage while you're in there."

"Okay." Brandi nodded and went in search of the bathroom.

Looking over her shoulder to make sure Brandi wasn't trailing her, Ava slipped through the kitchen and quietly pulled open the solid door that led to the attached garage. She closed it behind her and took a deep breath. Her hands were trembling as she took a few steps forward, leaned down and threw back a corner of the massive grease-laden cloth tarp on the concrete floor. This was one of the main reasons for her interest in this house, the built-in cellar in the garage floor. Cellar wouldn't really qualify for what it was, though. It was more of a small in-ground storage space or storm shelter. Its concrete ten by six foot walls were perfect for storing smaller items and tools. And of course the things Ava stashed in there.

She bent down to turn the knob on the combination lock that kept her little hiding spot locked up tight. 10-5-13, the month, day and year she began running. That day would be seared into her mind for as long as she lived. Going quiet for a second more, Ava listened to make sure Brandi hadn't gotten curious and come searching for her. It was still silent on the other side of the wooden door. She pulled the round lock base which set it free from the thick metal prongs. After removing the lock she reached around and lifted the top of the hiding place. It was made like the hood of a car— you could prop it open with the accompanying thick, metal pole. The six steps that led into her hidey-hole were made of concrete and she took two at a time to get to her items. Nervousness always swamped her when she approached the oversized black duffle that sat on a small work bench at the back of the storage space. Not that anyone knew the secret spot was in the floor of the garage—the previous owners weren't around anymore. They'd moved to Maine, or some other New England state with cooler temperatures and loads of fresh lobster. Once more Ava listened for sounds above her; still nothing. It was always the same when she checked on the black duffle; her fingers didn't seem to belong to her as she pulled the zipper back and revealed the contents of the bag. How almost $2 million could fit inside a duffle like that was beyond her. But it did. The banded stacks of one hundred dollar bills lay haphazardly in the interior like they were waiting for someone to take them on a shopping spree. That wouldn't happen. This wasn't her money to spend. Sure she'd spent some of it to buy her home, but that was all she'd take from the money that had cost someone their life…not just hers.

As Ava began to zip up the bag her eye was caught by the shiny silver object stashed with the money. The overhead light of the garage shone down just right and made the metal come to life in an almost sparkling glint. Her hands moved of their own accord, reaching in to take hold of the object. Money shifted around and brushed her hands as she pulled it free of its confines. *Protection.* That's the only reason she had this. She didn't much care for firearms but in case her past came back to find her, she'd at least have a fighting chance. The weight of the 9mm pistol wasn't as heavy as she remembered last week. It was her ritual to check on her hiding space once a week. It'd become like a religion for her to unlock the space and make sure everything was in its place.

Pulling herself from a multitude of inner thoughts, Ava gently placed the gun back in with the money and quickly re-zipped the duffle. She jumped up the steps, pulling the metal pole from the lid of the hole and dropped it back in place. She secured the combination lock and twisted the dial to make sure no one would accidentally find their way into her stash.

"Ava?" She could hear Brandi's muffled voice on the other side of the door leading into the kitchen.

"Shit," Ava cursed under her breath. She hastily pulled the corner of the tarp back over the floor, concealing her secret. Just as she had it covered, the door to the kitchen was flung open with a curious Brandi standing there.

"Are you covering up bodies out here?" Brandi leveled her with a comical stare.

"Nope. There's a huge oil stain on the concrete. I was just making sure it was still covered up," Ava lied.

"You're so weird. This is the south. Oil stains are like works of art here."

"You're the weird one."

"So I've been told several times."

"Let's get the rest of the living room painted and then I'll buy you dinner." Ava led the way back through the house and away from the things she wanted to keep hidden.

"Just because you buy me dinner, does *not* mean I'm putting out."

"Oh come on." Ava joked, happy that Brandi wasn't asking more questions about the tarp in the garage.

"Fine. Dinner and a movie and you have free reign into the panties." She held her arms out and offered herself in a dramatic gesture.

"No, thanks. But to boost your ego…if I did bat for the other team, you'd be the first one I'd go for." She winked at her best friend, thankful she'd found someone who'd give as good as she got.

"But you're going for Luke, right?"

"I'm going on a date with him Friday," Ava admitted.

"You should totally fuck him."

"Jesus. Do you not have a filter?"

"No, I don't. Besides, if you don't ride that stallion, some other southern belle will." Brandi acted like she was holding invisible reins and began whinnying like a horse.

"Can we please not talk about riding him? It's just a date."

"You have to seize the moment. Clearly he's attracted to you and you're hot for him."

"That doesn't mean I'm going to drop my panties on the first date, Brandi. I do have morals you know."

"I don't. If that man asked me out, I'd have his man meat in my mouth before we left the damn parking lot."

"Okay, that's a visual I didn't need."

They dipped their rollers into the paint pans once more and went about the job in comfortable silence. About ten minutes into the session, the *ding* of the doorbell caused both women to jump and shriek, paint flying everywhere.

"Who the hell is that? It's nine-o-freaking-clock!" Brandi threw her roller down and headed for the door.

"Wait…" Ava froze. This was it, they'd found her. All the planning and preparation she'd done to become invisible and it only took them two fucking years to sniff out her trail. Her heart slammed against her ribcage as her breathing sped up. Tunnel vision swamped her until all she could make out was Brandi's form heading for the front door. *Oh no*. What if they hurt her friend? What if they did the whole "shoot first, ask questions later" thing? The last thing they'd want was a witness who could identify them. Ava had to think fast before she caused her only friend in this world to become hurt or worse.

"I've got it." She all but pushed Brandi out of the way to get to the door before her.

"Holy shit, spaz. You about knocked me over." Brandi stood rubbing her arm where Ava had banged into her.

"I'm sorry. It's my house after all; I'd like to answer the door. Why don't you go grab me another glass of tea from the fridge?" Ava was trying to think on her feet. She needed Brandi out of the room in case there were some unsavory characters on the other side of the front door.

"Yeah, okay. But next time try not to beat the shit out of me just to answer the door. I like a little slap and tickle every now and then, but that's only from members of the human race who let me go fishing for trouser trout." Brandi laughed and disappeared into the kitchen.

Ava put her hand on the door knob and closed her eyes. If this was it, she was prepared to go. She'd been happy the last two years. She'd been able to do what she loved and had a good life during that time. She took one last cleansing breath and pulled the door open swiftly. Might as well get this over with.

Her eyes bugged out of her head when she took in the person waiting on the other side.

"Luke, what are you doing here?" Her voice came out small and breathless.

Luke couldn't help that his eyes scanned Ava's body from her bare feet to the top of the messy bun piled high on her head. She was beyond gorgeous. She wore a black tank top that'd been splattered with white paint and a pair of ratty cutoff jean shorts that begged him to run a finger just beneath the frayed hem. Would her tanned legs feel as smooth as they looked? Would her breathing accelerate if he touched her so intimately?

"Luke?" Her voice was full of question and he snapped his gaze back to her face.

"Sorry, I was…" His sentence trailed off, leaving him a bit embarrassed that he'd been caught giving her the once over. What the fuck was wrong with him? He didn't become embarrassed over things. He was a tough guy, a *man's man*. A kick ass and take names kind of guy. Not a total pussy who melted when he saw a silky, gorgeous set of legs.

"Checking me out?" Ava gave a half smile and tucked a loose piece of hair behind her ear.

"You caught me." He looked past her and into the house. "May I come in?" Luke lifted his chin and motioned behind her.

"Oh, yeah. Where are my manners?" She stepped aside, giving him a good look at her bare feet. Pink. How did he know that Ava would be a pink nail polish kind of woman? "Brandi and I were just doing some painting," Ava explained with nervousness in her voice.

Luke stopped and turned to face her. He lifted his fingers to a lock of hair in her messy bun. "I can tell. You have some white paint in your hair." He rubbed her silky hair between the pads of his thumb and forefinger.

She whispered, "It's not white, it's called 'blissfully serene'." Her eyes connected with his, pupils dilating instantly.

Luke couldn't help but step closer. He leaned his face down to hers. "Then you have 'blissfully serene' in your hair."

"Whoa! Don't mind me!" Brandi came around the corner and broke the spell that'd woven between him and Ava. "Should I get out of here? Do you guys need some private time?" She chuckled.

Ava's cheeks filled with pink as she stepped back from Luke. "No, you can stay."

"Are you sure? Looks like the two of you were putting off some major steam there. I can get the hell out of here and let you burn this place down."

"Stay," Luke and Ava blurted out at the same time.

He couldn't be trusted if he was left alone with her. She was becoming the best kind of temptation and he wasn't sure he could ignore it for too much longer. It wasn't a matter of 'if' something would happen between them, but 'when.'

"We were just finishing up for the night. You could stay and have a glass of tea with us. Or I have a few beers in the fridge," Ava offered.

"Sure, that sounds great. I'll have a beer."

He watched Ava's backside as she stepped in front of him and disappeared into the kitchen.

"So, how're you enjoying life here in Biloxi?" Brandi asked.

"It's fine." He wasn't really into deep conversations. His life was kept private for a reason. This chick didn't need to know when he took a piss or scratched his balls.

"Here you go." Ava reappeared and handed him a longneck with the cap already gone.

He lifted the bottle to his lips and took a long pull from the frothy brew. "Thanks," he said as he lowered the brown glass bottle.

"We can go sit out on the deck, there're a couple chairs out there." Ava pointed to a set of sliding glass doors through the living room.

"Sounds good." Luke followed her.

"Ava, I'm going to take off. I've got work early in the morning." Brandi grabbed her purse and went to the front door.

The look of panic on Ava's beautiful face was almost comical. She didn't want to be left alone with him any more than he wanted a vasectomy with a rusty pair of hedge trimmers.

"Are you sure?" Ava pinned her friend with a 'please don't leave me' stare.

"Yeah, the boss wants me there early. I'll come by the salon and check on you around lunch time though." Brandi quickly made her escape and shut the door loudly behind her.

"I should probably go, too." Luke placed his beer on the lone end table in the room and turned to leave.

"You don't have to leave, Luke. Stay. Drink your beer." She sounded so sweet. But he knew better. Women like her weren't all sugar and spice. They were dangerous.

"Yeah, I guess I'll hang out for a bit." Against his better judgement Luke grabbed his bottle and followed her through the door and onto the deck.

The night view was spectacular. The moon was full and glowing in the sky, casting a luminous shadow on the lapping waves of the gulf just beyond her beach house. The sand right at the shoreline wasn't too visible except for the darkening the salty waves caused as they lapped up and soaked the sandy grains. Even he could appreciate a view like this. "Nice place," he commented and then took another drink to cool the thoughts racing through his head. They mainly included bending Ava over the wooden railing, jerking her tiny shorts down her legs, and burying his cock inside her heat. The body part in question twitched with excitement at his lascivious thoughts. *Down boy*, he thought at the appendage.

"I love it here. The sound of the waves lapping on the shore makes me feel like things might be alright for once in my life." Ava stepped forward, bracing her elbows on the railing and leaning over. The action made her tank ride up just enough that Luke could see a sliver of midriff peeking out, beckoning him to trace a finger across the smooth expanse of her skin. "It's not that I always *wanted* to live on the beach, but I think it suits me just fine." She turned toward him and he about lost it. The way the night air was lifting the loose hair around her face, the halo of light coming from the doors that were just behind her and the genuine smile on her face was enough to drive any man to lustful thoughts.

"It's good you like it." His mouth and brain weren't on the same page as the dumb-as-shit comment came out. He didn't want to do any talking right now; he wanted to do more feeling than anything. Feeling her writhe as he teased her wet center with his mouth, feeling her body start to slip toward completion as he plunged his fingers inside her center and feeling her buck wildly as he let her ride him with abandon. Yeah, that sounded better than this idle chitchat they had going on.

"I guess it is." She smiled and he felt his resolve slipping.

"I'm gonna get going, thanks for the beer." He stepped through the glass door and made a b-line for the front door.

"Hey, Luke?"

Damn, why did she have to say anything? Couldn't she just let him slip out so he could go home and relieve the massive ache residing in his pants? "Yeah?" his voice came out pained.

"Why did you come by?" Her eyes searched his.

He wanted to tell her the truth but he couldn't. "Just wanted to say hi." He shrugged while he lied.

"Oh, okay. Thanks for stopping by. I'll see you Friday for our date." She threw him a heart-stopping smile.

"If not before then. Goodnight, Ava."

"Goodnight, Luke. Sweet dreams."

He hightailed it out the door and didn't look back. When was the last time someone told him 'sweet dreams'?

How about never. Not even his piece-of-shit mother whispered saccharine words like that to him at bedtime. Hell, the good-for-nothing bitch wasn't around half the time to say anything at all. *Sweet dreams*. No, he wouldn't be having sweet dreams tonight. They would be ones filled with a thousand and one ways he could make Ava scream his name.

When he made it to his truck, Luke hopped inside and grabbed the listening device from his console. He didn't visit Ava to say 'hi.' He was there to plant a bug in her house. If he was supposed to keep an eye on her, he needed to know who she was talking to and when. He set the device on the channel that would pick up the bug he'd placed under the lone end table. He cranked up the volume to make sure everything was placed correctly. What he heard shocked the hell out of him.

"Damn you, Luke Daughtry. If you'd have just stuck around and taken care of this ache." Ava's voice came out a little scratchy through the device but Luke knew he didn't hear her wrong. She sure as hell said that. It took every bit of strength he had not to fling open the door of his truck, bang on her door and demand that she let him take care of her ache. Deciding it was best to just walk away, he started the engine and drove off. His thoughts began to race as he headed home. *I wonder if she'll slide her slim fingers between her legs tonight and call out my name when she comes?* He knew for damn sure he'd be doing that very same thing in about ten minutes when he arrived home. He couldn't wait to hear what Ava's name sounded like as he felt the sensations of orgasm creeping up his spine.

Chapter Five

**THE WEEK SEEMED TO CREEP** by as Ava did her best to control the excitement for her impending date with Luke. She didn't know what to expect, but the sparks that'd flown during their brief time together on her deck while overlooking the ocean were a pretty good indication of things to come. Did she want that? Did she need someone like him to waltz in and take her body by storm? She didn't *need* it but she sure as hell *wanted* it. It'd been way too long in the naughty department of her life. Even when she was in a relationship with her now ex, she hadn't felt the same pull as she did when Luke was in the same room.

Hell, he didn't even have to be in the same room for her breasts to become tender and her lace panties to be permeated with moisture. One thought about how virile and fit he was had her clenching her jaw trying to stave off the chills that racked her spine. It was inevitable that something explosive would happen between them; she was even looking forward to it. But it couldn't go any further than purely physical. It was for his own good. Getting emotionally attached wasn't an option. He would be the one plowed over when it all went south. And she had no doubts that it *would* go south. It was only a matter of time before she was located and had to skip town again. Luke would be left wondering what the hell had happened when it all went down. She couldn't do that to him. She wouldn't crush him and break his heart like that. She'd experienced enough broken hearts to fill up the Gulf of Mexico. Adding his to it wasn't on her short list of fun things to do with her life.

Just as Ava swept up the hair from her last client of the day, Luke strolled through the door looking more than sexy in a solid black t-shirt. His jeans were worn on the front of the thighs but not in a dingy sort of way. They looked soft to the touch and she had to stop herself from thinking about slipping to her knees, popping the button open and reaching in to see what he'd feel like in her hands.

"Need any help?" He once again caught her eye-fucking him. His smile told her as much.

"You're early." She emptied the handled dustpan into the trash can and reached around to untie her stylist apron.

"Here, let me help you. You've managed to get a knot in this thing." He grabbed the ties of the apron and began to work methodically behind her back. She could feel his warm breath moving her hair ever-so-slightly as he tried to undo the mess she'd created.

"Thank you," her voice came out in a lustful whisper.

"No problem," his was equally as breathy.

It was torture having his hands so close and not touching what she really wanted them on. Each time he'd try to maneuver the knot from its binding, he'd unintentionally brush a knuckle across the small of her back. She sucked in a sharp breath when it felt like at one point his actions were deliberate. "Sorry," he said.

"Don't be." He did it again just to hear her intake a breath once more.

He leaned closer to her ear. "Am I hurting you?"

"Not at all. It feels…nice."

"When I do this?" He began to run a finger from the middle of her spine to the indent right above the waist band of her jeans.

"Yes."

"What about this?" His hands dropped the ties to her apron and slid to her hips, the heat of his palms seeping through her clothing and causing sensations that she'd never dared to feel before.

"That, too." She tilted her head to the side and closed her eyes.

"Can I ask you something, Ava?" His voice was now rough and gravelly. Clearly he was feeling the same things that were coursing through her bone marrow.

"Uh huh." She nodded slightly and waited for his question.

"What would you do if I kissed you right now?" His lips—just centimeters from her ear—felt warm and ready.

"I don't know," she answered honestly. Being kissed never really got her engine running. It was just something that led to the good part—sex. She could take it or leave it.

"I'm willing to bet if I put my lips on yours, you'll go soft all over and your panties will be soaked." His fingers bit into her hips a fraction more.

"And what if that *doesn't* happen?" She knew better than to challenge him, but she couldn't help it. Luke wanted to play and she wanted to see how far she could push him.

"I guess we won't know unless I kiss you, now will we?"

Kissing was the ultimate intimate act. Sure, sex was pretty damn personal, but for someone to bestow a kiss on you meant they were willing to go further than anyone else. Did she want that?

Logic was tossed out the window when she heard herself say, "Then fucking kiss me."

"Fuck, yeah." Luke didn't even bother to turn her around. His hands left her hips and found their way to her neck. He grabbed her jaw with a little more force than she'd expected but it didn't matter, it felt right.

If she'd thought that kissing was only a precursor to sex, she'd been dead wrong. The moment Luke's lips touched hers, she was done for. He didn't go slow either.

There was an urgency with which he kissed her that relayed the same feelings she'd been brimming with ever since she'd met him. He'd also been one hundred percent right. Her entire body went soft and melted into his like a candle that'd been left in the scorching July sunlight. Low moans built in her throat as she pushed herself back into him, feeling how he was affected by what was going on. His erection pressed into her bottom and as if it had a mind of its own, it began to grind against him, pulling moans from his throat as well. He broke away suddenly and stepped back leaving her cold and bereft.

"I'm sorry; I didn't mean to do that." She crossed her arms over her sensitive breasts as she apologized.

"Yes, you did, Ava."

"Luke, please," She didn't know why she was begging. She needed something and he held the key to giving it to her.

He raised an inquisitive eyebrow. "Don't play with fire if you don't want to get burned, Ava."

"I'm not afraid of a little fire." She issued another challenge.

"This isn't your typical *little* fire. This one will torch you and turn you into a pile of ash," he taunted.

"Maybe I *want* to be burned."

"Maybe I *want* to burn you. But this isn't a good idea." He shook his head. An internal battle raged behind his eyes.

Ava felt deflated. He obviously didn't want her as much as he'd let on. Sure she'd given him an impressive hard-on, but most men would acquire one of those if a slight breeze blew their junk in the right direction. She stepped away, trying not to be hurt by his rejection. "If you don't want me, I understand. I'm sorry I wasted your time." The tell-tale burn of tears formed at the back of her eyes. She bit the inside of her cheek to keep them from spilling out and causing her more shame and humiliation.

Luke studied Ava's back as she turned away from him. Did she really think he didn't want her? Wasn't the fact that his dick was hard enough to cut glass show her that he was more than interested in what she was offering up on a silver platter? He wasn't done with her by a longshot.

Stalking toward her, he pushed her against the wall just a few inches away. The short gasp that left her lips was music to his ears. Grabbing both of her wrists he lifted them above her head and pinned them against the wall in one of his hands. He then pushed his obvious attraction against the lush curve of her ass. "Does that feel like I don't want you?" She didn't answer him. "Does it, Ava?" he asked in a more forceful tone.

"No, but…"

"But what? Do you think my cock gets this hard over someone I don't want?"

"I don't know," she whispered.

"Well, it doesn't, sweetheart. I'm trying to go slow here, but you're testing my ability to even think straight."

"I'm sorry," she whispered.

"Do you know what it's like to see you then have to go home and stroke my cock to the mere thought of you? Do you, Ava?"

She was silent for a few seconds and then answered, "Yes, I do."

Luke chuckled. "When I left your house the other night, did you lie in bed and touch yourself?" She nodded. "Did you slide your hands in your pretty little panties and feel how wet you were?"

"Yes," Ava hissed.

"How wet did the thought of me make you?"

"Luke…"

"Tell me. I want to know if you were so fucking wet that you couldn't help but fuck yourself with your own fingers."

"I did, damn you!"

"Did you scream my name when your pussy clenched around them?" Another nod. "You're not the only one. I went home and stroked my cock to the thought of you. When I came—and believe me, it was the hardest I've come in a *very* long time—I fucking roared your name, Ava."

"Oh, God," she moaned.

"So see? I want you, and make no mistake, I will have you eventually. But for now, we need to cool it."

"Okay," she agreed.

He released her shaking arms and backed away, his jeans fitting more snuggly than they had when he'd dressed earlier.

Ava was shell-shocked by the way Luke had reacted to her. His tight grip on her wrists should've pissed her off and made her feel weak, but it had the opposite effect. She felt safe and strong when he pressed her against the wall of her salon. Good thing there weren't any locals strolling by. They'd have gotten one hell of a show through the large plate glass windows at the front of her shop. Now she was wondering if by 'cool it' he meant they weren't headed out on a date for the evening. She'd understand if that was the case. She wouldn't be happy, but maybe he didn't want to do this whole thing after all. Possibly he thought it was too damn messy; guys typically didn't do messy. She was left in limbo trying to read his expressions.

"I'm guessing the date for tonight is off?" She finally decided to jump on the elephant in the room and give its ass a hearty slap.

"We're still going out tonight."

"I didn't know, since…the whole…the thing...happened." Ava stumbled over her words trying to find the right thing to say, instead sounding like a toddler with a speech impediment. Now the elephant was trotting around laughing hysterically at her.

"I didn't say I didn't want to take you out. I just think this whole attraction thing needs to cool off." He looked like it physically hurt him to say that. A little spark of hope bloomed inside Ava when she saw his regret.

"I agree. I don't want to complicate things too much."

"Yeah, that." He ran a hand across his jaw as if he were thinking hard. "Anyway, do you need help closing up here?"

"Um, no. I need to turn off the lights and lock the back door. We can go out the front." She walked to the back of the shop, throwing open the breaker box and began flipping the switches that controlled the interior lights. The back door was already locked up and the heavy metal bar placed across it, but she made sure to double check just in case. She didn't want any surprises while she was working. "All done. Should I leave my car here and ride with you?"

"Wouldn't be much of a date if I asked you to follow me somewhere," he snorted.

"I suppose not. Alright then, I'm ready if you are." Ava motioned to the door and followed Luke out. She stuck the thick metal key in the industrial lock and waited until she heard the grating *click*, signifying it was locked. She yanked on the handle just to be sure.

"Ready? I'm parked across the street." Luke pointed to a newer model Chevy pickup truck.

Ava nodded and let him lead the way. He didn't seem like the kind of guy who'd have the money for a $50,000 truck and this vehicle had to cost *at least* that much. It wasn't as if she was judging him, but as far as she knew most self-employed contractors didn't make a ton of cash. Maybe she was wrong, though. Luke waited by the passenger door of the extended cab as she walked to him. Like a southern gentleman, he opened the door and offered her his hand for assistance climbing in. This guy was a walking contradiction. One minute he was gruff and a bit forceful and the next he was practically laying his jacket down over a puddle so she didn't get her glass slippers muddy. Ava wasn't sure *what* to think of Luke Daughtry at this point.

Her eyes followed his muscular body as he rounded the hood of the truck and slid into his own seat. The air in the cab was filled with tension so thick, you could practically see and smell it. Speaking of smelling things, Luke was heavenly. Was it his cologne or soap that made him smell so good she wanted to lick him like her own personal lollipop? He didn't start the truck immediately which put her more on edge. Ava continued to stare out the front window so she didn't see regret when she finally decided to glance his way. It felt like hours before he spoke.

"Ava." He said her name and it snapped her attention to him.

"Huh?"

"Seatbelt." He pointed to the fact she hadn't bothered to slip on her seatbelt.

"Oh, right." She slipped it over her chest and *clicked* it into place. It took a bit of wiggling around to make it comfortable; her breasts were still sensitive from being aroused by Luke.

"Thanks." He then started the engine and pulled away from the curb.

Ava wasn't sure what sort of conversation she should start, if any. They'd kind of skipped past "how are you, how's your day been" and to "take off your clothes, let me fuck you into oblivion" in a matter of thirty minutes. The awkwardness she'd expected when walking to his truck had materialized and here she sat, hands twisting in her lap, wondering why she'd agreed to continue this date after all that'd transpired.

Luke drove his truck down the two-lane highway leading out of the city limits and to his home. Ava sat silent beside him and he suspected she felt just as uncomfortable as he did. Things had gotten out of hand quickly back in her shop and he knew he was to blame. She'd taunted and challenged him but he should've been the one to put a stop to it. He knew better. This wasn't a fucking vacation for him. It was a job. An extremely well-paying job that he needed to do and get the hell out. But it was okay to have a bit of fun while you worked, wasn't it? If Ava was on board with the idea of having a fling then it shouldn't really be against company policy. He chuckled to himself. *Company policy.* The people he worked for didn't own a multi-billion dollar cooperation. They were goddamned criminals. Who gave a rat's ass if he had some fun on the side? They didn't need to know about it. They had their own agenda in the big scheme of things anyway; he was still trying to figure out what exactly it was. But now wasn't the time to stew over those facts. He'd promised Ava a date, and he would follow through.

"You can talk, you know." Luke let out a husky laugh.

"I really don't know what to say." She shrugged and continued to stare at the road ahead of them.

"I don't either. How about we start over?" he offered.

She shifted in her seat to face him. Her small hand darted out. "I'm Ava, I run a small salon and I've lived here for two years." She gave a smile that would knock a normal man flat on his ass. Luke wasn't a normal man and he happened to be sitting down already.

He extended his free hand and took hers. "I'm Luke, and I'm a pain in the ass. Nice to meet you, Ava." He offered her a genuine smile, something he wasn't used to doing. In his line of work, it was all about giving someone the *illusion* of security. Make them feel safe and hit them when they least expected it. But with Ava, it came naturally to give her at least something real.

"I won't disagree with you, but you're the nicest pain in the ass I've ever met."

"I'll take that as a checkmark in the pro column."

"Where're we headed?" She looked around and noticed the tree-lined gravel driveway up ahead.

"My house. You mentioned something about southern homes. Thought you'd like to take a walk back through time."

Her eyes lit up with excitement. "Really? Wow, this is so great. I've always wanted to take a tour of one. I've just never had the time."

"You have the time now. I'm glad you're excited about it. Fair warning though, I'm in the process of fixing it up so it's not one hundred percent yet." That was one thing Luke hadn't lied about. His grandmother really had passed away, but it wasn't recently. Millie had been gone for six years. She'd left her estate to Luke but he'd been too damn busy to do anything with it. When he located Ava in Biloxi, it was the perfect cover for this job.

"It could be mostly in ruins and I'd be fine with it. Thank you for bringing me here," she said just as the two-story plantation home came into view. Ava sat forward to get a better look as they drove closer. "Luke, this is spectacular." She looked at him like he'd handed her the key to unlock another dimension.

"It kind of is." He was proud of the home and its history. It'd been in the family since before the Civil War. After this job was through, he wasn't sure what would become of it. His dad would stick a boot in his ass if he sold it; *that* was for certain.

"I can't wait to go inside. Does it have the original furniture still?" She was practically bouncing in her seat. Who knew a house would make Ava come alive like that?

"Most of it's in storage for now. I'd like to have some of it worked on and restored back to its original glory."

Before Luke could put the truck in park and shut the engine off, Ava was unbuckled and had her door open. She bounded out of the vehicle like a child running down the street to catch up with the ice cream truck. Something pulled in his chest as he watched her take in the visual splendor around her. He wasn't a man who felt many emotions. Shutting himself down was part of his job; he didn't become attached to things and people. They were all disposable in one way or another; that was just a way of life for him. His mother enforced that lesson at a very young age. She'd showed him that even though you had people who loved and cared about you, it was okay to walk away and act like they didn't mean jack shit. So he'd adapted that way of thinking when he'd decided to go into his current field of work.

"Can I see the inside now?" Ava pulled him from his past and back to the present.

"Sure, come on." His key ring twisted around his finger and he climbed the few steps to the front door. He looked back at a glowing Ava and felt the pull just a little bit more. It was one thing to be attracted to her in a purely sexual manner, but to have strange feelings begin to break through…he had to squash them before something bad happened.

"Wow, I love this place!" Ava exclaimed while venturing from room to room in the quintessential 19th century plantation home. With its high ceilings and arched entryways, Ava felt like she'd been transported back to a time when petticoats and ball gowns were part of daily life. But the one thing that took her breath away was the grand staircase that greeted her as soon as she walked through the front door. The bottom was wide but as the steps ascended, they narrowed. The hand-carved railings and spindles were so intricately done, she felt sorry for the craftsman who'd had to sit and whittle them out once upon a time. Above the foyer hung a brilliant crystal chandelier. "Is that original?" she asked Luke, pointing to the fixture above her head.

"It is. When my grandmother moved in it still held candles to light the entryway and the foyer. But she had it redesigned to allow for electricity."

Ava spun around and watched as the gleaming sunlight from the arched window above the door streaked through, causing the chandelier to throw off glittering rainbows all across the hardwood floor. This was like something out of a movie. Even though—like Luke had said—things weren't one hundred percent, it was still stunning in her eyes.

"Would you rather live in a place like this, or your beach house?" Luke questioned.

"I think they both have their special qualities. But I would live here, hands down." Ava laughed.

"Because of the space?" He took a seat on one of the wider steps at the bottom of the staircase, propping his elbows on his knees.

"Not at all. I love the history of it. If these walls could talk, I'm sure they could keep us entertained for days upon end." She felt herself becoming wistful at the thought.

"I'm sure they could. Come on, I'll show you my favorite part." Luke surprised her by standing and grabbing her hand, tugging her gently behind him. He took her through another arched doorway and soon they were out in the cool evening air.

"I can see why it's your favorite." Ava stepped forward and was standing on a wrap-around porch. Semi-dilapidated wooden rocking chairs lined the porch and Ava thought she'd seen one of them move slightly with the breeze.

"I like to sit out here and think." Luke met her as she leaned against the railing.

"You're so lucky to have a place like this in your family." Her voice cracked a bit and she tried to hide it by clearing her throat.

"Do you have a family home?"

"No. My parents are long gone. They died in a plane crash when I was nine. I lived with an aunt and uncle until I turned 18. I got a scholarship to attend cosmetology school and moved to Chi…California." She caught herself before she spilled the beans about where she was actually from.

"Sorry to hear that." Luke's voice was full of sympathy.

"Don't be. I don't remember much about them. Dad worked for some investment firm and my mom was always out with her girlfriends. I was basically raised by a nanny." More sadness crept in. "Anyway, that's all long gone. I don't really want to ruin the night by talking about my woes. Sorry if I depressed you on the first date." The sad thing was, none of the story about her parents was real except the part about them being deceased. She'd made up an elaborate tale about them and eventually it seemed real even to her.

In the shadowed night Ava could see Luke move closer. He pinned her to the railing with his hips and cupped her cheeks in his rough hands. "You didn't depress me." Before she knew what was happening, his lips were softly pressed against hers. This time the kiss didn't hold any sort of urgency. He was slow and deliberate with his ministrations as he tenderly explored her closed lips with his. But Ava wanted, no, needed more. She parted her lips and accepted him inside, silently begging him to deepen what he'd started. Instead, Luke backed away just a bit.

"You're seriously killing me here, Ava."

"I know we've just met and this is technically our first date. I don't do things like this. In fact my last relationship was over two years ago." She knew she was rambling.

"I can't have the kind of relationship you want." Luke ran a hand through his hair and let out a groan of frustration.

"That's the thing, I don't want one," she admitted truthfully.

"What *do* you want?" He eyed her quizzically.

"I want to see why we have this crazy chemistry. Maybe if we do this, and get it out of our systems, we won't feel like we're so out of control around each other."

"So a 'hit it and quit it' type of thing?" he asked.

"Sure, if that's what you want to call it. No strings. Just you and I putting this thing to bed, so-to-speak."

"Are you sure that's what you want?"

"One thousand percent certain." Even though Ava said it, she really wasn't sure. Every woman dreamed of a fulfilling relationship. Not just a fling that fizzled out once one person got bored with the other. But she wanted Luke, her body craved him. She needed to see why her own body betrayed her when she was near him. She wanted to feel what it was like to have all his sexual attention placed on her. He was a focused, driven man. She wanted those things lavished on her for even just one night.

"Okay," he stated firmly.

"Okay?"

"Yes, okay." He stalked toward her again and didn't take his time claiming her mouth. His lips nearly crushed hers and he slipped his tongue past the seam of her lips to meld with hers. It wasn't fair that a man possessed the ability to kiss like that. He was essentially a hitman to her libido, he had her in his sights, and when he took the shot, she was done for.

Luke's body came alive when his lips connected with Ava's. There was no doubt about his attraction to the sexy blonde who exuded innocence and mystery. She wasn't like the other women he'd been with, no, she was special. He didn't want to admit it, though. His brain kept telling him that this was the worst idea he'd ever conceived in his entire life. But that didn't stop him. Maybe he was thinking with his 'little head' instead of the big one but it felt good when his body hummed with pure arousal around her.

As the kiss deepened, Luke felt Ava's hands bunch in the fabric of his t-shirt. She pulled him closer and he felt the heat of her hand all the way to his toes. He wanted more. There was a different heat he needed now. He broke the kiss and grabbed ahold of her face in both hands.

"Are you certain you want this?" The question came out before he had a chance to think about it. He hoped she didn't change her mind. Sure, he'd live, but the blue balls would send him careening into a shitty mood. Ava nodded. "One last chance. You can back out and I'll take you home. But if you say yes, I'm going to make sure I worship every part of your body tonight."

"Stop talking. If I didn't want this, I would've been gone thirty minutes ago."

That was the green light for Luke. His hands couldn't move fast enough to roam her still-clothed body—he would take care of that soon, too. The visual he had of her naked and willing sent chills down his spine and a more urgent ache through his shaft. Each hand slid down her slim sides taking in the slight curve at her waistline, and grabbing onto her hips. Both hands dug in, showing her that for tonight, she was his. She'd know it soon enough. Trailing back up, Luke grabbed the hem of her shirt and gingerly pulled it over her head revealing a pink satin bra. Her rounded breasts pushed against the material—nipples revealing just how turned on she was at the moment.

"Fucking gorgeous," Luke said in an almost pained tone.

"Touch me," Ava breathed as she reached around her back and undid the clasp to her lingerie. She let the straps slide down her arms and then removed the garment completely.

Luke could only hold his breath and stare at the beauty before him. He'd seen breasts before but Ava's were impeccable in every way. Firm and rounded with dusty pink nipples that seemed to be reaching for him. He had to act. Lifting a hand he softly touched one — Ava sucking in a breath as he issued light touches to one and then the other.

"You don't have to be gentle." She looked him in the eyes.

Those were the words that unleashed his inner beast. Fingers that had so gently explored now took to pinching and flicking the buds causing Ava to fill the night air with her breathy moans.

"I bet you could come just from this." Luke pinched and twisted, loving how her back arched to offer him more. "Maybe if I added this." His other hand went down to stroke her mound through her jeans.

"Yes," she hissed, pushing her lower half into his hand.

Luke watched as her eyes rolled back and then closed. She was already on the brink and that made his cock stand up and take notice. He'd give her this release but then it would be time to feel her come apart on him. He tilted his head down and asked in her ear, "Are your panties soaked?" Ava again nodded her answer. "I know they are; I can feel how hot and wet you are through your jeans."

"Please…" Ava begged.

He pressed harder on her center and twisted one nipple to the sounds of her gasps. "Come for me, sweetheart. Flood those panties with wetness for me," Luke grunted.

"I'm so close." Her breathing accelerated, showing Luke *just* how close she was.

"Can't wait to have my cock inside you when you come. I bet it feels like heaven. All hot and wet. I'm going to bury myself so deep in you, you'll feel it tomorrow."

"I'm coming!" Ava shouted and he pressed more firmly on her pussy. Her cries permeated the air around them; Luke feeling his own need ratcheting up a thousand notches.

"That's it, rub yourself on my hand," Luke felt her hips move quickly as she worked herself through the orgasm. "Fuck, you're soaking my hand through your jeans." He was desperate. He needed to be inside her worse than he needed his next gulp of air. Nothing was sexier than a woman in the throes of release. He'd seen plenty of it—

but Ava outshined all of them. It was like watching pure magic unfold right before his eyes.

Her eyes snapped open and a blush crept over the apples of her cheeks when she was fully sated. Was she *embarrassed*? "I'm sorry," she whispered.

Why was she apologizing? "What in the hell are you sorry for?" Luke was confused.

"I just…I think…I don't know," she huffed.

"Sweetheart, that was the hottest thing I've ever seen." Luke was still in awe of the way she looked when she came apart for him.

"Really?" Ava was still unsure of herself.

He stepped closer—if that was even humanly possible. "I don't know what sort of man you've had in the past, but if he didn't think that was amazing, he's a fucking douche bag."

Even though it was dark outside he could tell Ava was smiling at his comment. What sort of man wouldn't think that was spectacular? He sure as shit did. But Ava still didn't look convinced. He'd show her.

"Turn around," Luke ordered. She obliged. When she was faced away, he reached around her and unsnapped the button on the denim that covered way too much for his liking. The zipper was next, rasping down causing an echo of the grating metal around them. Ava began to shiver. He stopped for a moment. "Are you cold?"

"No, your hand…it feels so good."

Luke didn't reply. He answered her by hooking his fingers in the waistband of her jeans and dragging them down her muscular legs. On the way back up to her sweet spot he caressed her smooth stems, hearing her moan her approval. "Can't wait to touch you," he sounded desperate even to himself.

"I *want* you to touch me."

So he did. He cupped her soaked flesh from behind and felt her need coating his hand. "Fuck," Luke bit out.

She was so damn ready for him. But he wanted to take this slow. Getting inside her and blowing his load in less than thirty seconds wasn't how he wanted to do this. So he decided to toy with her for his own sanity. One finger traced the wet seam of her lips as he moved it back and forth, avoiding her swollen clit. He knew if he grazed it too much, she'd go off like a spangled rocket. She was already squirming like she was on the brink.

"Hurry," she groaned like she was in pain. If she was in the same limbo he was, there was no doubt she ached. But Luke needed to taste the sweet nectar coating his fingers. He pulled them from her lips and raised the soaked one to his mouth.

Her flavor burst on his tongue, telling his cock it was time to finish this. "So fucking sweet." He sucked the remainder of her flavor off his finger and unzipped his own jeans. Ava wiggled her ass in front of him in invitation. Not yet. Reaching for his wallet, he pulled out a foil packet and ripped it open with his teeth. In less than ten seconds his cock was sheathed and ready to explore her depths. His muscles bunched as he took hold of his erection and guided it to her entrance. He hoped this wouldn't be over too quickly.

"Need you inside me, Luke," Ava pleaded.

"Just a sec, I don't want to embarrass myself," he chuckled.

Ava reached back to find his hand which was still wrapped around his erection. She pulled him forward and forced him to insert the tip of himself in her wet heat. Fuck it was already *too* good.

"More," she demanded.

That was all it took for him to lose control. "Grab the railing, and hold on."

She did as he said and when she was steady, he jutted forward, burying himself inside her. "Fuck you're tight." She didn't say a word. Only stood there bent over with his cock, balls deep. "Am I hurting you?" Sweat beaded his forehead while he waited for her reply.

"A little. But don't stop."

Luke needed to move. He wanted to feel the scraping of his shaft along her inner walls. Taking his time he languidly pulled out until only the head was submerged. "How's that feel?"

"Good, so fucking good." Ava trembled. Damn he needed it fast and rough. He shot forward and a scream left her throat. "Again!" she shouted. So he did. Each time he pulled out of her and shoved himself back in it was torture. This wasn't going to last long at all. He wanted to feel her come all over him before he reached his peak.

Reaching around, Luke found her clit and began to tease it with his fingers. Her pussy fluttered in response.

"Are you going to come for me, sweetheart? Is your tight little pussy going to milk the cum out of my cock?" He loved dirty talk. Clearly she did as well. Each time he bit out crass words, her body livened even more.

"Yes, make me come!" She met him stroke for stroke as his cock moved in and out of her. Her fingers digging into the wood of the railing in front of her told him she was feeling pretty damn good. "I feel it. Oh, God!" She groaned as he reached a new spot deep inside her.

"Come on me. Make that pussy throb on me." He worked her clit faster, feeling it swell beneath his fingers. "That's it. I can feel you. Fuck, your pussy is gonna come isn't it?"

"Yes!"

"You want me to come with you, baby?"

"Oh, God yes! Come with me!" Her voice took on a high-pitched wail as her orgasm slammed into her.

Luke felt her squeezing him, and damn it was sublime. "I'm gonna come, too!" His own orgasm began to crawl up his spine as he worked in and out of her pulsing core. When the release hit, he roared into the night air like an animal set free from its caged confines. Nothing in his life was equal to that moment. It was pure unadulterated bliss being inside her and feeling her come alive for him.

He didn't want to leave her body; he wanted to stay there forever, buried in her moist center. But he couldn't stay. That reality hit him harder than a riptide carrying you out to sea. "Gotta take care of this." He pulled free from her still-clenching core. The heat leaving him didn't make things any happier in his mind.

As he walked through the house to dispose of the condom, his head was spinning. What did he just do?

He fucked a job. What if his employers found out? Would they be elated to know while he was on the job he decided to play around a bit? Chances were they'd be livid. He thought being inside her would rid him of the tension and ache he'd developed since laying eyes on her. If he thought that now, after being with her, he was a moron. Nothing would get rid of the ache now that he'd had just a small taste of the forbidden fruit still standing out on his porch.

Chapter Six

ONCE AVA RIGHTED her clothing, she stood in the night air waiting for Luke to return. Even though the breeze was starting to cool her off, she still felt like an inferno burned in her core. The blood coursing through her veins remembered Luke's touch even though he'd been gone for well over ten minutes. Had he regretted what they'd done? Was he in there hoping she'd make herself scarce so he wasn't left with the awkward scenario of having to deal with her? Those thoughts should've taken the afterglow down a few notches, but alas, they didn't. The craziest thing to come from all of it was that she'd thought by some insane chance the attraction would lessen. Not so much. If anything, it had heightened once she connected with him on the most primal of levels.

Ava stood there hearing only the rasping chirp of crickets around her. Her hands drifted over the railing—the same railing she'd held in her firm grip when Luke had taken her someplace she'd never been before. A smile lifted both corners of her mouth as she relived those moments over and over in her mind. Her hands began to clutch the weathered wood tighter as each breath and crass word he'd said replayed like a Technicolor film. Where was the pause button for your brain when you needed it? *Luke might be inside trying to figure out how to make me leave right this second,* Ava thought. But she hoped that wasn't the case. From experience she knew men could be distant creatures after the carnal act of pleasure was consummated. They could forget you existed and begin to push you away like you weren't even a blip on their radar. *What if I wasn't good enough?* She continued to beat herself up in her own mind.

"I can almost hear you thinking from here," Luke broke through her thoughts with his low gruff voice. Ava spun around to see him leaning against the door frame, arms crossed over his bare chest. *When did he take his shirt off?*

She folded her own arms and rubbed her palms against her still heated skin. "Just thinking how beautiful it is here. So serene." She drudged up a lie to cover her insecurities.

"Liar," Luke called her out which surprised the hell out of her.

She'd learned quickly how to stretch the truth to stay hidden. How was it that he could read her so well? "Luke, I'm sorry about what happened." She wasn't sorry. In fact she was the furthest thing from sorry. If sorry was the South Pole, she would've been standing beside Santa and his tiny Elves making toys at the North Pole.

Luke stalked forward until he stood toe-to-toe with her. In the dark he placed one finger under her chin and gently lifted her gaze to his. Even in black of night only lit by the moon, she could see the shimmering blue of his eyes gazing at her like she actually mattered. "I'm *not* sorry. And if you are, I've clearly done something wrong," he stated with authority.

Ava shook her head, "You didn't do anything wrong. It's me; I don't know how to act after this."

"You don't know how to act? What does that even mean?" He let her chin drop, walking back to the doorway with tension bunching his muscled shoulders.

"I don't want to get into it. Maybe you should take me back to my car." She walked forward and tried to push past him to no avail. He was built rock solid. The complete opposite of her. Where he was tight and firm on every plane of his body, she was soft and curvy. She didn't dare try to shove him out of the way; she'd more than likely hurt herself in the process. So she stepped back once more, hoping the distance would sway him from pushing the issue.

"I don't care if you want to get into it or not, Ava. Forgive my way of putting this but I just had my cock buried deep inside your body. I think you owe me an explanation why you feel awkward about it now." Okay so he wasn't going to drop it.

"I'm not trying to be a brat here, Luke."

"You're sure as hell acting like one." He laughed, making her anger rise to the surface.

"Yeah, well, maybe I am. So what?" She didn't have much of an argument. She *was* being a brat and she knew it. But that didn't stop her from trying to explain just a bit more. "I haven't had the best experiences with men. I'm sure you don't want to hear my issues though since, as you so eloquently put it, I just had your cock inside me." Her laugh bubbled up before she could stop it. What a silly thing to say. But Luke was right.

"Maybe I *do* want to hear it."

"Then you've lost your mind." Another laugh came out. "Fine. You want to know why I'm insecure about this? Here's the reason. I was in a relationship before I moved here. We dated for three years and in the beginning things seemed great. Wonderful, in fact. But as time went on, he became a control freak. He had me followed where ever I went, he monitored my phone and online use and he did things…" She trailed off and turned away, not wanting him to see her relive the horror her ex had put her through. She'd shoved all of that to the back of her mind when she'd bought that bus ticket two years ago.

However, Luke surprised her by coming up behind her, wrapping his warm arms around her. "Tell me, please?" His voice held genuine concern.

Ava stayed silent for a few moments, willing the tears to go away. "Every time we had sex, he would roll over and light a cigarette. And with that cigarette, he would burn me," she admitted.

Feeling Luke tense up behind her and squeeze her just a fraction tighter, Ava tried to break free of his hold.

"Don't," he held her. "Don't try to run away, Ava."

"I shouldn't have said anything," She shook her head while tears streamed down her face.

It felt like Luke held his breath while he contemplated what she was telling him. "How long did this go on?"

"Only the last two months we were together. I always made excuses why I couldn't sleep with him. I tried to keep it from happening."

"How many times did he do it?" It sounded like Luke was interrogating her.

"Eight times. I made sure we weren't together more than once a week."

Luke spun her around. "Thank you." He looked into her eyes. "Thank you for telling me." She nodded. "Are you working tomorrow?" he asked, throwing her for a loop.

"No. I closed the shop this weekend because of the Founders' Day Parade, why?" She cocked her head to the side in curiosity—feeling like an inquisitive puppy as she did so.

"I'm not taking you back to your car tonight," Luke stated matter-of-factly. "You're staying the night with me." He intertwined his fingers in hers. "I'm taking you upstairs. I want to touch every inch of you while you're laid out on my bed."

Ava sucked in a breath, her faded arousal sparking to life abruptly. Every response and argument died on her tongue as Luke all but pulled her through the house. When they reached the grand staircase he shocked her once more by sweeping her into his arms. Her head immediately rested on his shoulder as she let out a sigh of contentment. Feeling safe wasn't something normally assimilated into her daily life. She always had an eye on everything and one foot out the door. It was pure survival—an instinct she'd developed over the past two years. But right now, feeling Luke's arms under her, feeling his heart beating a thick staccato in his chest; she felt safer then she had in a very long time.

Luke held her secure as he carried her up the staircase and down the hall to the left. It was dimly lit but she could see urgency shading his handsome face; coincidently, she felt the same way. His bare feet patted the hardwood floor and soon they were in front of a door. Luke toed it open to reveal a room that stunned her. *This is his bedroom?* Ava thought. Luke softly put her on her feet as she looked around.

"This room is amazing." She spun around, taking in the splendor before her. Against one wall rested a massive antique bed, its intricately carved four posts reaching high, almost touching the even higher ceiling. The furniture was all original, dating back to the same era as the home itself.

"Doesn't look like much of a guy's room does it?" Luke looked unsure of himself for the first time since they'd met.

"No. But I love it." Ava smiled. It was cute how he was leaning against the wall looking like he was waiting for her approval. Maybe it was time she surprised *him* for a change. She slid off her shoes and walked barefoot to where he was standing. His gaze raked over her body, making her feel the weight of his stare.

He raised an eyebrow. "What are you doing?"

"Just coming over here to see you."

"What if I don't want you right here? What if I want you over there," he pointed to the bed, "in my bed?"

Ava felt sure and playful. "What will you do to me over there?"

"What do you want me to do?"

Ava didn't feel like she was winning this little game of cat and mouse. Seduction wasn't her strong suit. But she did have an answer for him. "Everything," she whispered as she made eye contact in the barely-lit room.

Luke's only response was to grab her face and begin to explore her mouth with his. Again Ava felt each stroke of his tongue to the depths of her soul. He swept in and out, causing a fucking motion with his tongue as he walked her backwards to the bed. He broke the kiss before the back of her knees hit the mattress.

Luke began to lift the bottom of her shirt. "I need to see every inch of you." He pulled the fabric over her head and tossed it to the floor. Once her upper body was on display, Ava became self-conscious about the burn scars littering her otherwise pristine skin. She reached down to cover them with her palms but Luke stopped her midway. "Don't." He warned.

"I don't want you to see them. Can we turn the lights off?" Damn she hated how insecure she sounded.

"The lights are staying on. I want to see *everything*. The good and the bad." His voice softened on the last word.

"Okay," she whispered.

Dropping her arms she waited while Luke raked his gaze over the ugly marks marring her skin. She was ready for him to become revolted at them but he didn't. Instead his fingers moved between the cluster of raised skin as if he were mapping out the pattern. "Do they hurt?" his eyes connected with hers.

Ava shook her head. "No. Not anymore." She smiled just a little bit.

"Good to know." He then dropped to his knees and began lightly pressing his lips to the affected area. Ava's eyes rolled back as he whispered kisses down on the area that made her feel less of a human being. She'd let the scars consume her for far too long. Not anymore.

When he was finished with his treatment, he stood to give her a soft kiss on her lips. "Now these." He quickly unfastened her jeans and pushed them down her legs, letting her step out of the rough denim. "You're every man's wet dream," he complimented as she stood there in nothing but her bra and panties.

"I need to see you, too." Ava pressed her palms against the firm skin of his chest and worked her way down to the button on his pants. She flicked it open and rasped the zipper down. Luke shuddered as she shimmied the jeans down his legs along with his boxer briefs. He stepped out of them and left her with a prime view of his assets. "You're a work of art," she mused.

"Touch me, Ava."

"Where?"

He grabbed her hand and wrapped it around his shaft. "Here." He laid his rough palm on top of hers and began to stroke himself with her help. "Feel that? That's what you do to me." Ava licked her lips in response. "I want you to taste me." He wasn't ordering her, he was almost begging, hoping she'd say yes.

"Lie down for me." She stepped out of the way to let him past her. She watched as he laid down on his back, his cock lying on his stomach waiting for her to do as she pleased. Crawling on the bed with him she straddled his legs and bent forward.

"You have no idea how sexy you look right now." He fisted the duvet as she once again took him in her hand.

"I could say the same about you," Ava didn't want to waste time. She kept her eyes locked with his as her tongue darted out and teased his slit.

"Goddamn. More," he grunted.

"Like this?" She felt daring. She became brazen as she opened her lips and took him inside her mouth.

"Yeah, just like that." His hips began to lift off the bed as she sucked and licked him closer to completion. "Your mouth is heaven." He spurred her to continue. "Do you want me to come?" he asked, the question coming out pained. Ava nodded while her lips were fastened around him. "Want me to come inside that sweet little mouth of yours, Ava?" Another nod. She wasn't stopping. She wanted to him to explode. She needed to feel what she'd done to him. "No." He reached forward and pulled himself free of her. She wasn't sure what was happening but soon found he'd turned the tables and she was on her back with him looming over her. "The only place I'm coming is inside you." Luke reached across the bed and grabbed a condom from the bedside table. Ava's eyes were focused on his cock as he rolled the latex over himself. He stroked himself a couple times before pushing her legs apart with one of his knees. He didn't tease her this time instead he thrust forward in one stroke causing her to scream out. "Yeah? You like screaming for me don't you?" He pulled out and shoved back in. "Scream again for me, sweetheart." He deepened his strokes.

"Luke!" Her voice wasn't her own as she screamed each time he pounded into her.

"Again! Scream my name!" he shouted.

"Luke! Oh fuck!" Her hands were now fisted in the sheets.

"Is this how you like to be fucked? Do you like me pushing my cock deep inside you, like this?" He plunged again and her entire body tightened up. "That's it. Arch that back for me." Her legs fell open a bit more. "Fuck. Are you trying to get me deeper?"

"Yes, please," she moaned.

"Spread them as far as you can. Take me in deep." She used her thigh muscles to move her legs apart as far as they would go, feeling Luke sink further inside her.

Ava's eyes closed as she reveled in the sensations that filled her. The connection they shared seemed as if it were even deeper than only a physical one. But that was crazy. She hadn't known him that long. There was no way she could be feeling anything for him. This was lust. Pure, carnal lust.

Luke must've sensed her pulling away. He slowed and leaned forward, his face only inches from hers—his warm breath fanning her face. "Look at me, Ava." She kept her eyes tightly sealed and shook her head. "Dammit, Ava. Look. At. Me." He thrust into her harder to get her undivided attention.

Her eyes flew open and connected with his. Something about that moment spurred her into the beginning pulsations of release. "Mmmmmm." She bit her lip to keep from crying out.

Luke reached down with his thumb and tugged her lip free. "Don't hold back on me. I want to hear every moan and scream from those delicious lips." Ava arched her back again as the orgasm subsided, she wanted more. "Oh no, you don't. I want another one. Give me one more, sweetheart."

"I can't," Ava whined.

"You can. And you will." He reached between them and began to massage her clit.

Sparks of a new wave washed over her, the feeling starting at the tip of her toes and working its way north. It had always amazed her how an orgasm could make you feel so out of control but so alive at the same time. Every nerve was focused on reaching that peak. Every ounce of energy was place on her body gripping that feeling. When her second one crashed into her, she felt Luke's thrusts become uneven. He was close. She knew it by the change in his breathing and the way his cock seemed to grow within her.

"Luke, come for me," she pleaded just like he had. She wanted to own his release as much as he wanted to own hers.

"Right now?" He pushed further in. "You want me to come for you right now, Ava?" His voice took on a hoarse quality, like he was trying to hold back and failing miserably.

"Yes. Come now," Ava demanded. She wasn't a taker; she gave more than she got in return, but for some reason, being in this bed with him in between her legs, she wanted everything he had.

His answer came in the form of an animalistic growl that echoed around them in the antiquated bedroom. The low tones bled from his throat, bouncing off the plaster covered walls, and landing in her head. She'd never forget the way he sounded in that moment. She'd never forget how it felt to make Luke lose control. In a way, she wanted to erase it because nothing could ever compare to this. She was ruined.

Luke was always an early riser. It didn't matter how tired he was, he'd get up before the sun peeked over the horizon and start his day. Hell, some nights he didn't sleep a wink due to his job. There wasn't a set schedule; he did what was needed to pay the bills. After this job was done with his current employer, he'd be able to sit comfortably for the foreseeable future. But there were still questions plaguing him. Ones that needed to be answered now that he'd gotten to know Ava on a much more *personal* level. He'd tried not to let being with her become a roadblock between him and this massive payday, but now, he wasn't so sure he could. And didn't he feel like the biggest pansy ass for thinking like that.

Leaving her in his bed all alone made him twitchy inside. She looked so peaceful lying there curled on her side, blonde hair spilling over the pillow like a halo of spun gold. When he'd glanced back one more time before leaving the bedroom, he had to blink to assure himself that this wasn't a dream. That the breathtaking scene before him was in fact an honest-to-God reality.

Last night was one of the best of his life by far. The crazy thing though? It wasn't about the sex. It was more than that. He didn't want to put a label on it now, or even ever if he had his way, but being around Ava was like breathing in the most glorious breath of fresh air. On the outside she was strong and resilient; a woman who could go toe-to-toe with anyone. But inside was a vulnerability that made her human. He'd learned a long time ago to shut down his emotions and do his job, but for some reason Ava was making him throw everything out the window. Luke wasn't going to think about that right now though; he'd take this one day at a time and in the end, he would wash the blood off his hands and walk away like he always did.

"Good morning," he heard a small voice—Ava's voice—behind him.

Luke turned around to see her standing in the kitchen doorway. Her lightly tanned legs were smooth and bare, only partly concealed by the t-shirt she wore. His t-shirt. Blood flew to his groin as he lifted his gaze to see her hair quite the mess and her face free of makeup. Had she been wearing it last night? He couldn't remember. "Morning. Did you sleep okay?" He didn't do the whole morning after thing so this conversation was beyond his realm of understanding.

"I did until you got out of bed. Where did you go so early?" She entered the kitchen and took a seat across the table from him. He immediately stood to grab her a cup of coffee.

"I took a morning run; had to clear my head a bit," he answered as he filled the ceramic cup with dark brown liquid. Truth was, he'd gotten a phone call and didn't want to her to overhear it if she'd woken up.

"You still on her?" the nameless man asked.

"Yep, what now?" Luke was all business with his employers. Most of them were assholes who didn't give a damn if you had an opinion about things anyway. There was no use arguing or trying to change their mind about something.

"Plans have changed. Stay on her for a few more weeks."

"Listen, I've got more shit to do than babysit for you," Luke bit out.

The other man grunted into the phone. "You want me to find somebody else to do this shit? I have ten other guys on speed dial who would do this shit for half your price."

That wasn't what he wanted at all. In fact, if they found out he'd lied about her being in Phoenix, they'd both find themselves at the bottom of a lake. "Fuck no, I've got this."

"Good. I thought you'd see it my way." The guy hung up.

What was it with these types and them hanging up? Must've made them feel tougher to do shit like that. But honestly, not much intimidated Luke.

"Earth to Luke," Ava cut through his mental replay of the morning's phone conversation.

He spun around with her cup of coffee in his hand. Setting it on the table in front of her, he leaned down and gently kissed her forehead when she looked up. "Sorry. I was thinking about some projects I need to start this weekend."

"Oh. Do you need any help? Since I closed the shop until Monday, I could stick around and lend a hand." She lifted the steaming cup to her lips and made a sipping sound as the hot brew hit her mouth.

Luke took a drink from his own mug, laughing internally at himself. This shit was way too domestic for his liking. Ava sitting across from him, drinking from a matching coffee cup; when had he sold out to normalcy? "You don't have to help," he chuckled.

"You didn't have to help me fold towels that day in the shop either, but you did." She shrugged. Okay, the woman had a point. "Or is it that you don't think I can do manual labor because I'm female?" Her lips lifted at the corners in a teasing smile.

"Oh, I know you can work hard. I saw the evidence of that last night," he teased back.

"You hardly made me work for an orgasm," she said without making eye contact. Was she embarrassed to talk about things like this?

"I *could* make you work for it, though."

"For you, I'd be willing to put in the time." Now she snapped her gaze to his, her amber eyes full of heat.

"Stop it, Ava."

"Stop *what*?" she feigned innocence.

"You know exactly *what*. If you keep up the mischief, I'll have no choice but to drag you over here and make you work the hardest you've ever worked for an orgasm," he warned.

"Told you already, I'm not afraid of a little work," she stated matter-of-factly.

"Oh, there's nothing *little* about this job, sweetheart." Luke winked.

"Then it's a good thing I have experience. Would you like to see my résumé'?" The saucy minx then stood and peeled his t-shirt off her flushed body. Tossing it to the floor, she stalked to where he sat and threw one of her legs over him, straddling his lap. Luke caught the scent of himself that still lingered on her from his shirt—that, mixed with her sweetness was doing nothing to help his self-control. There was also the fact that she was now grinding on his groin, showing him just how hard she was willing to work.

"Ava," Luke warned, although he didn't know why he'd protest such a thing, it was heaven having her like this.

"Yes, Luke?" She stopped her motions and cocked her head to the side like a curious puppy.

"Don't you think it's kind of early for this?"

Ava peeked over her shoulder and out the kitchen window. "Nope. There isn't a good *or* bad time to do this. But I can stop if you want me to." She went to stand back up and Luke pulled her to her previous position.

"Like hell you will." He grabbed her hips and began to move her back and forth over his lap. "I think you're trying to kill me."

Ava placed her hands on his shoulders and dug her nails in. The slight pain ratcheting up his need even more. "It would be a good way to die, wouldn't it?" Her head lulled back causing her mussed up hair to fall away from her face.

"God, you're fucking beautiful." Luke pulled his hands from her gyrating hips and grabbed both sides of her face. "Kiss me, sweetheart." When she did, he almost lost it. He didn't deserve to be with her. If she *really* knew who he was, she'd run and hide. It made him a bastard of epic proportions to sit here and let her do this. But that didn't stop him from reaching up and cupping her breasts in his coarse hands.

"Mmmm, your hands feel wonderful," she moaned as he molded and tweaked them.

"Do you want to come for me?" His cock was screaming, telling him he was the one needing to come. But he wanted her orgasm more than his own at the moment.

"I want to," she pulled her bottom lip between her teeth and bit down fairly hard. He wouldn't be surprised if she drew blood.

"Keep riding me and make yourself come."

"What about you?" She didn't stop her movements but looked at him when she asked. It tugged at him a little that she was worried about him.

"Don't worry about me, just show me how sexy you are by coming, sweetheart." Damn he couldn't wait to watch her again. Both times he'd seen her shatter they'd been in near darkness. It was the light of day now and he'd get a prime view of her angelic face when she fell over that precipice.

"Tell me to come for you," she demanded.

"Come for me." He couldn't help the need seeping from his voice.

"Again. Tell me," she breathed.

Luke could tell she was almost there but it stunned him she needed him to help her by being commanding. "Do it, Ava. Come."

She seemed to be struggling a bit. Her movements became uneven and her face scrunched up like she was trying too hard. "I can't," she said on a shaky sigh.

"The hell you can't. You're gonna fucking come."

"I...help me."

Oh, he'd help her alright. He couldn't wait to sink his fingers inside her and feel how soaked she was. One hand moved in between them and grazed her swollen flesh, her hiss of approval told him this was what she needed. "Tell me what you want." He wanted to tease her. Wanted her so needy that when he finally fucked her with his fingers, she'd grasp him so tight he'd blow his load in his pants.

"Inside me. I need your fingers inside me."

"What if I just want to do this?" Luke continued to play on the outside of her glistening lips, teasing and tormenting her.

"No. I need *more*." Ava shifted herself closer to his fingers trying to pull him in. "Damn it, Luke! Please!"

He knew she was getting frustrated but he wasn't ready to take her over the edge yet. Reaching around with his free hand, he placed it on the back of her neck. He pulled her head close enough that his mouth was only an inch from her ear. Opening his lips, he whispered, "I'm going to fuck you with my fingers in about fifteen seconds. I want to hear you scream my name when you come all over my hand." She frantically nodded. "Get ready, sweetheart."

Letting go of her neck he leaned back in the chair. He dug his fingers into her hip to steady her. The hand that'd been toying with her inched closer to her opening and his cock began to twitch even more. This was going to be rough watching her, but he could handle it. So he held firmly to her hip and sank two fingers into her. She immediately bucked and threw her head backward. Luke smiled as he watched her with intent. "Fuck, yeah," he groaned. His fingers explored her as he finally found the spot that would send her soaring. "Come on; show me how pretty you look when you give me that orgasm." Fingers delving even deeper, he felt the first waves as her walls began to clench around his digits. "There you go. All of it, I want it all." She began to ride his hand like it was his hard cock inside her. He wished it *was* right now. Male satisfaction coursed through him as her head snapped up and her amber eyes connected with his blue ones.

"I'm coming for you, Luke," she announced as her pussy grabbed his fingers tighter and she flooded his palm with moisture.

Yeah, watching this was worth not burying himself inside her. Hearing her screaming and chanting his name like he was a pro football player taking the field for game time. Smelling the sugary sweet scent of her pussy as she came all over his hand. And seeing her body glide over his lap with grace and beauty. Damn this was one of the best moments of his entire life. And he'd had some pretty good ones up until now.

When she recovered from the epic release, Luke pulled his hand free. "Did I make you work hard enough for that?" he teased.

"Maybe a little *too* hard," she chuckled, still trying to slow her breathing. She climbed off his lap and began to kneel in front of his chair. Her hands went to his fly, eyes never leaving his as she popped the button open and gradually pulled the zipper down.

Luke's eyes closed as she grasped him through his pants. She didn't have to do this, but he was sure as hell glad she was.

"How hard should I make *you* work for it?" Ava threw his own question back at him causing panic to rise in his chest. He was so close already it was a miracle he didn't shatter just from her pulling his zipper down.

"I think you should—" he was cut short by the shrill ring of his phone. "Fuck!" He stood so fast from the chair that he almost knocked it over. A worried look fell over Ava's face as he refastened his jeans. "Gotta take that," he stated as he grabbed his phone off the counter.

As Luke made his way outside for privacy he answered, "Daughtry."

"How's it going?" His partner in crime, Cole Matthews asked.

"Confusing as hell." Luke gave a half laugh.

"In what way?"

"Can't really explain it right now." He ventured further away from the house and into the yard.

"It'd be nice to know. Maybe I can help you clear things up."

Since he was almost to the gazebo, he stepped up and took a seat on one of the weathered benches. "They want me to continue to keep an eye on her. I'm not sure what their plans are just yet." Luke scrubbed a hand over his face in frustration.

"You figure out why they want her?"

"Not yet. Although I did figure out she used to date one of them. Seems he liked to be abusive and burn her with a cigarette after he fucked her." *Why in the hell would he tell that story?*

"How on earth did you figure out *that* piece of information?"

Shit. This wasn't going to end well. "Just came up in conversation." He shrugged even though the person on the other end couldn't see him. Luke hoped the guy believed his lie, though.

"Stay away from her, Daughtry," the guy warned.

"Yeah."

"I mean it. These aren't fuckers you want to mess with."

"I fucking get it, Matthews," Luke's voice rose and he regretted it as soon as it happened.

"Just do your job until this is over. Once you figure out what they want from her, then it's done."

"Alright."

"I'll call you in a few days." The guy hung up leaving Luke remorseful over what he'd done with Ava. It couldn't happen again. There was too much at stake here and letting his dick lead the way wasn't doing him any favors. Why did this shit have to be so difficult? He was supposed to get in, do a job and get the fuck out. But, no. He'd done the thinking with his little head and now he'd most likely have half the mob on his ass for it. He hoped to hell they didn't find out about him and Ava. But they'd had a good run. A night of hot sex, plus a morning of it; yeah, that was all he needed. He'd gotten his fill of her. The craving had now dissipated and he could focus on what his employer needed him to do.

Chapter Seven

AVA WATCHED AS LUKE sawed some boards to replace the rotten ones on the front porch of the plantation home. She shielded her eyes from the sun as it beat down on them, sweat already running down her back even though it was only ten in the morning. Letting out a tired sigh, she sat down on the steps and watched him work. There was something about a man doing labor like that. The way their muscles stretched and moved the bend of their back as they reached over to grab a tool, it was like sexual sensory overload. Luke shut off the circular saw and placed it on the makeshift work bench of plywood and saw horses. He picked up the cut piece and inspected it—holding it up and looking it over like he wanted to make sure it was absolutely perfect. Ava wasn't sure what to do. She'd offered to help but Luke was hell bent on her keeping away from the power tools. He'd said, "his is a man's job," which frustrated her to no end. In fact, she was still steaming from his comment. He'd been laughing when he said it, but that didn't really matter. She'd spent the past two years doing everything for herself. There wasn't a task she couldn't do.

"Still pissed?" Luke came over and sat next to her, laying the board on the grass below.

"A little," she huffed.

"I was only joking." Now he seemed genuinely concerned that she was upset.

"Why do men think using power tools is only for a guy? I bet I could walk right over there and do the exact same thing you just did," she threw up a bit of a challenge.

"Then by all means," Luke motioned to the work bench.

Ava wasn't about to back down. She stood from her perch and walked to where he'd been only moments before—putting an extra sway in her hip as she went. Hell, she'd show him she could do this and make him drool at the same time.

"Don't hurt yourself," Luke called.

"Pffft." Tucking a loose piece of hair behind her ear, she grabbed the saw and looked it over.

"Need help?" he snickered.

"Very funny. No, I don't need help." Okay so the damn thing was more complicated than she'd first imagined. But she was going to prove she could do this.

"Want me to have 9-1-1 ready?" Ava looked back and Luke had his phone ready in his hand. She shook her head and picked up the tool.

"Can't be that hard," she mumbled as her hand wrapped around the handle firmly. When it did, the saw powered on, scaring her and causing it to fly out of her hand to the ground. What she didn't expect was for two muscled arms to grab her from behind and pick her up off the ground.

"Easy there, Bob Vila, don't want you losing one of those pretty feet," Luke said as he kissed her neck.

"Stupid tools," she bit out.

"Not the tool's fault. It's the operator." Luke chuckled. He was still holding her firmly in his arms and Ava felt secure. "Maybe I should go make some tea," She wriggled out of his hold and planted both feet on the ground.

"Good idea. Let's take a break for a while," Luke suggested.

"Be right back."

Once inside she made her way to the kitchen and began searching for the tea bags and sugar. She riffled through cabinets, finally finding the bags but not the sugar. "If I were sugar, where would I be?" she mused aloud. Looking around she spotted a door. Most of these homes had some sort of pantry didn't they? "Ah, I bet you hold all the grocery secrets don't you?" Ava laughed as she realized she was talking to herself.

Deciding the door was the best option, she pulled it open and found that it wasn't a pantry, it was the door to the basement. A musty smell wafted up and over the decrepit wooden steps leading down causing her to sneeze a few times. What was the old saying? "Curiosity killed the cat?" She didn't need to know what was down there—even if there could be some really cool Civil War antiques hidden below those stairs.

Ava tapped her foot trying to decide whether or not it was a good idea to be nosey. Surely Luke wouldn't mind. After all, there might be something down there he could use to help restore the place. She looked back to make sure he wasn't coming in the house. When all was clear she took the first step, descending into the damp and dark basement. The steps below her creaked as she took one at a time. Once she reached the bottom, she looked for a light switch. The only illumination was a bleak amount of sunlight streaming in through weathered windows; not ideal for treasure hunting. But the need to figure out what was down there ate her alive. Walking further her hip bumped into something, pain shooting through her body. She felt around and managed to find some sort of desk lamp to switch on. Her eyes adjusted to the room and she noticed that she'd bumped into a table of sorts. It wasn't until her eyes completely focused that she realized what was sitting on the table.

"What. The. Fuck?" Eyes wide she stared at what was before her.

"What are you doing down here?" Ava jumped at the sound of Luke's gruff voice.

She spun around to see an angry stoic expression on his face. He wasn't happy about her little Jacque Cousteau moment. "I thought this was the door to the pantry." She tried to look apologetic.

"It's not," he bit out.

"Kind of figured that out." Laughter bubbled out.

"I didn't tell you to pilfer through my shit, Ava." Oh hell, he *really* was pissed.

"Luke, I'm really sorry. I thought there might be something down here you could use in your restoration efforts." She looked at the items on the table and turned back to him. "What's with this anyway?"

"None of your business." He walked past her and pulled a cloth over the items, covering them up.

"That's an awful lot of firepower on that table. Planning on fighting off zombies out here or something?" She wanted to lighten his mood.

"No. But there are wild animals that need to be taken care of."

"With a sniper rifle?" Her voice dipped as she said it.

"Go upstairs, Ava," he ordered.

She crossed her arms over her chest. "No. I want to know why you have something like that here."

Luke ran his hand over the cloth and spoke, "I used to be in the military."

"Oh."

"Yeah. Is that enough of an explanation for you? Or do you need me to write you a fucking novel about it?"

Ava didn't much care for his gruff demeanor. She spun on her heel and ran up the stairs. Sure, she was acting like an errant child, but they'd been joking and laughing all morning. What the hell had changed all of a sudden? So she'd found a high-powered rifle in his basement, was that any reason for him to go off the rails? As she ran through the kitchen she could hear Luke calling her name. No way was she staying there a moment longer.

"Ava, wait!" he yelled as she darted out the front door of the house. "Damn it!"

She continued to jog down the gravel driveway—hearing Luke's footfalls closing in behind her. "Leave me alone!" She looked back and saw he was coming closer. Damn, he could run fast and she was quickly running out of steam. Stopping, she put up both hands, signaling him to stop.

"Are you going to run all the way back to town?" He wasn't even out of breath. Damn him.

Ava's lungs burned as she doubled over, trying to pull precious air into her battered lungs. "Maybe," she huffed out.

"All thirteen miles of it?" Luke sniggered.

"Laugh it up," she said in a mocking tone. "I'm not staying here if you're going to be an asshole all day."

"You invade my personal space and expect me to be shitting glitter and rainbows?"

"You didn't tell me to stay out of the basement, Luke!" Ava shouted as she walked closer to him. His manly scent mixed with the sweat from him running had her libido doing backflips.

"Fair enough," he let out a sigh and ran a hand through his sweat-drenched hair. He looked around and back to her. "I don't want you to leave. But if you want to, at least let me drive you back." He looked sorry.

"I don't want to go." Ava stepped even closer.

"So you're staying?" He pulled her into him and she laid her head on his damp chest and nodded. "Good."

"It's so hot out here. Too bad you don't have a pool." Her mood was lightening but not too quickly. No wonder they said crime rose with the temperature. She was so overheated, crime was sounding like a wonderful consolation right now.

"No pool, but I have something else that might work." He grabbed her hand and began to walk across the vast property.

"Where're we going?" She looked around but all she could see were trees and emerald grass.

"Just trust me."

They walked about a hundred yards until they met the tree line at the edge of the property. "How are trees supposed to make me cool off?"

"Smartass," he joked, still pulling her behind him.

They trudged through the small forest and soon came to a clearing that opened up to a pond, sunlight glistening off the surface of the water like a sliver of glass. It was completely shielded from view by trees and tall grass. It was *amazing*. But a thought hit her. "I don't have a bathing suit with me." Ava began to nervously chew on her thumbnail, something that'd become a habit in the past two years.

She glanced over at Luke who was pulling his work boots off and tossing them to the ground. "You gonna stand there, or are you gonna get undressed?"

"You can't be serious."

"Extremely. Come on, don't be a wuss."

That was all she needed to decide. First her shoes were toed off, her shirt was pulled over her head and tossed to the ground, and then she shimmied out of her jeans. She chanced a look at Luke to see him watching her intently like a hawk watches its prey. Something about the way he was looking at her made her feel empowered. Her skin broke out in gooseflesh knowing he was eating her up with his eyes. If it wasn't already a hundred and five degrees outside she would've been burned up just with one look from his blue eyes.

Standing in the open in her bra and panties, Ava looked over to Luke who stood in only a pair of black boxer briefs. He flashed a mischievous smile and pointed his gaze to the water. What happened next was a blur as she saw him run toward her, grab her by the waist and hurl them both into the waiting water. The cool liquid hit her skin and caused her to scream as she went under. She gulped down a mouthful of water. Suddenly her body was being brought to the top, the sunlight hitting her in the eyes as she surfaced. The only thing she could do was sputter and cough as she tried to rid her body of the dingy water.

"You okay?" She couldn't quite see Luke when he spoke but his voice was laced with concern.

"No." She continued to cough. "Asshole!" She finally got her breath and splashed him with some of the slightly brown water.

"You should've seen your face. Priceless." He laughed.

"I'm sure it was. Yours would've been the same if someone tried to drown you." She couldn't help but giggle which ended up in a fit of laughter. The water around her rippled as her entire body shook with amusement. Ava suddenly stopped and looked around.

"Something wrong?" Luke pinned her with a stare.

"I, uh...lost something," she said as her head whipped back and forth, searching the surface of the water.

"What'd you lose? An earring?" Luke raised his eyebrows in curiosity.

"No. My underwear is gone." Her cheeks flushed with embarrassment.

"You mean this?" Luke pulled his hand above the water, holding her drenched undergarment.

"Give it back!" She lunged forward trying to grab it, but failed.

"I'm keeping it." Luke began to twirl the fabric around his finger in the air.

"Fine. If you get to keep mine, I get to keep yours," she threw out.

Luke didn't even hesitate as he bent down in the water and moved around. He then pulled his arm up and tossed his underwear to her. "Fair is fair. But I get that, too." He pointed to the lace covering her breasts. "Hand it over."

"Fine." Ava reached around to unhook her bra.

Sliding it down her arms she then tossed it to Luke. Looking down she could see her naked breasts bobbing in the water.

"Now *that* is fucking beautiful." Luke's gaze became heated as he took in her nudity.

Ava glanced down and instinctively covered her bare chest with her arms. It wasn't as if she was ashamed of her body, she just wasn't used to being out in the open, having her girly bits on display. "I think it's time to get out." Wading through the mud on the bottom of the pond, Ava made her way toward the bank. Luke didn't leave the water; only stood there and watched as she removed her now naked form from the water. He still had her bra and panties but it didn't matter, she didn't really want to put her dry clothing on over the soaked garments anyway.

The sun began to beat down on her while she pulled her jeans up her legs and tossed her shirt on. When her shoes were on both feet, Ava began to walk back through the trees, and headed for the house. Even though she'd grown up in Chicago among the towering buildings and the normal bustle of the city life, she looked around and wondered if something like this might be more suited to who she was. The fresh air, the abundance of space to run and do as she pleased—but that was a silly thought. This wasn't her home, it never could be. It was a fantasy, a wish that would never be granted.

She didn't really know Luke that well. Besides some extremely passionate encounters, Ava really had no idea who the man was. He'd said he was in the military, but wouldn't elaborate on his time there. She'd given him an opening to do so, but he clammed up and made her feel like an idiot. Maybe something terrible had happened to him? But she hadn't seen any scars or marks from where he would've been wounded. She had every opportunity to do so. Luke was one big mystery. A man who seemed to put his all into everything he did and then some. So why was he being so secretive and private about his early life? The lot of it was starting to cause unwanted stress. This was just a fling. A passing fascination between two individuals. There wasn't going to be a happily ever after. No white doves would be released in their honor. Plain and simple, it was sex. So why did that mere thought begin to cut her to the very core of who she was?

Chapter Eight

LATER THAT EVENING, Luke looked down on Ava's sleeping face as her head rested in his lap while he sat on the porch swing. The air had turned slightly cooler and it'd seemed like an ideal time to sit out here and watch the sun fade away into the oblivion that was night. Ava had helped cook dinner, which to his amazement had been the closest to normal he'd ever felt. His parents never did that shit. He'd have been lucky to get a bowl of Ramen before he went to bed at night. Having this angelic creature move gracefully throughout the kitchen made his ancestors' house feel like a *home* for the first time since he could remember.

As the swing moved back and forth in a hypnotic motion, he tipped his head back and closed his eyes, remembering the times he came to visit his grandmother when she lived here. They were always happy times. Summers filled with dips in the pond, scouring the property for discarded cannonballs from the war, and sitting around chatting with his grandma. When he'd let her know he was moving to Washington, D.C., she wasn't too excited about the idea. But it was a move he needed to make in order to further himself. If Grandma Violet knew the things he did now…let's just say she wouldn't be welcoming him with open arms. There would've most likely been a flour-covered rolling pin knocking him upside the head.

"Are you asleep?" Ava's smooth voice and her hand grazing his cheek pulled him out of his reminiscence.

"Nah, just thinking." He smiled and began to caress her cheek the same as she did to him.

"Care to share?" Damn her and that smile. It was becoming a weakness and Luke didn't admit weakness.

"Maybe another time. Ready for me to take you home?" He didn't want her to go, but surely she needed to get home.

"Do I have to go? It's like a slice of heaven out here. It feels like I can forget about everything and just…*live*."

"And you can't do that anyplace else?" He regretted the words as he said them.

Ava sat up and scooted to the other end of the swing. "On that note, time for me to go." Slipping her flats on, she stood and faced away.

"I'm an asshole, aren't I?" Luke leaned forward and braced his elbows on his knees. "I'm sorry." For some reason he felt the need to apologize when he'd wronged her; which was strange because normally, he didn't give a damn about people's feelings. But Ava was different. He didn't want to hurt her. He didn't want to see lines of worry crease her smooth brow. And he certainly never wanted to take part in drying her tears. If he was ever faced with that, he didn't know if he'd survive it. But this wasn't a fucking fairy tale. He wasn't the white knight riding in to save her from her troubles. No, Luke was the villain. The guy who snuck in like a thief in the night to upturn everything she held dear. She'd think this was her sunny sky, but eventually she'd find out that all he carried with him were bleak clouds that eventually turned into a whirlwind of disaster. Point blank, this wasn't going to have a happy ending.

Silence blanketed around them before she finally spoke, "At least you're one step ahead; most people don't know they're an asshole until they get hit in the face with their own shit."

Luke's shoulders bounced with amusement. "Never heard it put like that, but I guess you're right." He laughed louder.

"I'm always right." As she sat back down next to him on the swing, he took in her profile in the fading light. Damn she was a beauty. But something deeper pulled him in. Something he still couldn't describe held him to her.

Shaking the idiotic thoughts from his head Luke figured it best to stop looking at her. Distance. That's what he needed. He cleared his throat, "So…" suddenly he was at a loss for words.

"Yeah?" Ava pulled her legs onto the swing and faced him.

Nervousness swamped him like a teenage boy glaring at a pair of tits for the first time. He rubbed the back of his neck before speaking again, "Do you want to stay the night again?" Now why in the hell would he ask her to do such a thing? Wasn't the point of this thing to distance himself? But even he knew he'd rather take a jackhammer to his nuts rather than walk away from her.

"I can. If you want me to, that is." Ava gave him a questioning look.

Did he want her to stay again? Did he want to wake up with her lush curves pressed against his flesh? Did he want to breathe in the scent of her hair from behind as he pushed himself between her legs and made love to her until she dug her nails into his arms? Fuck, yeah, he wanted that. And he was going to have it. "Then it's settled. You're staying." He practically jumped off the porch swing and grabbed her hand.

"Slow down there, Sparky. No need to rush." She giggled.

"I beg to differ." Luke pointed at the clear outline of his erection pressing insistently at his zipper. "There *is* a reason to rush."

Ava had never seen Luke so uncontrolled before. He was tugging her behind him as he flung open the front door of the house. "Luke, slow down," she said as she turned to shut the door behind them. When she pivoted back around, two hundred and fifty pounds of hard male flesh had her pinned against the antique wood.

"Can't seem to slow down when it comes to you," he grunted as he pinned her wrists in his hands and held them to the door by her sides. For a brief moment panic took hold but was soon replaced with need. Luke would never hurt her. He wasn't that kind of guy. "Can't seem to get enough of you either," he pressed his face to the rapidly beating pulse point on her neck. "Your smell." He breathed in deeply. "Your taste." She felt his moist tongue dart out and run up the side of her neck, eliciting a shiver through her body. "But most of all," one of his hands left her wrist and cupped her between her legs, "the way you feel when you're coming all over my cock." He began to massage her through her jeans, causing her to cry out.

"That feels so good," Ava mewled.

"You have two choices. I'm either going to throw you over my shoulder, carry you upstairs and fuck you in my bed. Or I'm going to fuck you against this door. Which is it gonna be?"

"The door."

"The door it is." Luke reached for the hem of her top and yanked it over her head. Her pants were discarded next. She was still gloriously nude under her clothing since he'd confiscated her undergarments earlier in the day. "Every time I see you like this I feel like I'm looking at you for the first time."

"Please hurry," Ava begged. Her skin was like embers, just waiting for him to stoke the flames and send them both blazing.

Luke threw off his clothing in record time, grabbed a condom from the back pocket of his jeans and rolled it on with practiced precision. He then pressed his heated body to hers. "Say it, Ava. Tell me you want me to fuck you," he said in a gruff voice.

"I want you to fuck me, Luke."

"Tell me you want to come for me."

"I want to come for you."

"Damn right you do." Luke grabbed one of her legs and hitched it around his trim waist. "Are you ready?" he asked as he stroked her entrance with the head of his erection.

"More than ready."

"Good." Luke gave no warning as he thrust into her channel until he was fully seated. Ava cried out at the invasion—not because it hurt—but because it was delicious torture having him buried inside her. He reached down and lifted her other leg up and around him—driving himself deeper somehow. Ava's back screamed as he drove into her, shoving her body against the door. Something was different this time. It almost seemed like Luke was trying his hardest to drive some sort of demon away. But why?

Ava reached up and slid her arms around his sweat-laden shoulders. "Luke, please look at me," she asked softly, but he refused to look up. "I need to see your eyes," she began to plead with him.

"No, damn it!" Luke roared as he continued his mind-numbing motions.

What was happening? Why was there such an urgency radiating off his body? Something was disconnected in all of this, so much so that Ava felt herself slipping out of primal attraction and into vast worry for him. She had to do something. "Luke, stop!" she yelled. He froze in place, his face nuzzled in her neck and his cock still deep within her. She waited until his breathing lessened and he was ready to talk to her. "What is going on?" she asked.

"I'm fucking you against the door like you wanted, Ava." The words weren't ones of tenderness or caring. They were close to those of spite. "Isn't that what you wanted?" Luke's breathing increased and Ava felt him push forward. "This," he began to thrust again, "is what we have," *thrust*, "this," *thrust* "is what we do, Ava."

"No." She pulled her legs from his hips and planted them on the ground. With a shaky hand she laid her palm on his chest and pushed him away. Luke flashed a questioning glance but said nothing. He grabbed his discarded clothing from the floor and began trudging up the stairs. "Luke?" Ava called, but he didn't look back or answer her and soon he was out of sight. The door to his bedroom closed with an audible slam and she knew that things were over.

Not sure where to go from there, Ava quickly dressed and then made her way outside. Pulling her phone from her purse, she dialed Brandi's number.

"Jesus shit, Ava. Do you have any idea what time it is?" She heard the sleepiness in her friend's voice.

"I'm sorry. But I need help." Ava felt the heat of tears begin to sting the backs of her eyes. Brandi must've heard the crack in her voice.

"What the fuck did the bastard do?" The sound of rustling clothing and something being scrubbed against the phone told Ava that Brandi had gotten out of bed. "Do I need to help you hide a body?"

Ava couldn't help but laugh. "No. I just need you to come get me please."

"Are you sure I don't need to bring along a shovel and a tarp?" Ava heard the jingling of keys and the sound of a car starting on the other end.

"It's not *that* bad." Ava wasn't sure *just* how bad it really was. Something had caused Luke to shift from being a nice guy, to someone who reminded her of her past. She didn't need someone like that. She'd had enough of that in

Chicago and wasn't going down that road again. The stupid thing was she really liked Luke. He was fun to be around and genuinely seemed to like her too. But it was all an act. An act to most likely get into her panties just like every other card-carrying member of the douche bag population.

"I'll be right there," Brandi said before she hung up.

Wasn't this just great. What began as a beautiful weekend, turned out to be shit, just like the rest of her existence. It always felt like she'd finally gotten ahead and settled, but when she became comfortable, the other shoe always dropped.

Chapter Nine

"**DO YOU WANT TO TALK** about it?" Brandi drove down the two lane highway away from Luke's home while Ava stared out her window into the bleak of night.

"Honestly, I don't even know how to explain it, Brandi," Ava sighed.

"Did he hurt you?" Concern laced her best friend's voice.

"No, nothing like that. Everything was great this weekend. In fact it was the best weekend I've had in God knows how long."

"You're not giving me much to go on here," Brandi laughed.

Ava stayed quiet for what she'd thought was a reasonable amount of time. How did she explain what'd happened when she wasn't even sure herself? "Can we not discuss this right now? I'm beyond exhausted and just want to go home."

"Whatever you say, chief. But as your best friend, I'm gonna want details eventually. I don't like seeing you like this." Ava felt a reassuring tap of Brandi's hand on her knee, but only nodded in the dim lit interior of the car.

The miles ticked by as the two friends rode in silence back to Ava's beach house. The entire weekend with Luke was replaying in her head like a bad silent movie and all she wanted was to either hit the pause button or delete the damn thing altogether. The ignorant thing was that even the tiny thought of his touch sent her body spinning out of control. He was masterful at handling her, and damn it if that didn't piss her off. It wasn't fair that he could draw her in like she was a helpless fly, then snag her in his web and devour her whole. Mentally kicking herself wasn't going to be enough punishment in the coming weeks. The best she could hope for was to work her ass off to try and rid her brain of his touch and him in general. But Luke Daughtry wasn't someone you could just forget. He made an impact like a damn meteor crashing into the earth. It would be a while before she'd be able to move without feeling him on her and inside her.

Monday morning Luke sat on the same porch swing he had the night before with Ava. It was stupid but he could still smell her floral fragrance floating around him as the slight breeze blew in his direction. He'd fucked up. And that wasn't a good thing since his job was to keep a steady eye on her at all times. He'd never meant to shove her away like he had, he only wanted to emotionally distance himself so he could think straight and do the job he was being paid to do. Now all he could think about was making amends with her and hoping she'd let him in again. If she did, he needed to set some ground rules. Clearly they'd gotten in way over their heads by sleeping together. And if she redeemed him by some twist of fate, he'd have to make sure to never cross that threshold again. It would be dangerous for his plans; and come hell or high water, he would complete his task and walk away.

Finally deciding it was time to start his epic groveling, Luke threw on some different clothes and made his way to his truck in the driveway. What he didn't expect was for someone to be standing there waiting for him. *Cole Matthews.*

"I thought you were an early riser?"

"Not today. What're you doing here?" Luke stood a few feet away and crossed his arms over his chest.

"Boss man said I needed to come and help you keep an eye on things."

"Already pegging me for incompetent, I see."

"Hell, Daughtry. You know as well as I do this has to be done right."

"Would've been nice to get a head's up. I don't need a fucking babysitter." Luke hit the unlock button on his key ring and went for the door. Before he could grab the handle to pull it open, the other man stepped in front of him, blocking his way. "I'm not in the mood for your shit today, Matthews," Luke growled.

"Seems we have something in common then."

"Yeah, okay. I fucked up but I'm trying to fix it. So get the hell out of my way so I can do just that."

"Make sure you *do* fix it, or both our heads will be on the chopping block. I love you, man, but if someone is getting tossed under the bus, it's gonna be you," Cole chuckled.

"Don't worry about it. I've got this under control."

The other man stepped out of Luke's way and started to walk away from the vehicle. "Emotions are messy. Just make sure you don't get yours involved. You know how this's gonna end, you've seen it already."

"I don't need a reminder." Luke yanked the door handle so hard he felt his arm muscle protest.

So they thought he couldn't do his job. Big fucking surprise there. Those motherfuckers didn't know him very well if they thought he needed someone to come down to Mississippi and wipe his ass for him. Yeah, shit had happened in the past; that was nearly ten years ago. He'd learned his lesson about how human emotions could fuck you over, and he didn't plan on letting that happen again. Control over the situation was what he needed in order to see this thing through. He'd have that as soon as he got Ava back in his sights and made her forgive him. What the hell would make a female forgive you for fucking up anyway? Flowers? Chocolate? Hell, it'd been years since he needed to pull the chick card. As he started his truck and drove down the gravel driveway, he mulled over the options. Ava didn't seem like the type of woman to swoon over material things like jewelry or fancy things. She was a grassroots girl. One who would more than likely be enamored with something simple. This was going to take some planning on his part but he was nothing if not meticulous with his actions. He'd wow her and then she'd have no choice but to forgive him.

"Good morning, Chase," Ava greeted her first client of the day. The awkward redheaded, freckle-faced twenty-one-year-old smiled as he made his way over to the styling chair.

"Mornin', Ava. How was your weekend?" He sat down and stared at Ava in the mirror.

She tried her hardest to be pleasant and friendly but none of those things described how she really felt on the inside. Exchanging pleasantries was about as far as she wanted to go on this dreary Monday. If the first day of the week wasn't bad enough already, the storm rolling in outside made it much worse. "Better than some, and worse than others." She tried to keep things vague. Not that she'd spill her problems to a client anyway, but giving any sort of solid answer about her weekend was far from her mind.

"You gonna be at Bo's on Friday? It's their 20th anniversary." Chase was a good kid, but he'd always rubbed her the wrong way for some reason. Ava had a feeling he was once again getting ready to ask her out.

"Probably not. I'm not much for public gatherings." *Or running into Luke by chance,* she thought.

"You outta come. It's gonna be a good time. Free wings and beer from seven to nine." He watched her as she spread the cutting cape over his body. "I sure could use a date," he winked as she snapped the cape around his neck.

Ava knew he meant well, but the kid was nine years her junior. It wouldn't be considered robbing the cradle but it was pretty damn close to the mark. "Thank you for the offer, Chase. But I don't think so." How many times did she have to turn him down for him to get the hint?

"Sweet little thing like you needs a man to take care of her," Chase said matter-of-factly.

Fury bloomed inside her already aggravated body and this was the last straw. Without thinking of the ramifications, Ava grabbed the leather-backed chair and spun the kid around so she could look him in the eyes. "First off, I'd think again if you think for one second I'm a *sweet little thing*. And secondly, I don't need anyone to take care of me, least of all you. So how about you stop thinking one day I'm finally going to give in and go *anywhere* with you." She was fuming as she saw he wasn't paying a lick of attention to the words coming out of her mouth, but instead had his eyes trained directly on the small amount of cleavage revealed at her chest. "Are you fucking kidding me?" She stood up straight and pulled her top up to cover what was being shown. It wasn't that her shirt revealed much at all though, Chase was being a pervert like always. "Look, you little shit. You need to learn some manners and tact. If you want a woman to be interested in you at all, you need to start listening to her instead of drooling over her tits." Ava reached forward and yanked the cape from around his neck. Just as she went to pull her hands away, Chase grabbed one of her wrists and yanked her down on his lap.

"I like a woman who plays hard to get," he cooed.

Ava tried to stand and pry herself from his grasp. "Let me go."

"Come on now, we could be really good together." Chase thrust his hips up to show her he was ready and willing in the southern region of his anatomy.

Bile began to rise in her throat at the thought of what he might do to her. After all, she was alone in her salon and she highly doubted anyone could hear her scream. She struggled more as he held tighter to her body. "Don't fight it. I bet you'd like it once you had a taste," the sick little fucker whispered in her ear and had the nerve to lick her earlobe. Not being able to remove herself from his punishing grasp, Ava let her body go lax. "See, I knew you'd want it." He took her hand and placed it on the front of his jeans. "All for you, baby," he chuckled.

The only thing she could do was play along until she could manage to either get the hell out of there or have the opportunity to shove her knee into his crotch and make him sing like a soprano. "You're right. I've wanted you for so long, Chase. How about we take this to the back, out of sight from prying eyes?" Ava tilted her head to the large windows to the front of the shop.

He didn't make a move to stand up. "What are you gonna do when you get me back there?" his voice dipped low. How disgusting, he was actually getting turned on by this shit. But she had no other choice.

"It's a surprise." Ava tried to keep it inexplicit. Just the thought of telling him anything sexual had her wanting to lose the yogurt she'd forced herself to eat for breakfast.

"I want you to tell me. Go ahead, tell me what you're gonna do to me back there."

Ava closed her eyes and willed herself to not throw up. Taking a deep breath she forced the words out, "I'm going to…"

"She's not going to do anything to you, asshole!" Ava's head snapped up to see Luke coming right for them. "I strongly suggest you let her up or I'll make sure you eat out of a fucking straw for the rest of your life." Relief hit as Luke came closer and wrapped his coarse-skinned hand gently around her bicep.

"And who the fuck are you?" Chase stood from the chair as Luke pushed her behind his big frame.

Anger pulsed off Luke in waves as she backed up a bit more in case things got physical. "I'm the guy who's going to make sure you're bleeding when you walk out that door. If you're lucky, I'll only break a couple bones." Luke began to stalk toward Chase while Ava watched with horror.

Chase threw his hands up in surrender. "Okay, look man. I'm sorry."

"I'm not the one you need to be apologizing to." Luke bit out.

"Ava…I'm sorry…I shouldn't have…" he stammered.

"Now, get the fuck out of her shop. If I ever hear of you coming in here, or even looking at her while out in public, I will rip every limb from your body while you scream like a little bitch. Is that clear?" Luke said with a deadly tone to his words.

"Crystal clear." Chase scurried past her and Luke and darted through the front door.

Trembling with fear and adrenaline, Ava backed herself against the wall and slid down. Landing on her butt, she pulled her knees to her chest and tucked her head down. White hot tears began to erupt as she shook with so many emotions. In the two years since she'd lived here, she'd never been so afraid that someone would actually cause her harm. But today made her realize no matter where she ran to, she would never be safe. As she sat there bubbling with emotions, Ava could hear Luke's soothing voice cutting through the fear induced haze.

"Ava, sweetheart. Look at me," he kept his voice low and calm. When she didn't look up, he gently placed a finger under her chin and lifted her eyes to his.

"Hey, everything's fine now. I'm here."

Instinct told her to throw herself into his waiting arms, but common sense made her pause. After what'd happened between them last night she wasn't sure just where they stood. "Thank you," was all she could manage to croak out between her sobs.

"Don't ever thank me for protecting you. I'm just glad I came in when I did. Are you okay? Let me look at you." Luke helped her stand on shaky legs. He seemed to be taking stock and making sure she wasn't injured. She'd hate to see what he would've done to the forceful freckle-faced kid if he'd managed to harm her in any way. The thought was rather comforting. "I wanted to rip his fucking head off for touching you." Ava shook her head. She didn't need the police involved in her life for any reason. If Luke had beaten the hell out of Chase, it would've caused a shit storm in her life. "Let's get you out of here. You don't need to be here right now."

Ava stepped around him and walked to her chair. "I can't leave. I have more appointments today." She grabbed a tissue to dry her face.

"Put a note on the door and lock up. I'm not letting you work when you're upset. This isn't up for discussion."

After what'd happened the night before, Ava wasn't sure where she and Luke stood. Even though he'd swooped in to save the day, there was still this odd tension between them. Before she went anywhere with him, it was necessary to clear the air. Having something like this hanging over their heads like a dark raincloud just wouldn't do.

"Luke, we probably need to talk." She turned to his now relaxed body and let out a sigh.

Luke rubbed a hand over the back of his neck and into his mussed hair. "You're probably right."

"I don't know what happened last night, but the way you acted really hurt me." She didn't mean it to sound like she was being a whine bag about it, but it came out that way anyhow.

"I never promised you anything beyond what we were doing, Ava," he defended.

"And I never asked you for anything else. I don't want a relationship. But I do want to be treated like a human being and not like a piece of convenient ass." Her voice rose a bit and she regretted it. Being afraid of Luke wasn't the problem; she was only scared that saying the wrong thing would push him away further.

"I would never think of you in that way, you have to know that."

"But I *don't* know that. You pulled a one-eighty last night. It was like you weren't even the same person I'd been spending time with all day. What the hell happened?"

Luke's shoulders dropped like he was giving in, or maybe even giving up. Ava didn't like that at all. No way was she letting him duck inside himself and throw up more walls. "I don't know."

"Don't give me that line of bullshit. I'm pretty good at seeing through people and you're as transparent as a piece of Saran Wrap."

"The truth is I'm overwhelmed right now. I'm trying to work on this house and then I met you. Things got out of hand pretty damn quick."

"So I'm the problem?" Ava questioned.

"No. I didn't say that. You're not a problem, at least not to me."

"Then tell me how I can help make things better for you. I enjoy spending time with you, Luke. I don't want this to ruin what we have." Desperation crept into her voice. She didn't want to need him in her life, but after the mostly amazing weekend they'd shared, she wasn't ready to let him just waltz right out the door.

"I enjoy spending time with you, too." One side of his mouth kicked up and an adorable boyish grin then spread over his handsome face. Ava finally noticed the dark circles under his eyes and it hit her that he might've been up all night tossing and turning just as she had.

"It doesn't matter how long this thing between us lasts. Days, hours or even months. I just want to be around you. If that's asking too much then I'm sorry."

"I don't think you're asking too much. Because I want that, too."

"Then I say we put last night behind us and start over. I'm willing to do whatever it takes to be able to spend time with you." She felt like she was bargaining but she'd do just about anything at this point to ensure Luke would stay in her life for even a little bit longer.

"Just as long as you know I can't and won't make you any promises." Regret crossed his face as he waited for her response.

"Nothing in life offers a guarantee anyway."

"Then I think we have things settled. Now, grab your things, you're coming home with me for a few days."

Chapter Ten

FOR ONCE LUKE didn't question himself when he drove them back to his home. Like he'd told her at the salon, it wasn't up for discussion. She was either going to come willingly, or he'd toss her over his shoulder and pull a caveman move to get her there. Hell, every Neanderthal instinct went into high gear when he'd walked into her shop and seen that dickweed latched onto her, trying to take advantage of her. That shit wasn't going to fly. Knowing damn well he didn't have any rights to her didn't matter. What *did* matter was the clear fear and discomfort written all over her color-drained face. When he'd walked in and saw her like that, the primal urge to protect and keep her safe bubbled to the surface like a volcano full of molten magma. The only thing keeping him from dismembering that ginger prick was knowing that the police would've been called in. He didn't need the Five-O on his ass. What he needed was to get her out of there to somewhere she felt safe. The only place he could think of was his house.

"I hate to ask, but can you take me to my house so I can grab some things, please?" Ava asked as he drove through town. "If you don't want to turn around it's okay. I can have Brandi bring a few things."

Luke didn't hesitate in pulling off the side of the road and doing a U-turn. Maybe that made him whipped or maybe that just made him a nice guy. But *'nice'* wasn't what anyone would use to describe him at all. Trying not to think too much into it he grabbed her hand and pulled the back of it to his lips. He laid a light kiss on the baby-soft skin. "It's not a problem." Then he continued down the highway in the direction of the coastline.

"I won't be long," she assured him.

Luke could still see she was shaken up from the ordeal earlier and that pissed him off. How could some dipshit come in and try to take advantage of a woman who clearly couldn't protect herself. That was a sobering thought. Wasn't he basically doing the same shit? Wasn't he here to keep an eye on her and invade her privacy by planting a listening device in her home? Yet again he'd come to the realization that he was indeed a *special* kind of bastard *and* a hypocrite.

"Do you want me to wait here?" Luke pulled his truck into the driveway and parked a few feet from the garage door.

"Um, you can wait here. I'll just be a few minutes." Ava's exhausted attempt at a smile had his chest hurting.

"If you need anything I'll be right here," he offered.

He watched her hop down from the cab of his truck and walk around to the side entrance of the garage. Once she was out of sight he flipped open the console and removed the false bottom he'd installed. The black receiver was still sitting in there nondescriptly so he grabbed it and switched it on. The frequency was already set to match the one in Ava's home. He wasn't sure what sort of information he expected to hear since she wasn't going to be in there long, but any info at all could help him keep an eye on her as his employer had requested. Scratch that…demanded.

At first there wasn't much noise except for some rustling around; more than likely Ava packing some things in a bag. But after about two minutes he heard the familiar ringing of a cell phone. Luke turned up the volume so he could eavesdrop on what would be a one-sided conversation on his end.

"Hey," Ava answered. "Yeah, something happened with a client." He heard her take a deep breath. "No, I'm fine. Just shaken up." A few moments went by before she spoke again, "Brandi, really, I'm okay. Stop worrying about me." It sounded like she'd plopped down on the sofa which was extremely close to the end table where he'd planted the bug. He could now pick up Brandi's voice well enough to decipher the entire conversation.

"I don't like this, Ava."

"I'm going to stay with Luke for a few days. I need some time off."

"I don't know if I trust him, though. Especially after what'd happened last night," Brandi huffed.

"We talked about it and worked it out. I think things are fine now."

"You think? Or you know? Those are two completely different things, Ava."

"Look, I like him. We're really good together. I don't want to analyze it too much."

"But you know what they say: 'if it seems too good to be true…'"

Ava finished the saying, "'It probably is.' But what if it just *is* good? Shouldn't I take a chance on it? Wouldn't I be stupid *not* to?"

"You have more balls than I do. And as your best friend it's my job to warn you and tell you you're being a dumbass." Luke heard Brandi laugh.

"And as *your* best friend I'm supposed to tell you to back off bitch." Ava snorted which had Luke smiling. He'd never heard her snort when she laughed. It was kind of cute.

"Well, I've done enough warning you away from the sexy beast. I guess I'll let you get your freak on now," Brandi hooted.

"Yeah, thanks. I'll call you tomorrow and let you know how things are going."

"Sounds fab. Love ya, babe."

"Love you, too." Luke heard Ava sit something down near the bug. Must've been her phone was his best guess.

Suddenly he felt himself being swamped with guilt over what he'd been doing. Even deep beneath his twisted heap of a soul, he knew there was some sort of good guy lurking. He'd not seen hide or hair of that guy for what seemed like forever, but wrong was wrong. It didn't matter how you tried to justify it. Switching off the receiver, Luke crammed it— with a little more force than usual— in its hiding spot.

"Damn it!" he cursed as he pounded the heels of his hands into the leather cover of the steering wheel. Things were way off track. He wasn't supposed to be as close to Ava as he'd gotten, but backing off now would cause suspicion. He couldn't risk it. Seeing things through was the only option.

Leaning forward, Luke curled his arms around the steering wheel and rested his head. "What the hell am I gonna do?" he muttered.

"About what?" Ava's silky voice startled him. He hadn't realized she'd opened the passenger door.

He needed an answer and quick. Ava stood there beseeching him with her beautiful amber irises. "Oh, I was sitting here thinking about a couple of projects I need to get done. Probably stressing myself out over nothing." He smiled.

"Okay. Do you want me to put my stuff up here or in the back?" She stood there looking so innocent and lovely that it almost hurt physically to look at her.

"In the back." He unbuckled his seatbelt and threw open the door. "I'll help you."

"Why do men always think we're helpless?" Ava laughed.

Once he made his way around to her side of the truck he noticed the four bags at her feet. He looked from them to her face. "Moving in already?" He raised an eyebrow.

"Well that one," she pointed a slim finger to a hot-pink medium-sized duffle, "Is nothing but underwear. I figured since you like trophies, I'd need extra to keep up."

Luke's voice dipped lower as lustful thoughts invaded his body and brain. "What if I don't let you wear *anything* while you're staying with me?"

"Is that a threat? Or a promise?" Ava stepped closer, her sugary floral scent enveloping him like a blanket of blissful sensations.

"Which do you want it to be?" Damn he needed to touch her. To reach out and feel her creamy silken skin beneath his fingers.

"I want you to choose." Her voice shook as she moved in and her chest brushed his. It didn't matter if she was standing ten feet away or mere millimeters, his body recognized hers and knew the promises it held. Even though it was like opening Pandora's Box every time he touched her, he craved it like he'd die if he didn't have just one more touch.

"How about we take this to my place?" Luke wanted nothing more than to act out every vehicular sexual fantasy at the moment but Ava deserved better than a quick fuck in a truck cab.

Her facial expression went from extremely heated to lax in a matter of seconds. "That's probably a good idea." He could tell she was filled with disappointment but she'd have to get over it. His plans for the evening would perk her right up.

"Did you get any work done on the house today?" Ava began what she hoped was neutral conversation as they drove to Luke's house.

"No. I was up most of the night so I slept in."

"I was, too. Well, not the sleeping in part, but the insomnia issue." She tried to make it known that he wasn't the only one having trouble sleeping after what'd happened between them the night before.

"Then tonight we'll work on a good night's rest." Luke grabbed her hand and twined their fingers together. His promise of sleep was a bit of a letdown though. There were far too many things she'd rather be doing with him than sleeping.

Since it was early afternoon Ava decided to take in the visual splendor of the landscape around her. Mississippi wasn't so bad. The heat was more than excessive, and the weather—being so close to the Gulf—was somewhat bipolar at times, but all in all, it was a beautiful state to live in. She only hoped her past didn't rear its disgusting head and ruin everything she'd built over the past two years.

She knew better than to get too comfortable, but there was always that tiny part of her that wished this was the place she could permanently plant her roots.

Luke turned the truck onto the long gravel driveway leading to the plantation home. Ava became concerned when he stopped and yanked the gear shifter on the steering column into the 'park' position. "What's going on?" She looked around and then to Luke.

"I'd like to show you something," he said as he opened his door. She watched him round the front of the truck and come to the passenger side where she sat with her door closed. He opened it for her and offered his hand to help her down.

"You're starting to worry me." Ava tried to put humor in her voice but trepidation seeped through.

"Then stop worrying and come with me." Luke grabbed her hand and began to pull her along with him across the expanse of lush grass. Soon though he stopped in front of a tree. "My ancestors planted this tree right before the war." He pointed at the towering slice of nature. "Come here."

Ava followed and soon she was standing in the cool shade of the most magnificent weeping willow tree she'd ever seen. The flexible branches draped over each other like a cascading waterfall spilling green onto the earth below. Each branch was covered in tiny leaves that caused a bushy effect and almost made it seem as if the outside world didn't exist. The rough textured trunk was thick and sturdy, telling her that it had indeed been rooted in its home for many years. She envisioned Luke's family digging a hole for what was once just a sapling needing love and attention to make it grow. Ava fluttered her eyes closed and thought of the many picnics that might've been had here on days-gone-by. The laughter of children circling around the base as they played hide-and-go-seek in the sweltering Mississippi summer months. And the stolen affections of a couple who sought shelter under this tree from prying eyes while locked in a passionate embrace. This wasn't just a tree; no, it was a symbol of the history on this property. A reminder of good times and trying times.

"Want to see the best part?" Luke's question pulled Ava from her dreams. She nodded and trailed him as he wound around the other side. "Look," he motioned to a carving about eye-level.

"What is that?" She stepped closer.

"My great-great-grandparents were married here. After the ceremony, they carved their initials in the trunk."

Ava lifted her hand and ran a finger through the ancient grooves. "This is…I don't even have words to describe this, Luke." She turned to see him watching her, some sort of strange emotion playing on his face.

"You're the first person I've shown it to."

"Really?" She couldn't believe he hadn't brought anyone else here to share something this special with. Stepping toward him, she wrapped her arms around his midsection and hugged him tightly. "Thank you."

"I knew you'd appreciate it. You seem to find beauty in the smallest of things." His arms encircled her body, returning the gesture she'd given him.

"In life I like to see the smaller parts that make up the picture. The things most people miss because they're too busy trying to see everything as a whole. If they'd only slow down and appreciate the little things, they'd find so much more joy around them."

Even though she'd had a rough past couple of years, she adopted that motto. It didn't matter who you were, life would throw something in your path that caused you to trip. The only way to survive was to look at things with a different perspective. Only then would you see that maybe what you'd thought were road blocks, were merely stepping stones to get to a better tomorrow.

Ava found so much comfort wrapped in Luke's warm embrace. If she could stay there forever she just might consider it. But this was the real world, not some fantasy that prevented you from getting hurt if you found yourself in too deep. If she wasn't careful she'd find herself so deep that she'd be near the earth's core soon.

"Your take on life is refreshing. I wish I knew what caused you to have such an outlook." Luke lightly kissed the top of her head.

"Not really something I want to talk about." Ava hoped he wouldn't press the issue. She didn't want to ruin this sublime moment with more lies. And that's what they would be. Lies to cover her reason for being in Biloxi. Lies that would hurt Luke if she told them and then he found out the truth. No, she wasn't going down that road.

"I respect that." He pulled away enough to tip her head back and look into her eyes. He stared for what'd seemed like an eternity and surprised her by saying, "You wear contacts?" His face was full of confusion.

Ava pulled away and turned her back. "Yes."

"They look like they change the color of your eyes." She could feel him getting closer behind her.

"They do." Her answers were clipped as she hoped against hope that he'd drop it.

"What color *are* they normally?"

"It's not important."

"I think it is. Seriously, Ava, what color are your eyes?" He grabbed her shoulders and spun her around, looking deep into her currently tawny colored eyes.

Ava let out a resigned sigh, "They're blue."

"Oh. Well, I'd love to see your beautiful blue eyes someday," his voice was as sweet as molasses with its southern drawl and sugary words.

"Maybe someday." She shrugged while letting him tug her into another embrace.

"But what I really want is to kiss you right now." He tilted her head back.

"No one's stopping you." Ava smiled up at this dazzling creature of a man, wondering why on earth someone as incredible as him would want someone like her.

But it didn't really matter. They were in their own hand-crafted bubble and he was once again getting ready to kiss her breathless. When his slightly moist lips pressed against hers, she automatically opened her mouth in invitation for him to take things deeper. Luke could never be close enough. She could never be full of his taste, aroma or sounds. The more she had of him, the more she wanted. It was a blessing and a curse being with him. She'd thought she could work him out of her system like any other bad habit. But she couldn't do it when he was kissing her like he was starving for her. Because the fact of the matter was, she was just as hungry for him as he was for her. It didn't make sense. Nothing truly made sense anymore when she thought about it. It wasn't just Luke, it was her entire life. The way things had been so good lately, how she'd decided that maybe she wouldn't have to run anymore, and how she'd finally found a sense of peace when she woke up each morning. The times she looked over her shoulder were far and few between, she didn't feel as if she needed eyes in the back of her head so much now, and knowing she had at least one confidant in her life—her dearest friend Brandi— made each day more special. Luke was just icing on her bliss-filled cake.

"I'm starting to believe that you think too much," Luke said when he finally released her from the toe-curling kiss. His face held concern, but it was the awe and affection that gave her pause.

"Can't help it." Ava let out a girlish giggle that was so unlike her.

"I guess I need to ask what you're thinking about, don't I?"

For once she didn't want to hide from him. She was willing to tell him exactly what was on her mind. "I'm just…happy." Ava let out a contented sigh.

"Happy is good." Luke wrapped his arm around her shoulder. "Let's head to the house. I need to feed you and hold you for a while."

"Sounds like the perfect evening."

Chapter Eleven

THERE WASN'T A MOMENT of the evening that Ava didn't find herself smiling like a loon. Luke took the time to cook dinner—some sort of chicken and cheese casserole his grandmother used to make—and she found herself enjoying the quiet company while they ate dinner on the back porch. Contentment snuck its way in as she listened to him talk about his time in this house when his grandma was still alive. The summers he spent learning every recipe she'd stashed in her cookbook. The times he and she would get into a flour tossing fight while baking her award-winning peach pie. And the days when she'd gotten sick and he'd stayed with her until she took her last breath. Ava could see the emotions playing out on his face like a slide show and felt her own emotions bubbling to the surface. He'd obviously loved his grandma very much. It was evident in the way he spoke about her. Ava found herself wishing she'd met the woman who'd shaped and molded such a huge chunk of Luke's life.

"Tell me about your family." Luke picked up his glass of iced teas and took a long drink.

"Not much to tell really. My parents owned a small bookstore. Pretty mundane stuff." Ava shrugged. She wasn't lying this time. It wasn't like he could look her parents up and find information on them.

"Do you talk to them much?" Luke prodded.

"No, they were murdered when I was in Cosmetology school." Ava held back the tears that threatened to spill over. She'd never forget the phone call she'd gotten from her aunt on the day her parents were killed. She'd been finishing up with a client while completing a level of training at the hair academy. In just a few seconds her world went from hopeful to bleak.

"I'm sorry." Luke reached over and wrapped her hand in his. The gesture comforted her more than she wanted to admit.

"It was tough the first few years without them. You get used to seeing them and talking to them on the phone. It finally sunk in when I picked up my phone to call my mom one day and realized she *wouldn't* be answering."

"Damn, Ava."

"I spent a couple years being scared that whoever killed them would come after me. The police said it was a random break-in, though. I didn't even go back to their house after that. My aunt wanted me to go and get some of my parents' things, but I couldn't bring myself to set foot in the place where such a horrific thing happened."

"Can't say I blame you. Did they ever catch the person who did it?"

"No, the case went cold about six months afterwards. There were tips called in to the police department, but they couldn't form any solid leads. Plus, with it being Chicago, it was nearly impossible to nail down a suspect." Ava snapped her mouth shut and hoped Luke didn't catch her slipup. She looked away to hide the fear in her eyes at her mistake.

"*Chicago*? I thought you were from California?"

"Oh, did I say Chicago? Sorry, I guess I got mixed up," she laughed hoping he'd drop it.

Luke chuckled but when she looked over at him she could see suspicion lurking in his eyes. *Damn it.* She'd been doing so well hiding her past. Luke had caused her to drop her guard and screw up. "Must be the day I've had. The whole incident with Chase…my brain needs a break." Another excuse; one she hoped he'd believe.

"That's understandable. It's getting late. How about we go lay down?" Luke grabbed his empty glass of tea—the half-melted ice cubes clanking around the bottom like a couple of Yahtzee dice in the game shaker—and reached for her hand. She'd expected him to lead her up the grand staircase to his waiting bed, but he did nothing of the sort. Instead he walked into the newly renovated living room and pulled a folded blanket from the back of an antique armchair. Ava gave him a quizzical look as he turned around with the fluffy item draped over his arm.

"What's that for?" she asked as she reached out and ran her hand over the inviting fabric. The silky texture of the blanket felt like home. Like something she'd want to wrap herself in while sipping a cup of hot cocoa on a cold winter's night.

"It's for lying out under the stars." He smiled as he leaned toward her. His lips pressed a gentle kiss to her forehead and she damn near melted on the spot. "Come on." He tugged her behind him and back through the kitchen.

The night heat hit her as she followed him out the back door and onto the wraparound porch. Memories flooded her as she remembered what they'd done on this very porch just a couple nights ago. Her fingers ached to grab ahold of the railing again and let Luke take her body until she begged for mercy. But it seemed he had other plans for tonight. Ones that involved lying on a blanket, staring up at the sky. It was romantic in a way, but not the scene she'd envisioned when he said he wanted to "lie down" with her.

Fireflies sparkled all around as Luke searched out the perfect spot to spread the blanket. Glancing around, Ava wondered why he'd finally chosen a spot beneath a towering magnolia tree. "Um, it's going to be hard to see the stars under a tree," she said while chewing on the cuticle of her thumbnail.

Luke didn't say anything as he situated the blanket, stretching out the corners so they were perfectly symmetrical. Ava stood by and watched him kick off his shoes, pull off his socks and tug his shirt over his head. "I wasn't planning on watching the sky. I'd rather watch you."

"I'm not interesting enough to watch. You'd probably get more enjoyment from stargazing."

Luke stepped closer and grabbed the bottom of her shirt, gently tugging it upward. "You underestimate your qualities." She lifted her arms so he could remove her top entirely. "I, for one, think you're worth watching." Luke brushed his knuckles along the flat surface of her exposed stomach. "And touching," he reached up and grazed her already erect nipple through her lacy bra, "and tasting."

Ava closed her eyes as he leaned down and ran his warm tongue between her still restrained breasts. "That feels amazing," she breathed.

Luke wasn't in a rush. His every movement was meticulous in a way that had her anticipation mounting with each thud of her heart. His fingers walked over her skin like feathers floating on a slight breeze. His mouth worked to drive her mad with lust and the small sounds that escaped from his throat had her whimpering with enough need she thought she'd faint.

"Let's take care of these." Luke moved one finger inside the waistband of her jeans, stroking her skin ever-so-lightly and made quick work of the button and zipper. He knelt and pushed the denim down her legs, leaving her standing in nothing but her skimpy undergarments. Once her feet were free of the clothing she instinctively crossed her hands over he lingerie-clad breasts. Luke stood and pulled her arms free. "Don't do that," he scolded in a non-threatening tone.

"But we're outside. What if someone sees us?" She looked around anxiously.

"There's no one here but us. And don't ever hide any part of your body from me, Ava. You're breathtaking."

Ava wished he'd stop saying sweet things like that. She didn't want to admit how much they affected her. "Okay," she agreed.

Luke shoved his jeans down his legs, his boxer briefs with them. He didn't say a word as he laid down on the blanket staring up at her. Ava couldn't help but appreciate the way his body looked in the silver moonlight beaming down like a spotlight on his flawless physique. His chest gleamed with a light sheen of sweat from the warm summer night, his rippled abdomen caused her mouth to flood and dry up all in the same breath, and his cock…Ava shivered at the thought that soon she'd have that inside her again.

"Come down here, sweetheart. I need to touch you." Luke extended his arms up in invitation for her to join him. Need was etched across his handsome face as she lowered herself onto the blanket and lay on her side next to him. He shifted to face her, his hand reaching for hers, locking their fingers together, "Tell me what you're thinking," he whispered.

"I don't want to say." She was rather embarrassed at the thoughts flitting through her head like nervous dragonflies.

"Tell me."

Her eyes met his and she *did* tell him, "I'm thinking about how bad I want you inside of me." Her cheeks heated at her own admission.

"Want to know a secret?" Luke took his hand from hers and tucked a loose lock of hair behind her ear.

"Yes."

"I'm thinking I can't wait to be deep inside you, feel you tighten around me and scream my name when you come for me."

"Please." Every time she was with him in this capacity she found herself begging. She didn't normally implore for anything, but Luke brought out something inside her that she normally kept hidden.

"Let me feel you," he said as he trailed his hand down her body. She instinctively rolled to her back and let her legs fall apart as he stroked her over the top of her panties. "Damn, you're so hot here." He put more pressure on her already swollen clit through the thin material. She couldn't control the soft moans that escaped her lips as he pushed her panties to the side and ran his fingers through the wetness gathering at her center. "Do you know how happy it makes me when I feel you like this?" She didn't answer his rhetorical question. Just hearing his excitement over the fact that she was *beyond* turned on made her inner walls clench and more moisture seep onto his fingers. He continued to pet her, but didn't make any moves to enter her with his fingers. "I don't want anything inside you tonight but my cock."

Luke rolled to his back and pulled Ava on top of him. She sat astride his body and the thick length of his erection sat nestled against her waiting warmth. "Let me take these off." She moved to stand and he tugged her back down.

"Leave them on." Luke once more pushed the lace to the side. "I want you to ride me, Sweetheart." His hand wrapped around his shaft and stroked a few times before he gave her the go ahead. Ava reached out, took him in her hand and stroked, feeling his silky skin glide through her palm.

She lifted her body up, aligned herself with the swollen head and slowly began to sink down on him. Just as he entered her, Luke grabbed her hips and halted her motions. "Stop." He sounded like he was fighting himself.

Ava's heart skipped a beat as she knelt looking down at him. "I'm sorry." She didn't know what she was apologizing for, but by the look on Luke's face, he was apprehensive about something. Did he see someone on the property near them? Did he all of a sudden decide he didn't want to do this with her? Every insecurity danced in her head like a ballet of insanity.

"Damn it. I forgot the condom," Luke sighed.

"We can…I mean…" She wanted to tell him that she trusted him. But the words wouldn't come out.

"Ava, I don't want you to think I'm making you do something you don't want to." He looked up at her with what she thought was affection.

"You're not pressuring me. I'm safe and I've been on the shot for six years."

"I'm clean, too."

She leaned down. "I want to feel you, *all* of you. Nothing between us," she whispered seductively in his ear. "I want to feel you come deep inside me." She wasn't embarrassed to tell him that. It wasn't that she was experienced in the matter; if Luke agreed to it, he would be the first man who'd ever done that with her.

"Fuck." He reached down and began to stroke his shaft again. "Tell me that again."

Ava became brazen all of a sudden. She didn't know what came over her as she reached down, yanked her panties to the side and took Luke's erection from his hand. Lowering herself, she began to rub the head of his cock through the gathering wetness between her thighs. "I want to ride you, Luke. I want to feel your cock as it slides in and out of my pussy. I want to feel you as you fill me with cum."

"Jesus. You'd better stop talking like that or I won't make it inside of you," Luke groaned.

Ava wasn't waiting any longer; she'd had enough teasing and felt an extreme urgency to get to the good part. She brushed his cock a few more times across her more than ready center and lined him up with her waiting entrance. Her eyes flickered shut as she sank down—inch by delectable inch—until he was fully seated inside her. The feel of his intimate flesh in contact with hers had her so close to the edge of bliss already. Taking a few calming breaths she finally opened her eyes to see Luke was struggling, too.

"Better than I could've ever imagined," he said, grasping her hips and holding her to him. His grip seared her flesh as he dug his fingertips into her skin as if he were holding on for dear life in a raging storm.

Ava slid her hands down and placed them on top of his; his fingers trembling just as hers were. How empowering was it to know a man like Luke was hanging onto his control by a hair? In her mind, it was the most powerful feeling she'd ever known so she took advantage of it. Bracing her hands steadier on his, Ava began to rock back and forth, feeling the sublime friction of his skin on hers. With each motion the sensations amplified and their breathing echoed in the tepid night air. Luke dug his fingers deeper into her flesh and pumped his hips upward, finding a brand new spot that caused Ava to arch her spine and throw her head backwards. Her hair tumbled over her shoulders and tickled her skin each time she swayed back and forth over his erection.

"You're what fantasies are made of," Luke's voice was strained; something she understood very well. If she'd even tried speaking right now, she'd come across sounding like one of the tree frogs chirping above them. "I want to see you come like this. Can you come for me?"

Ava could only straighten her neck and nod. "Good. Ride my cock; come all over me."

She began to ride him faster, her movements becoming uneven. Luke held tighter, keeping her steady. "So close," she whispered, hoping he would hear her.

"That's it. Do it. Come, sweetheart," he crooned until she rocked enough that the beginning flutters of her release overtook her.

Once more her head lulled back and cries of unadulterated pleasure spilled from her lips. Luke helped her keep her rhythm as the sounds of their coupling filled the expanse of space around them. She heard his breathing change as her pussy pulsed around him. The thought of him emptying himself inside her with no barrier heightened the sensations and she knew another orgasm was on the horizon.

"Tell me now if you don't want me to come in that sweet little body of yours, Ava," he grunted.

"Come inside me," she cried.

"One last chance." He was holding back to make sure she was okay with what they were doing.

"Fucking come inside me!" Ava's voice was demanding and she wasn't going to apologize for it.

"Fuck, yeah. I'm gonna fill that tight little pussy up. You ready?" Ava frantically nodded as her second orgasm ripped through her. Luke shouted as his release tore through him while Ava let out a keening wail. If someone heard them, they'd think they were in some sort of pain. On the contrary. They were in the throes of the most heavenly moment either of them had ever felt. As Luke's hips thrust upward, Ava could feel the warmth of him spilling into her depths. It was the most intimate she'd ever felt with anyone; it both scared and exhilarated her. She wondered if Luke had ever done that with anyone else.

After she was spent she collapsed forward onto Luke's chest. His ribcage moved her up and down as he worked to get normalize his breathing. He stroked her sweat-dotted back as she lay there, not knowing what to say. The only sounds besides their breaths were the chirping of crickets and the noisy tree frog above them. She'd expected Luke to say something other than, "I've never done that before." He sounded hesitant to share his revelation.

Ava lifted up and tucked her hair behind her ears. She reached out and stroked his jaw, the stubble from his five o'clock shadow pricking her palm. "I haven't either," she admitted.

"Damn, you're so amazing." He pulled her back down and sealed his lips to hers. It was as if he were trying to tell her something in his kiss that he couldn't relay with words alone. She didn't question it, only soaked in the sensations like a sponge.

This thing between them wasn't long-term and she was fully aware of that fact. There was nothing written in stone that they'd even be together next week. So Ava reveled in being with him tonight. She would take what she could get because no promises were made. Promises were something she wasn't even sure she wanted. Most of the time they only led to heartbreak and pain. She'd had enough pain to last her a lifetime. If anything, she'd keep her heart locked away for safe-keeping and pretend this thing between her and Luke was still only a passing fancy.

Chapter Twelve

AFTER THEIR VORACIOUS session of what Luke could only describe as the best sex of his life, he held Ava against his chest and listened to her soft breathing. He shouldn't have taken things this far. He should've backed off after the fight they'd had the night before and threw in the towel. But knowing he still had a job to do weighed heavy on his mind. Not to mention, Matthews showing up was a reminder that this was all going to end eventually. The best bet was to keep up this charade and walk away when everything was said and done. Ava understood; she'd said so when they spoke about this thing between them. So Luke wasn't sure why he was kicking his own ass over everything.

"Don't fall asleep." Luke chuckled as he stroked Ava's naked back.

"But you're so comfy." she yawned and tried to lift up.

"I didn't say you had to move." Luke pulled her back down, her lace-clad breasts pressing against his chest.

It was strange how perfectly she fit next to him. Where he was hard muscle and masculine, she was soft and lush, and oh so feminine. She held herself with a tough exterior but Luke could see she was like a marshmallow on the inside. He wasn't like that. Emotions for him were something of myth. When you showed people your emotions, they used them against you. They'd chew you up and spit you out like you were just another disposable scrap of garbage in this shit-laden world.

"Are we staying out here all night?" Ava asked as she lifted her head. Even in the silver moon's glow she looked like an ethereal creature—a mirage. Maybe this *wasn't* reality. He might wake up tomorrow and find there really was no Ava. That thought caused his heartrate to increase and anger to simmer beneath the surface.

"Only if you want to."

"I think I need a shower." She rolled her body off his and began to stand. "Are you coming in?" Her petite hand extended down in offering to him.

"Yeah." He stood as well in all his nude glory. They began to pick up their discarded clothing, but a sound compelled him to stop and listen closer. "Ava, come here. *Now*." He suddenly felt the urge to protect her. They weren't alone; that much he could gather.

"What's wrong?" Her face showed signs of concern but he didn't want to spook her. Even though she was worried, she did what he said and drew closer to him. Luke didn't say anything as he continued to take in the sounds around them. "Luke, what's happening?" she whispered.

"I need you to be quiet." The tiny hairs on the back of his neck stood to attention, alerting him that something was off. He quickly and quietly shrugged on his jeans while listening.

"Hey, man, it's just me." Luke's shoulders relaxed at the sound of Cole's voice. The fucker picked the most inopportune time to stop by for a chat. "Did I interrupt something?" The other man approached and Luke could finally make out his form in the dim outdoor lighting.

Luke pushed Ava behind him to shield her mostly naked body from the other man. "Don't come any closer," he called. He then reached down and grabbed Ava's clothing, handing them to her. "Get dressed," his voice came out clipped as he shoved the garments into her hands. He used his body to buffer her while she hurriedly pulled on her pants and shirt so the other man didn't have the chance to lay his eyes on her.

When she was fully clothed, Ava looked up at him. "Who is that?" She nervously tucked her hair behind her ears and began to chew on her thumb again.

Luke grabbed her hand and removed her finger from her mouth then kissed her forehead in a reassuring gesture. "Just a friend. No need to worry."

"Just a friend?" Cole came closer and laughed. "I'd say I'm a little more than that, wouldn't you agree, Daughtry?"

Luke faced him and gave him the best "shut-the-fuckup" glare he could manage. He needed to think of something to say so Ava wouldn't be suspicious of him or Cole. "He's my cousin," Luke blurted out with confidence.

"That's right, cousins." The other man backed up his story, for which he was grateful.

Ava—being the friendly person she was—stepped around Luke and approached the other man with her hand extended. "I'm Ava, Luke's…friend."

Cole grasped her hand and gave it a quick shake. "Cole Matthews," he introduced himself as well.

"Nice to meet you, Cole. Luke didn't tell me he had family still around." Ava looked back to Luke.

"I'm not from around here. Just passing through while on a job."

"Oh? What sort of work are you in?" Luke admired Ava's conversation abilities but he wanted this particular one to end.

"I'm in the cleanup business. When people make big messes, I'm contracted to come in and clean them up." Luke shook his head at Cole's response. Funny thing was he wasn't too far off the mark with his answer.

"So like big corporations?" *Damn* she kept on prodding for answers. Luke felt unease settle in his gut.

"Pretty much." Good, Cole kept up the ruse. "Would you mind if I steal Luke for a bit? I have a business proposition he might be interested in."

"Yeah, sure. I'm going to go take a shower." Luke watched as Ava bent over to pick up her shoes. He also took in the fact that Cole eyes were centered right on her ass. That right there made him want to walk over and kick his *'cousin'* in the dick. Ava of course was oblivious to it all.

"Towels are in the linen closet in the bathroom. Feel free to use my stuff." Just to show Cole he wasn't playing around, Luke pulled her in for a tight hug before she headed up to the house. When she was inside and the door shut behind her, Luke switched to business mode. "Let's go somewhere we can talk. I don't want to chance her coming out and overhearing us." He yanked on his socks and shoes.

Luke decided the gazebo was the best option for a night chat. It was far enough away from the house, but close enough he could see if Ava was coming back outside. He grabbed one of the wrought iron patio chairs, flipped it around and sat with his chest to the back of the chair.

Cole did the same as he looked over his shoulder to make sure they were alone.

"What the fuck are you doing here tonight?" Luke didn't feel like beating around the bush. He wanted to know why the hell Cole wasn't staying away like he was supposed to.

"Checking up on you. Have they called you recently?"

"Not for a few days." Luke ran a hand through his sweat-soaked hair. "I told you I'd handle this, didn't I?"

"Yeah, you did. But I ran into an issue. The hotels in the area are booked due to some festival. I need a place to stay while I'm here."

"Hell, no. You can't stay here." Luke shook his head.

"You know damn well they want me to stay close."

"I don't give a flying fuck what they want. The answer is no." Luke stood his ground.

"Fine. Guess I'll report back about you two then." Cole shrugged and pinned Luke with a stare.

"You've got be kidding me. You're gonna pull some grade school tattle-tale shit because I won't let you stay here?" A laugh blurted out before he could control it.

"You know damn well you're breaking the rules, Daughtry. They will come down on you so fucking hard you won't even remember your name."

"What the hell do you expect me to do?"

"Stop sticking your dick in her and do your fucking job." Cole's voice rose a bit more.

"I don't know if I can do this job anymore," Luke sighed in resignation.

"You don't have a choice. You walk away now this whole thing blows up bigger than shit. You know it and I know it. They aren't messing around this time."

"Fuck."

"I just have one question for you and I want total disclosure."

"Yeah?" Luke didn't know what Cole wanted to ask but he braced himself for the worst case scenario.

"Are you in love with her?"

"Fuck no!" he answered instantly. "Jesus, I don't do that shit. Love is a word used by delusional people to explain their raging hormones."

"Okay. I just wanted to know."

"I'm trying to stay close to her. If that means I have to fuck her to complete this job, then so be it."

"Not really a hardship, I'd imagine. That girl is something else." Cole whistled.

"I suggest you back the hell off before I come over there and knock your pearly whites down your throat," Luke warned.

Cole threw his hands up in a sign of surrender. "Hey, man, I get it. You're marking your territory. I promise to stay out of your way as much as possible. Which room do you want me in?" Cole stood and stretched his back, the sound of his spine realigning echoed in the gazebo.

Luke didn't respond; he only began the short walk to the house. Damn it, this was a complication he didn't need right now. But Cole was right, if they found out what he'd been doing with Ava, this would turn from a controlled situation to complete chaos in no time. Now he had to deal with keeping track of her *and* Cole. What a way to end what *had been* shaping up to be a fun-filled night with Ava in his bed.

"Hey, I was beginning to think you weren't coming back in," Ava said to Luke as he came into his bedroom and sat down on the end of the antique bed. The frame creaked with the weight of his body.

"Cole's staying here while he's in town." Ava noticed an irritated quality to his voice.

"Okay. I can leave in the morning." She didn't want to leave, but if he wanted her to go while his cousin was in town, far be it from her to stand in the way of family time.

"You're not going anywhere. I wanted to warn you, that's all." Luke stood from the bed where he'd been removing his shoes and disappeared into the in-suite bathroom.

She sat there trying to come up with reasons why he'd 'warn' her about Cole staying. The only thing she could come up with was the obvious so she stood from her comfy spot and found him brushing his teeth at the sink. "Is he some kind of ladies' man? If so, don't worry, I don't have any interest in him." She wanted to make sure Luke knew she wouldn't be jumping on the Cole wagon anytime soon.

Luke spit out the toothpaste in his mouth and rinsed with a handful of water. He dried his face with the towel from the rack nearby and turned to her, "I didn't mean you would want to jump his bones, Ava." He added a small laugh.

"Then why would you warn me?" She went back into the bedroom and sat in the center of his large bed.

"He's nosy. Asks a lot of questions. Didn't figure you'd want to be caught with your pants down, so-to-speak."

"Thank you for looking out for me but there's only one person here who I want to have my pants down around." She punctuated her comment with a sweet smile hoping he got the hint. It wasn't a usual thing for her to be so hungry for someone, especially when she'd had a huge helping of him not even an hour ago on the lawn. Heck, even the thought of what they'd done sent shivers racking her body.

Luke stripped down to his underwear and climbed on the bed in front of her. For a few brief moments all he did was stare at her. He didn't make a move to touch her and she wondered if something was wrong. "Everything okay?" She pulled her hand up to chew on her nail.

Luke reached forward, stopping her before she had a chance to bite down on her own finger. "I just want to look at you for a minute."

"Ah, maybe you'll have to pick me out of a lineup one day and you're committing me to memory just in case?" She certainly hoped that wasn't true.

"No, I can't get over how damn beautiful you are." Every word he spoke had such sincerity behind it. It wasn't forced and it didn't feel like he was slathering on a thick layer of bullshit just to appease her. He was being one hundred percent real.

"You're not so bad yourself." She chuckled, reaching out to cup his stubble-laden cheek in her soft palm.

His head tilted to the side molding into her hand like it was meant to be there. Warm breaths tickled her wrist as he did nothing but look directly into her eyes. What he was seeing, she'd never know. "Come here." He reached out and pulled her into his lap. Her legs stretched out beside him, her front connecting with his. "Are you okay?" His question threw her.

"What do you mean?"

"I mean are you okay with what happened…what we did earlier?" This side of Luke was an enigma. The moments when he showed insecurity and vulnerability were more frightening than the ones when he showed his more dominant side. But she was beginning to develop feelings for both sides of the man underneath her.

"Of course I am. It was…perfect." She sighed wistfully as she thought back to the intimate moments they'd shared. She honestly couldn't have thought of a more perfect interlude.

"It was pretty damn special."

"It was," she echoed him.

"You're probably tired. Let's get some sleep, okay?" She'd be lying if she said she wasn't disappointed a bit by his suggestion of sleep, but she was tuckered out from the eventful day she'd had.

"Sleep sounds wonderful." Ava climbed off his lap and went for the door.

"Where the hell are you going?" Luke jumped up and met her.

"Downstairs. The couch is down there." Pointing to the door she looked over to Luke who had a look of pure confusion on his face.

"You're not sleeping on the couch."

"I'm not? I thought you'd want me to sleep there." She didn't know if he wanted her in his bed tonight, he'd never said as much.

"Hell, no. I want you in my bed so I can hold you."

"Okay." Ava smiled and went back to the bed. She threw back the blankets and slid herself in. Luke walked over and stood beside the other side but didn't make a move to climb in with her. "Oh, am I on your side?"

"No. But you're wearing way too many clothes to be sleeping in my bed." He shoved his underwear down his legs and slid under the covers with her.

"Didn't know this bed had a dress code," she said while lifting her t-shirt over her head leaving her breasts exposed.

"It does. The dress code is naked so I can touch you if I wake up in the middle of the night." He reached over and grazed the back of his knuckles across her sensitive nipple.

Ava sucked in a breath at the contact and closed her eyes. "Luke," she breathed.

"These need to go, too." He pulled on the waistband of her sleep shorts. It didn't take her long to shed those as well and drop them off the side of the bed to join her shirt. "Dress code accomplished." He grinned.

There was only one lamp in the room and it sat on the nightstand on Luke's side of the bed. With a light click it was turned off and the room was bathed in a slight glow from the moonlight peeking in through the slit in the curtains. Ava startled when she felt Luke's hand graze her breast once more. "I thought we were sleeping?" she questioned as she held back the moan that wanted to escape.

"We are." His hand now cupped her tender swell and squeezed slightly.

"This doesn't feel like sleeping," she joked.

"What does it feel like?" His voice was low and gravelly, a tone that told her he was turned on.

"It feels like you're touching me." He stopped and pulled away. "No, don't stop." Her words came out strangled. Soon his hand was back but this time it trailed a path down her stomach and drew lazy circles right above her aching sex. "Touch me, please," she whispered in the dark.

"Where?"

"Lower." He dipped one finger lower and continued his circles around the wet flesh of her swollen clit. Her back bowed as he teased and tormented her with his finger and soft pants fell from her lips as she tried to keep herself in check. But she needed more. He must've sensed her building frustration because he scooted closer, grabbed one of her thighs and pulled it from the other. "Spread your other leg wide for me." She immediately did as he instructed and he rewarded her by sliding his hand over her folds. "Do you have any idea how hard it makes me knowing you're all spread out, waiting for me?"

"No," she answered honestly. She'd never been desired to the extent that he was claiming. It was causing excitement and nervousness to rain down on her like a torrential downpour.

"Feel that?" he grabbed her hand and wrapped it around his hard as steel cock. "You do that to me," he growled.

Ava reached down and pressed his hand to her center. "You do that to me." Her head rolled toward him so she could see his face in the moonlit room. "I want you." She'd grown past the point of being shy about her desires. Luke elicited some sort of sex crazed maniac in her and she wasn't about to apologize for it.

Luke took no time at all in throwing back the sheet that concealed their bodies and settling himself above her. She lay there with senses that were hyper-alert, every single nerve ending firing on all eight cylinders. His heavier weight settled next to her as he used his hips to mock thrust against her ready and waiting flesh. She'd tried to control her reactions to him but it was a losing battle equivalent to the Battle of Troy. Luke was the one sealed in the Trojan horse, waiting to destroy her senses with the wicked things he did to her body.

"I want to take this slow, sweetheart," he said as he leaned his head to hers and brushed his warm lips to hers. "I want to savor this body." He ran his palm down her side, tickling slightly as he went.

Ava began to squirm with need. She'd thought of herself as a patient person. After all, patience was a virtue.

That thought made her giggle to herself. *From the position I'm currently in, it doesn't seem like I have many virtues left.*

"Hey," Luke pulled her attention back to his rugged face. "Stop swimming around in that head of yours. Just feel." He grabbed his hard length and placed it at her entrance. With a slight push of his hips he entered her only about halfway but she needed so much more. The desire to be filled completely by him clawed at her like a catnip crazed feline, accosting its favorite scratching post. What seemed like hours ticked by as he used her agony to torture her by only allowing her to have him bit by bit. Ava's hands reached down to grab the firm muscles on his ass and pull her to him. "Ava," his voice held a hint of warning, "Stop forcing this. I want to make slow sweet love to you. Can you handle that?" his tone softened.

"Yes," Ava whispered while her eyes filled with unshed tears. She didn't want them to spill onto her cheeks and show Luke how she felt. This whole thing between them wasn't about emotions; it was just two people being together in an intimate capacity. She had no business trying to sort through the myriad of feelings swamping her.

Just as she relaxed a fraction more, Luke took the opportunity to slide the rest of the way into her warm waiting body. Her breath caught at feeling all of him within her. Sex never was an emotional thing for Ava. She didn't care one way or another about it. And towards the end of her relationship with her previous boyfriend, it became evident that sex was just another way for him to control her. There was no way in hell she was letting that happen again. Focusing on just the physical feeling was what she'd intended to do, and was succeeding currently.

"Not sure I'll ever tire of this," Luke punctuated his words with deliberate, languid strokes in and out of her depths. His unhurried pace seemed to chip at her resolve even more as she felt the sensations building in her heated core. How Luke was able to take her from freezing cold to boiling in a matter of strokes was beyond her. But she welcomed it with open arms. "Tell me what you need," he began to grind his pelvis against her clit each time he immersed himself him her wet heat.

Ava didn't want to tell him that what she really needed was something he couldn't give her. Safety, a future…no,

Luke couldn't guarantee any of those things. They were wants that she'd stuck in a small box in the back of her mind. The box was locked up tight with zero hope of breaking the code. The day she fled from her old life in Chicago was the day everything she'd ever hoped for and dreamed of went missing in action.

"Ava, focus on me. On this." Luke drew her attention back to what he was doing to her body. He continued his ministrations—taking her further to the peak she wanted to dive off of.

Their heavy breaths dusted around them like a cloud that couldn't be waved away. Their combined moans called to her and with each second she felt her body come alive even more. The way Luke slid his bare flesh in and out of her was something to behold. God, she wanted this tender moment to last a lifetime.

"Sweetheart, I'm close," Luke sounded as if he were gritting his teeth. She wasn't quite there yet though.

"Do it for me, please," she pleaded.

"Not unless you go with me." His control was slipping; she knew by the tensing of his muscles.

"No. I want to see you when you come."

"Jesus." He rose up enough to prop himself on his elbows, his face only inches from hers. "Tell me to do it, Ava."

She lifted her hands and stroked the sides of his stubble covered cheeks. "Come for me, Luke." Her voice was tender and caring. He didn't reply, only locked gazes with her and sped up his movements slightly. If she wasn't paying such close attention to how his body felt, she would've missed it. Still he held back for some reason. Why? She wasn't sure. But Ava wanted him to use her body for his pleasure only. Maybe it was to prove to herself that he was just like all other men, selfish. Or maybe she wanted to watch the emotions play across his face when he tipped over the edge. She didn't have to wait too long to experience the latter either. With a final thrust of his hips, a low growl that escaped his throat and his head tossed back, Ava saw everything she wanted to as Luke poured himself inside her body.

Once he was spent, he slowly rolled from atop her body and lay next to her. She managed to roll her body over so she was looking at his more than handsome face.

"Why did you let me do that?" He brushed a few hairs from her forehead.

"I wanted to see you." Luke pushed at her shoulder until she was on her back once more. "What are you doing?" She watched as he pressed against her side and began to lift her leg over his thigh.

"I'm not letting you go to sleep when you're aching like you are now." His hand slid down her body and began to toy with the sensitive flesh between her legs. "Move your other leg out a bit so I can touch you."

"You don't have to do that." She was serious. As much as she loved the thought of him taking the time to pleasure her, she felt it was unnecessary.

"But I *want* to do it." He didn't waste any time plunging two of his rough digits into her delicate folds. He pulled them out and rubbed moisture over her sensitive clit.

"Mmmmm," she whimpered arching her back.

His fingers traveled back inside and he began to fuck her with his hand. "Do you have any idea how sexy it is to know my cum is inside you right now?"

"Oh, God," Ava groaned. Damn she loved the foul things that came out of his mouth.

"That I'm spreading it around with my fingers and soon you'll come all over my hand?"

"Luke, I need…" she struggled for the words.

"Relax. I know what you need." The fucking motion of his hand picked up speed and his breathing did as well. "I want you to let go for me, sweetheart. I want you to give me everything you have. Can you do that?"

"Yes," she whined as her release teetered on the edge.

"Let me have it, give me what I want." Luke's rough voice spurred her orgasm into hyper-speed as she felt her pussy begin to flutter around his fingers. "*More*, I want more, Ava."

Soon she was giving him all she had as the quakes spread over her body and her sex pulsed in steady waves around his hand. He heightened the sensations by giving her more of what she wanted. Screams tore from her lips as her eyes unfocused. All she could make out was the sounds of Luke urging her on. When her body decided it had no more to give, she went lax in what felt like a heap of bones on the bed beside him.

"Now that," he kissed her softly on the lips, "was fucking beautiful." Luke rained down small kisses on her neck, both breasts and even her bare stomach as she lay there trying to recover. Her eyes fluttered shut and the last thing she remembered before sleep overtook her was Luke saying, "Sweet dreams, my gorgeous girl."

Chapter Thirteen

SOMETHING STARTLED AVA awake during the middle of the night. She wasn't a very sound sleeper anyway, but the noise she'd heard made her sit straight up in bed. Her heart beat rapidly in her heaving chest as she sat there listening again. *Thump.* The noise was back. *Thump.* There it was again. Five times she counted the strange sound and finally she decided to do some investigating. Glancing over at a slumbering Luke, she decided not to wake him. She'd go downstairs and try to find the source of the thumping sound on her own. Quietly sneaking out of the bed and pulling on her t-shirt and shorts, Ava walked to the door and pulled it open. Her gaze kept going back to the amazing man lying amongst the rumpled sheets—only his torso covered with the white fabric. Her body warmed instantly as she took in his frame with the incandescent glow of the silver moonlight. No, she wasn't going to wake him. She could handle this on her own. So she opened the door—hoping Luke wouldn't wake from the sound of the antiquated hinges grating on each other—and stepped out into the darkened hallway. Her bare feet didn't make a sound as she traveled over the smooth hardwood and found herself at the top of her favorite thing in Luke's home…the grand staircase.

Grabbing the unfinished railing Ava let her hand glide over the planate surface as she took each step one by one to the lowest level. Once her feet left the last step and were secure on the floor below, she stood stock still and craned her neck to listen. *Thump*. Whatever it was sounded like it came from the kitchen. She soundlessly padded to the source and stood in the doorway, glancing around in a room that, like the rest of the house, was illuminated only by moonlight. The *thumping* noise sounded again by the doorway that led outside. Ava tip-toed over to it and looked down to where the wood of the door met the floor. Laying there gasping for air was a bird. Its wings flopped around like it was trying it's best to escape its confines but it wasn't getting very far. Having loved animals, Ava picked the creature up and held it out in the rays of moonlight that streamed through the glass window in the door. The poor thing was still gasping for air as she held it gently and looked it over. It wasn't going to make it. After she'd come to that reality she unlocked and opened the back door to take it outside. At least it would be free while it took its last breath. Just as she went to step outside, Ava heard the *thud* of footsteps coming up the basement steps. *Shit.* She quickly ducked behind the door. Clearly it wasn't Luke; he was still upstairs sleeping soundly. So it had to be Cole. Why she was hiding she didn't know. But her circle of trust didn't extend very far and she wasn't about to be alone with someone she'd met only hours earlier.

The poor bird flopped around in her palms while she stood hidden and soon it took a breath and went still. She listened as the footsteps came closer to the door and could hear Cole talking on his phone.

"Yeah, I'm here. Don't worry; I've got my eye on things." Cole let out a laugh. "Not sure how deep he's in but the fucker is going to be shocked, that's for sure." There was silence before the door opened and then, "Nah, I'll have it all tied up soon. You know I'm the best at making sure loose ends don't unravel too far."

Ava pretty much stopped listening after that part. What was he talking about? Was it something to do with his job? Or was he discussing Luke? So many scenarios played through her head. Ava wasn't a trusting person—not after the shit she went through a little over two years ago—but for some reason she trusted Luke. If he *was* in trouble, she'd want him to know.

The door swung open so violently Ava didn't have time to stop it. She felt the heavy wood batter her body and let out a yelp.

"What the fuck?" Cole's voice sounded on the other side. He pulled the door shut and Ava stood there holding her head where it'd smacked her. "What the hell are you doing back there?" he bit out, his expression was full of suspicion. She tried to focus her eyes but everything looked blurry. "Is that a dead bird?" She'd forgotten all about the deceased animal in her free hand.

"What the hell is going on down here?" Ava heard Luke's voice.

"I don't know, man. I flung open the door and she was hiding behind it," Cole explained.

"Ava, sweetheart, look at me," Luke said softly, lifting her gaze to his. "What the heck is that? Jesus, a dead bird? Do I even want to know why you're holding a dead bird?"

"It was trapped," Ava tried to explain.

"Let me have that thing." Luke wrenched the animal from her hands and flung it out the back door. He looked at her face which held a bit of sadness. "Oh, no. We are not having a fucking funeral or a candlelight vigil for a *bird*."

Ava rubbed her head and winced. "I didn't say I wanted a funeral for it. But it deserved better than to be tossed out the door like that."

Cole snickered beside her. "Look, I'm heading back to bed. You might want to put some ice on that bump." He left the room and Ava was standing there with a worried Luke.

"Here." he pulled out a chair from the small kitchen table. "Sit down. I'll make an ice pack." Sounds of rattling ice trays and a bag being opened was all she could hear while Luke worked to make a pack to help her head. When he was done he pulled up a chair next to her and held the bag to her injury.

"Thanks," she groaned.

"What were you doing down here anyway?" he asked.

"I heard a noise. I think that bird got in here somehow and was injured. I didn't mean to wake you."

"It's fine."

Ava waited for a bit before bringing up the one-sided conversation she'd overheard Cole having. "Luke, I heard Cole on the phone. I think you're in trouble," she whispered, not wanting the other man to hear her if he was within earshot.

"What makes you think that?" Luke sat back and crossed his arms over his bare chest. Of course her girl parts had to come to life right now. Ugh. But she pushed those feelings aside and told him what she'd heard. Luke didn't interrupt or try to interject anything until she was finished. "It's nothing. He has all kinds of problems with his work. Probably some dickhead got out of line again," Luke defended.

Ava trusted him so why would she question what he was saying. He knew his cousin better than anyone, she supposed. "Okay. I just wanted to make sure." She felt the ice melting in the bag and pulled it away from her head. "I think I'm going back to bed. I'm tired and of course have a brain ache now." Luke took the pack from her and tossed it into the kitchen sink.

"I'll be up in a bit."

Disappointment swamped her knowing he wasn't coming back to bed with her right away, but maybe he had something he needed to do. So she traipsed through the house, up the staircase and back to Luke's bedroom. Slipping under the sheets she lay back and let her eyes drift shut while catching Luke's scent in the bed. Everything smelled like him. It was one of the most heavenly aromas she'd ever inhaled. Damn, she sounded like a creepy stalker now.

"Fuck," Luke bit out after he heard Ava close his bedroom door. He sat at the table and leaned forward, propping his elbows on the antique wood.

"Problems?" Cole walked in and took a seat across from him.

"She heard you talking, you know. I told you to be careful. What about that didn't you understand?" Luke was pissed. He'd laid the ground rules for the other man but he didn't seem to give a damn.

"How the hell was I to know she'd be up at three a.m. trying to save a damn bird?" Cole sat there with nonchalance all over his face.

"What were you doing downstairs?"

"Making some adjustments." He stood. "Want to see?" He opened the basement door and motioned to the bottom.

Luke stood and followed him. "Why the hell not."

The men descended the steps into the damp basement. Cole flipped on the overhead light and bathed Luke's worktable with illumination. He then threw back the cloth covering that hid the items underneath.

Cole picked up the high powered rifle and aimed it at a far wall. "Your wind-gauge was fucked up. I took it apart and readjusted it. See for yourself. It should turn a lot better now." Cole handed him the gun.

Luke sat the firearm on the table, pulled the bipod into position and leaned down, putting his face to the cheek piece. He peered out the scope and twisted the wind-gauge. "Yeah, you're right. It needed that." Luke laid the piece of equipment back on the table.

"Where's your other stuff stashed?" Cole asked as he rounded the table. "I looked but didn't see anything but this one."

Luke let out a laugh. "Sorry, buddy, that's for me to know and you to wonder about. Anyway, I'm beat, I'm gonna head back upstairs. Do yourself a favor and stay out of my shit," he said over his shoulder.

"You wound me, man," Cole laughed.

Luke had known Cole for about ten years, but that didn't mean he appreciated him digging around in his stuff. One rule Luke had was the one where no one was allowed to touch his tools *unless* it was him. Those were the tools of the trade and Cole knew better than to put his meat hooks all over them. Luke switched off the small light and made his way back to the kitchen. He went over to the sink, bracing his hands on the edge and peered outside. Letting out a puff of air he grinned and shook his head while thinking about Ava and the dead bird. *Silly woman.* He chuckled out loud at the absurdity of her feeling bad about the dead creature.

Chapter Fourteen

THE NEXT MORNING AVA woke to the sound of her phone ringing so loud it could've woken all of Mississippi. She rolled over and snatched it off the nightstand. *Brandi*. Before she answered it she chanced a look behind her; nope, no Luke. He must've gotten up early to go for a run.

"Good morning," Ava greeted her friend.

"I thought you were supposed to call me last night?"

"Damn. I must've forgotten. I'm sorry."

"Yeah, well it's good to know you weren't hacked into bite-sized chunks. How are things going?"

She heard the sound of Brandi taking a sip of something. Probably coffee which was something Ava had a hankering for, *big* time.

"I'm still in one piece. Although Luke's cousin showed up last night. He's quite strange."

"Oooh, is he hot?"

"Would you stop it? I didn't realize you were so hard up."

"Are you kidding? I could rub against every fence post between here and Texas and it still wouldn't relieve this damn tension," Brandi complained.

"And I'll never look at a fence post the same way. Listen, I'll call you back later. I want to grab some coffee and wake up more."

"Alright. But if I don't hear from you, my ass is driving out there with guns-a-blazing."

"Deal. Bye." Ava hung up and tossed her phone back on the nightstand. She swung her feet over the side of the bed and quickly made her way downstairs.

Searching the living room and kitchen she didn't see any sign of Luke or Cole. She shrugged and grabbed a mug down from the cabinet. As the coffee poured into her cup she happened to look out the window above the sink and saw Luke with a shovel. He tossed it down by a tree and bent down to lower something into the hole. *What if he's really a serial killer and hiding bodies out there?* Ava thought. But that was insane; Luke wasn't a killer. He was just a sweet southern guy who she'd grown extremely close to in a short period of time. Besides, the hole wasn't big enough to hide an entire body. Maybe a hand or foot, but not the whole thing. Ava laughed at the thought.

As she filled her cup and took it to the table to enjoy, Luke walked in, brushing soil from the front of his jeans. "Damn it's a hot one out there," he commented.

"It's Mississippi. Comes with the territory." Ava chuckled.

"Smartass." He bent down to kiss the top of her head.

"So, what were you putting in that hole? You suddenly decide to have a green thumb?" Ava laughed again.

"Nope. I was burying a body." Ava's head shot up and goosebumps covered her body. "Relax, it wasn't a human body."

"Oh. Then what was it?"

"Your dead bird." Luke shrugged like it wasn't a big deal, but it was a *huge* deal to her. He'd taken the time to dig a hole and make a grave for the unfortunate winged creature.

Ava laid her hand on his arm. "Luke, that was so sweet. Thank you." She leaned over and pressed a soft kiss to his warm cheek.

"It was nothing."

"*You* may think it was nothing but *I* happen to think it was kind and considerate." She took her empty mug to the sink and leaned her butt against it. "What are we doing today? You don't want me to open my shop, so what sort of things do you have to keep me busy?"

"I could think of several ways to keep you busy. Most of them would involve screaming orgasms," he teased.

"Ugh, get a fucking room," Cole said as he strode in. Ava's face flamed as he pinned her with a heated stare. Damn she didn't like him. "Hey, man, I've gotta head over to Gulfport for the day. I'll be back later." Cole slapped Luke on the back and then left.

"What's he doing in Gulfport?" Ava asked.

"No clue." Luke stood and headed through the house. "I'm gonna take a shower. Get dressed."

"Where're we going?"

"Town. Grocery shopping to be exact. Figured you could help me."

"Okay," she called as he took the steps two at a time.

How strange that Luke wanted her to do another domestic thing with him. He still didn't seem like the kind of guy to love any sort of domestic duties. Oh well. Ava wanted to grab a few things anyway. She tromped up the steps and into his bedroom where the steam from the shower was escaping the bathroom through the open door. Riffling through her bags she pulled out a summer dress that would keep her cool for the day. The heat was about to get to her. Of course she was used to the weather now, but it didn't make her like it. She changed quickly, slid her feet into a comfy pair of flip flops and went back downstairs. She'd just mill around while Luke finished with his shower.

Finding a narrow hallway with a high ceiling, Ava walked down it and ended up at a closed door. Her better judgement told her to turn back but the curious side of her told her to open the door and see what was in there. So she did. She grabbed the antique brass knob, twisted it and pushed the door open. Stale air surrounded her as she stepped into the sparse room. It was a bedroom — half the size of Luke's, with only a bed and a wooden chair sitting close by. Two of the spindles on the chair were missing but that's not what caught her attention. The matte black pistol laying there caused her to take a step back. Cole had taken up residence in this room. But why would he have a gun in here? The hairs on the back of her neck stood to attention as she neared the chair and crouched down to get a better look at the menacing firearm. It still had the serial number intact so that meant it wasn't hot. Well, it *could've* been stolen but a *good* criminal would've filed the number off to keep heat off themselves. She'd seen plenty of that in her old life back in Chicago. She knew the basics of the trade and this gun didn't look like it had 'fallen off the back of a truck'. It looked closer to a police issue weapon. Ava sucked in a sharp breath. Was Cole law enforcement? *Oh shit*. Did he know who she really was? Ava lifted her hand toward the gun and ran a finger over the semi-rough surface. The grooves bit into her finger like shark teeth trying to devour her entire being. Panic began to bubble up in her stomach and bile rose at the thought that Cole might be here to hurt her.

"What are you doing in here?" Luke's voice cut through the haze in her brain.

She couldn't help her reaction as her nerves jumped so hard and landed her on her ass. "I was…" she couldn't even finish her sentence.

"Ava, you need to stop snooping around." Luke grabbed her under her arms and pulled her upright. She turned around to look at his face. "What's wrong?" He asked.

She turned around to the chair and pointed at the black menace lying on the wooden chair. "Why does Cole have a gun?"

"A lot of men carry guns. It's nothing unusual." He blew it off.

"But that one is law enforcement issue," she said with a shaky voice.

"How do you know that?" Luke raised an eyebrow in curiosity.

How was she going to explain she knew all about guns? She couldn't. If she even tried, she'd blow the story she'd so perfectly constructed. That wasn't happening. "I've watched a lot of crime shows." She hoped he believed her stupid lie.

Luke placed his hands on her shoulders and lowered his face to meet hers. "Cole has a gun, big deal. I have a gun in the basement, right?"

"Yes," she said nodding.

"So, like I said. It isn't a big deal. Now, let's get out of here and grab some supplies. Okay?" he cajoled.

"Okay." She took one last look at the pistol before following Luke out the door and shutting it firmly behind her.

She still didn't like Cole. Something was off about him and she intended to figure out what that something was. She needed to get ahold of Brandi to have her do some digging. Ava didn't own a computer for fear that her online activity could be traced. Her phone was a prepaid one she changed out every month; new number and all. She wasn't taking any chances. One wrong move and they would be able to pinpoint her location and move in. She'd spent the last two years being cautious and it wasn't going to stop now. Hopefully Brandi would be willing to do some digging around and find information on Cole.

Jesus, if Ava didn't stop snooping around, Luke's cover would be blown in no time. Damn Cole Matthews and him leaving his shit out where anyone could see it. The man knew better. But he was a fuck head who had no regard for being caught. Luke made sure his shit was hidden at all times—besides his rifle in the basement. And that was an easy lie to pass off. Ava believed him and he hoped it stayed that way. But currently driving his truck down the two lane highway while watching the beautiful creature stare out her window, he considered telling her everything. But he just couldn't do that. It would devastate her and make her hate him. He would keep his secrets for a bit longer and hold on to her while he could. He only hoped Cole didn't open his fucking mouth and let everything hang out.

"I was thinking...since Cole is staying, maybe we could invite Brandi for a barbeque or something," Ava said sweetly.

"Yeah, that sounds like a good idea. When were you thinking?" He tightened his hands around the leather of the steering wheel. He didn't really want her friend there, but if it made her more comfortable he'd concede. Maybe she'd forget about what she'd seen earlier.

"Tonight? I mean, if that's okay with you?" She peered over at him. How the hell could he say no to an angelic face like that? He couldn't.

"Sure. Why don't you give her a call once we get to the grocery store? Maybe she'll want to bring something. I'll give Cole a shout and let him know what's going down, too. I have a couple calls to make anyway."

"Oh, okay." She shrugged.

They drove in silence for the remaining ten miles and when they got into town, he found the local grocery store. He parked a couple rows from the front entrance and cut the engine. "Here." He handed Ava a couple hundred bucks in cash. "Go on in and grab what you need. I'll be out here making my calls and I'll come in and meet you."

She took the bills from his fingers and leaned over to give him a swift kiss. "See ya soon." She smiled.

Luke watched her walk toward the front of the store—glancing around as she did. Her hands latched onto a shopping cart and soon she was out of sight as she disappeared through the automatic sliding doors. When she was completely out of sight, Luke grabbed his phone and hit the speed dial button for Cole.

"Trouble in paradise already?" Cole answered with a laugh.

"How stupid are you?" Luke bit out.

"Whoa. What the hell did I do *now*?"

"You left your sidearm out where anyone could see it. She fucking found it, Matthews." Luke wished the other man was right in front of him so he could do a little homemade plastic surgery on Cole's face with his fist.

"Shit," Cole cursed.

"Yeah, *shit*."

"I'm sorry man. It's my spare. I sure as shit didn't think she'd go in my room."

"I didn't either. But she's got a curious side to her. You have to be more careful. If she discovers who we are, she'll run. If she does that, we're fucked."

"Roger that. Listen, I'll be back this evening sometime. I have some info you might find interesting," Cole offered.

"Be back around six. Ava wants to have a barbecue with you and her friend Brandi."

"Oh, hell. The domestication gets even better. I never thought I'd see the day when Luke Daughtry played house with one of the women folk," Cole hooted.

"Man, shut the fuck up. You know damn good and well this is just part of the job. The payday is what I'm after. If I have to play house, then so be it."

"Yeah, yeah. Keep telling yourself that. I'll be back before six. Be sure to have on your 'Kiss the Cook' apron," Cole chortled as he hung up.

Fucker. Sometimes he wanted to punch the guy so hard his head would spin around on his neck. Time to make the other call—the one he dreaded the most. Luke reached inside the center console and pulled up the false bottom. The burner phone was still in there. He grabbed it up and hit the same number he'd dialed for the past couple months.

"I was beginning to think you forgot you're on a job," the gruff voice answered on the other end.

"Nah, I just can't stand talking to you." Luke wasn't in the mood for this guy's bullshit today.

"Watch it, buddy. I'm the one making sure you get your money when this is all over."

"Speaking of which, when *will* this all be over? You've had me babysitting for quite some time." Luke was getting restless.

"Well, there have been some interesting developments. Seems you told us a big one when you said the bitch was in Phoenix." The other man began to hack. Luke hoped he had the black lung from smoking, served him right.

"How ya figure she's *not* in Phoenix?" He wanted answers.

"Sent some boys down there to scope things out. They've spent the past week scouring the city and the suburbs. *Nothing*. So either you're fucking with me, or my boys need to find their way to the bottom of Lake Michigan."

Shit. "Yeah, I lied. I wanted to see if you were serious." He kept his tone steady while he talked.

"Then how's about you tell me the truth."

Think, Luke, think. "Savannah, Georgia." He threw out the city on the fly. It was seven and a half hours from Biloxi which would give him plenty of time to get things in order if need be.

"Yeah, I didn't much peg the little bitch for the dry heat of Arizona anyway. Savannah sounds about right."

"Now what?" Luke asked.

"Now you do what you're doing and wait for my call."

"That's not good enough." More information was what Luke needed. "How about you tell me why you're keeping her alive? Maybe I can help you figure out how to find what you're looking for," he offered.

The other man laughed and began to cough. Luke pulled the phone away from his ear until the man was done. "Just keep an eye on her. Oh, and one more thing…"

"Yeah?"

"If you even think about sticking your dick in that hot piece of ass, I'll make sure you choke on the damn thing as you're sinking to the bottom of Lake Michigan," the other guy warned and then hung up.

Well, Luke had fucked up on *that* front already.

Wasn't much he could do about it now. He stashed the phone back in its spot and grabbed the keys out of the ignition. He'd already been out here for fifteen minutes and he didn't want Ava getting suspicious. Time to do some more domestic shit—as Cole liked to call it.

"I know it sounds crazy but the guy gives me the creeps," Ava said to Brandi on the phone while reading the back of a Pop Tart box. Why she was reading it, she didn't know. It wasn't like she'd paid much attention to nutritional facts in the past. But for some reason it was captivating today.

"I'll see what I can find," Brandi promised. "What time is dinner tonight?" Ava could hear her friend clicking around on the keys of her computer already.

"Probably around six. You can bring a dessert if you want to."

"You know I don't bake. I do good to boil water."

"Then just pick something up on your way to Luke's house."

"Fine. But only because I love you." Brandi chuckled.

Just then Ava saw Luke out of the corner of her eye.

"Gotta go. Luke's here now."

"Alright, see you later."

She hung up the phone just as Luke approached the shopping cart. He looked in at the still empty buggy and gave her a curious expression. "Are we having air for dinner?"

"I didn't know what you like to eat." She shrugged. Hell, she'd let him fuck her to oblivion and she had no clue what his favorite food was. How pathetic.

"I'm a man, I like meat."

Ava's cheeks warmed at the thought of what kind of meat he really liked. "Okay, to the meat section it is." She whipped the cart around, nearly smacking Luke in the family jewels as she spun it.

"Damn, watch out. I'd like to keep that intact if at all possible."

She smiled and walked past him saying, "I kind of like it in one piece too." There was that brazen personality shining through once more.

"And they say men are the ones who think about sex every thirty seconds."

Ava stood before the case filled with all varieties of red meat known to mankind. She had no clue what to pick—luckily Luke was right there to assist. "How do you know which ones to choose?" She bent over and picked up two different types of steaks. They sat safely in their Styrofoam trays, covered with clear shrink wrap. "Do you like the bone in? Or bone out?"

Luke straightened and pinned her with what could only be described as a leer. "I prefer the *bone* in." His gaze raked down her body.

Ava tossed the packages of meat back in the cooler case and let out a sigh. "How can a person make grocery shopping filthy?"

"Hey, we haven't even visited the produce section. I bet there's some fun to be had there." Luke began laughing so hard he was gasping for air.

"You're like a teenage boy trapped in a man's body."

Luke didn't reply he only stood there snickering. Ava found his inner boyish charm quite fascinating. It didn't coincide with his normal tough guy demeanor. But either way, she liked it. Maybe a little too much.

They walked around the store laughing and earning dirty looks from other shoppers as they made jokes and played with the cucumbers and cantaloupes in the produce section. Luke wanted to know what he'd look like with a pair of boobs so he shoved two melons under his shirt and presented himself to Ava.

"Oh. My. God. Now I *know* you've lost your mind," she laughed.

It was refreshing to play around and joke with this part-Neanderthal. Of course she enjoyed the caveman in him as well—especially in the bedroom.

"Do we have everything we need?" Luke asked as Ava rolled the metal buggy to the front of the store.

"I think so." She did an inventory of the items in the cart and snapped her head up. "Wait. I forgot sour cream for the baked potatoes."

"I'm on it," Luke said and hurried to the back of the store.

Ava stood there waiting for him and noticed something rather odd. A man stood at the front just beyond the five checkout lanes, leaning against the scratch-off lottery ticket machine. He kept a close eye on her but she did her best to pretend she wasn't paying attention. He was clearly studying her though; she could feel his gaze piercing her as she stood there with her hands grasping the red handle of the cart in a death grip. His hair was buzzed short and she could make out a jagged white scar above his left ear. His eyes were wide set with eyebrows that seemed to grow together in the center. His eye color was unclear though since she was still a good ways away. Nothing about his clothing screamed, '*I'm not from around here*' as he stood there taking her in. In fact, he looked like a local with his cut off t-shirt and jean shorts. Although she did notice some sort of inked creation on his left forearm.

"Hope this's what you needed." Luke came back just as she was feeling extremely uncomfortable standing there.

She looked at the white container in his hand and said, "Yes, that's perfect." When she glanced back to the spot where the creepy man had been standing, he was gone. "Let's go." Her tone came out clipped.

"Everything okay?" Luke touched her arm and she jumped. "Hey, what's going on?"

"I'm fine. I just want to get this stuff and go." She rolled the cart through one of the checkout lanes and began to throw the items on the black conveyer belt. When everything was rung up, she paid with Luke's cash and hurried from the store. Luke was struggling to keep up as she made it to his truck and began to toss the bags of food over the side of the bed.

"I wish I knew what was wrong. Maybe I could fix it." He picked up a couple bags and helped her load them.

"Sorry, I'm just tired. I guess my crankiness has reared its ugly head."

Luke didn't respond as he finished the task and got in to start the truck. She startled as it roared to life but quickly put everything out of her mind. So what odd things were happening? Maybe she'd just gotten way too comfortable and paying the price now by being paranoid. It figured things would turn out like this. Maybe the man in the store was just a normally creepy guy. Maybe he didn't recognize her like she'd though he had. But she didn't want to stick around to find out. Who knew if he was still around watching her? All she wanted was to go back to Luke's place and talk to Brandi later that evening.

Surely her friend would have some answers, right?

Chapter Fifteen

"**ARE YOU SERIOUS?** You didn't find *anything* on him?" Ava stood at the kitchen counter slathering potatoes with butter and rolling them in sea salt.

Brandi wrapped the spuds in foil and laid them off to the side. "Nope. Not a thing."

Luke and Cole were in the backyard firing up the grill so she knew it was safe to chat with her friend. "That doesn't make sense. If he were a business owner, he'd have to have some sort of public records, right?"

"I don't know, you tell me. You own a business and you don't have records of your name." Brandi pointed out.

Shit. The woman had a valid point. "It's not the same."

"Isn't it? I really wish you'd confide in me a little more. I don't know what's going on and I want to. You moved here two years ago and yes, I've been your friend, but I need more, Ava."

"Why is this such an issue now?" Ava brushed a stray hair from her forehead.

"Because you're like the pot calling the kettle black right now. You want to dig into Cole's life, but you refuse to divulge any info about you before you moved here."

"I went through some really bad shit. I've told you this already, Brandi."

"Yes, you have. You know what, forget I said anything. You must have reasons for keeping secrets and I should be a good friend by leaving you alone about it all." Thank God she was backing off.

"Thank you." Ava handed Brandi the last potato and washed her hands in the sink nearby.

They'd fallen into companionable silence when Brandi decided to speak up again. "So, Cole is a sexy motherfucker."

Ava's mouth gaped. "You cannot be serious."

"Of course I am. Look at him." Brandi pointed out the window at the man in question.

Ava peered out and glanced at Cole. She felt wrong for even looking at another man, but she and Luke weren't exactly an item. So she guessed it would be alright to take a gander. Look, don't touch. Not like she'd touch Cole with a ten-foot pole anyway. But he was good-looking in a Backstreet Boy kind of way. He wasn't built like Luke though; his muscles weren't as defined, he wasn't near as tall as Luke and he gave off more of a preppy vibe than anything. His short black hair looked like it'd been trimmed not too long ago and the guy definitely used some sort of moisturizer on his skin.

"I think you should hook me up. Let me get a little action on the baloney pony for a bit," Brandi said as she ogled Cole over Ava's shoulder.

"I'm not hooking you up with anyone. If you want to ride that, be my guest. But you'll have to go out there and proposition him."

"Don't mind if I do." Brandi dusted off her hands and was out the door. Ava witnessed her best friend sidle right up to Cole, whisper something in his ear and soon he was taking her hand and leading her back into the house.

"We're going to go have a talk." Brandi came in with a huge smile on her face. Cole was right behind her and had an equally devious grin.

"Need any help in here?" Luke came through the door a few seconds later.

"Nope, I have it all covered." She placed a baking sheet with the foil wrapped potatoes in the oven. "Seems your cousin and my best friend are getting to know each other."

"She literally walked out there and asked him if he wanted to fuck," Luke tittered.

"Good Lord. She lacks this thing called tact."

It wasn't long and they could both hear the tell-tale signs of Brandi and Cole getting it on in his room. The headboard of the bed was banging against the wall, Cole was grunting and groaning and Brandi's vocalizations made it sound like a porn movie was being filmed on-location.

"I can't listen to this. I'm going outside." She made her way through the door with Luke right behind her.

"I wonder if that's what we sound like." Luke began laughing.

"That's not even funny," she replied.

"Don't you ever wonder about it, though? If you sound like a rabid animal in the heat of the moment?"

"I haven't given it much thought until now." She turned and cocked an eyebrow at him. "You'd know better than me. *Do I* sound like a wild animal?"

Luke came closer and wrapped his arms around her. The faint scent of barbecue grill smoke and something that was uniquely him enveloped her senses. "Maybe a little." Ava tried to squirm away. "But there's this little sound you make, right before you come," he whispered close to her ear, "It makes my head spin and my cock hard enough to jackhammer concrete." His tongue darted out and licked the shell of her ear.

"You'd better stop talking like that," Ava warned.

"Why's that?"

She wriggled free of his grasp and pointed to the grill only a few feet away. "Because as much as I'd like to let you hear that sound again, I think dinner is burning."

Ava watched him whip around and stare at the plumes of white smoke escaping the closed grill. "Shit!" He ran to the contraption, threw back the lid and grabbed the oversized meat tongs. He began flipping the steaks. "Oh, good. We don't have to eat like gods tonight." He sounded relieved.

"Eat like gods?" she questioned with extreme confusion on her face.

"Yeah. Burnt offerings." Damn. That incredible smile of his had her wanting to bow at his feet and worship *him* like a god. When he finished with the meat he closed the lid and looked at her with those stunning blue eyes. Somehow the sunlight made them seem like he had stuck sapphires in his eye sockets.

"What's wrong?" Ava wasn't sure why he was looking at her so strangely.

"Nothing. I just want to stare at you all damn day."

"You'd get bored after a while." Why was she becoming self-conscious all of a sudden? Maybe it was the way he didn't just see her outer appearance; he saw deeper. Like he was mapping out the nooks and crannies of her soul.

"Trust me, I could never find myself becoming bored with you."

Ava shook her head. "You shouldn't say things like that."

"Why not?"

"Because I don't deserve to have things like that said about me, Luke."

His expression changed from playful to downright stern in a matter of nanoseconds as he took long strides to get to her. "No. Don't you ever think you're not deserving of something. I don't want to hear that come out of your mouth again. When I tell you that you're the most beautiful woman I've ever laid eyes on, you'd better damn well believe it."

Ava wasn't sure what to say to that. She stood there in awe that someone like Luke would think that way about her. No, she didn't think she was anything special, but the way he spoke to her, looked at her and touched her made her feel like she was this mythical desired creature. She half wondered if he knew she felt the same way about him. "How did I get so lucky in finding you?" she asked.

Luke turned away. "Let's not talk about it." Something in his mood changed, causing her to wonder what she'd said wrong.

She stepped close behind him and wrapped her arms around his midsection, feeling his muscles bunch as she rubbed his stomach over the top of his shirt. "I shouldn't have said that."

"Ava, I don't want you to think this can go anywhere past where it is now." He brushed his hands across hers.

His words stung a bit. Sure, she'd been fully aware of their intentions when this all began, but now…she wanted more. "I feel like there's something here. Something more than what we have. Don't you feel it?" She wasn't letting this go.

Luke spun in her arms and cupped her face in his hands. "Yeah, I do. But that doesn't mean we need to act on it. Can't we just be content with this?" He was pleading with her. Behind those blue eyes he held himself back. For what reason, she didn't know. But she wanted to. She was willing to stick it out to see if maybe he'd change his mind eventually.

"I guess so." She wasn't happy with her own answer. Squaring her chin and giving him an ultimatum was on the tip of her tongue but the chances of ruining what they had now were too great. If this was the only way to have him, then yeah, she'd hang on.

Damn it. Why did he have to go and jump into this thing with both feet? Luke knew it would backfire on him eventually and right now, it was all imploding in on itself. In his arms was this magnificent woman who he'd give his left nut to be with. But there wasn't a future for them. In fact, Ava didn't have a future and it was his fucking fault. He was using her. Using her for his own gain. When she found out who he really was, she'd hate him and he couldn't blame her. Hell, he hated himself at the moment. If he didn't have a job to do, he'd pack his shit and get the hell out of Dodge in the next five minutes. But even the thought of driving away from her sparked a pang of emptiness in his chest. No, he wasn't leaving; he couldn't. He'd stay here and finish this and then he'd be gone.

"Something smells good out here." Brandi and Cole sauntered out of the house with shit-eating-grins on their faces.

"It's about time you two decided to join us," Luke was glad for the reprieve from talking about feelings and shit with Ava.

"We were discussing the finer points of Biloxi living," Brandi giggled.

"And by *finer points* I assume each other's sex organs?" Luke hooted. He felt Ava snickering while he held her in his arms.

"Yeah, yeah." Cole rolled his eyes and smoothed his hair down.

Luke wasn't thrilled that Cole had fucked Ava's best friend. But the man was a grown up and could make his own bad decisions. Luke wasn't there to play babysitter with the other guy. As long as Cole did his job, Luke would keep his boot out of his ass.

Ava broke free of his grasp and walked over to her friend. "Let's go check the food inside while they finish out here."

"The meat should be done in about five minutes," Luke pointed out.

"Okay." She gave him a sweet smile—one of the ones that cleared the blackness away from his heart just a little more each time he saw it.

Cole didn't speak until both women were behind closed doors inside the house. "So…" he shuffled his feet and had a guilty look like a kid who'd just gotten caught sneaking Oreos.

"Have fun?" Luke began tending to the food on the grill once more.

"Brandi's something else."

"Just remember the shit you told me. I'm throwing it right back at you," Luke warned.

"Nah, man. It was just some fun. Everyone needs to blow off some steam every now and again. Isn't that what you're doing?"

Luke didn't like the thought of Cole saying Ava was just a way to blow off steam. His caveman instincts took over and he nearly growled at the other man. "No, it's not."

"Come on. There are two fine pieces of ass in that kitchen. Who wouldn't want to bend them over and make them scream?"

"I'd watch it if I were you." Luke took a deep breath and counted to ten. He hoped like hell Cole would shut his mouth.

"We could swap," Cole chuckled.

That was it. Luke had no tolerance for the other man's crass comments about Ava. Without thinking of the consequences he spun around and grabbed Cole by the shirt. "Look, motherfucker, I told you to shut your goddamned mouth!" His face was only inches from Cole's as he shouted. "You don't know how to follow directions do you?"

"What's gotten into you?" The deep brown of the other man's eyes seemed to be taken over by the black of his pupils. "Where's the hardass Luke Daughtry I used to know? Are you pussy-whipped already?"

"I told you to shut your trap." Luke held tightly to Cole's shirt.

"So you're gonna let some little blonde bitch lead you around by the dick because she's such a good lay?"

Before Luke thought twice he released Cole's shirt, reared his arm back and cracked the other man in the jaw with his fist. Cole fell to the ground in a heap as he stood over him.

"What the hell is going on out here?" Ava came running from the back porch with a look of terror on her face. She immediately dropped to her knees and surveyed the damage to Cole's face. "Luke, why did you hit him?"

Luke was too pissed to even talk at that point so he kept his mouth shut. But he saw something in her eyes that he hated himself for putting there. Fear. She was scared of him.

"What the fuck?" Brandi came rushing out with a look of shock on her face. "Ava, what happened?"

"I was looking out the window while you were in the bathroom and Luke punched Cole."

Luke's feet were planted firmly but when Brandi walked up and shoved at his chest, he almost fell back with the force of her movements. "You want to fight? Huh? How about you fight me?" She kept shoving until his back hit the grill behind him.

Ava stood from the ground and yelled, "Everyone stop it, please!" Luke's heart sank as tears began to flood her eyes.

"Ava, sweetheart, please don't cry." Luke stepped around her pissed-off friend and tried to console her.

"Don't you fucking touch me." She shook her head and backed away, ripping his heart to shreds even more.

A previously unconscious Cole groaned and lulled his head from side to side on the grass below them.

"Fuck," he bit out.

"Brandi, go grab a bag of ice and a towel," Ava instructed her friend.

"Ava, look at me." Luke spoke softly trying to get her to listen to him. The contempt for him that'd been so clear in her eyes was replaced with concern for the other guy as she bent down to help Cole to his feet.

"Let's get you inside and put some ice on your jaw."

"Ava?" Luke tried to get her attention again but she ignored him. Just fucking perfect.

He watched her lead Cole inside the house, leaving him in what felt like solitary confinement outside. Rubbing a hand over his face he mentally kicked himself for losing his cool like he had. What the fuck was he thinking? Why couldn't he just turn his cheek to what Cole was saying? The guy was always cracking jokes and being an asshole. It wasn't any different than any other day. But today it wasn't funny because he was talking about Ava. Luke plunked his big frame in a lawn chair, leaned forward, and braced his arms on his elbows letting his hands dangle in front of him.

"Guess you're in the doghouse now." Brandi came out sat beside him. She extended her arm and handed him a beer with the cap already popped off.

"I fucked up." He sat back and took a long pull from the dark brown bottle, letting the yeasty liquid quench his thirst and quell the anger inside him.

"Can I ask what happened?"

"He was talking shit about you and Ava. There's a lot of things I can handle, but that wasn't one of them today."

"What kind of shit-talking was he doing?"

"The bastard suggested we swap." Luke groaned at the thought of another man's hands on Ava.

Brandi let out a hooting laugh and took a sip from her own bottle of beer. "You're a nice guy and all, but I don't think Ava's the swinger type."

"I don't doubt that."

"Why did it bother you so much, though?" The crazy woman just wouldn't let up.

"I don't want another man *looking* at her, let alone putting his hands on her." He wasn't ashamed to admit that fact. If Cole had even attempted to touch Ava he would've made it so the other man wouldn't have use of his hands for the rest of his life.

"Yet you don't want anything serious with her? That doesn't make a lick of sense." Brandi shook her head.

"Nothing makes sense anymore."

"Look, if you want this to just be a fling, by all means, keep doing what you're doing. But I can tell you, that beautiful woman in there deserves a whole lot more than some guy fucking her and tossing her away when he's done." She sighed. "I don't know much about Ava before she moved here. But from what I gather, it was some bad shit. She's guarded her heart and body since she's been here. I've watched dozens of men try to catch her eye but she didn't spare any a second glance until you."

"She deserves better than me." There, he'd finally admitted it. He should've felt better but he didn't.

"That's a bullshit excuse and you know it."

Damn he wanted to just lay everything out on the table and pay the penance for his sins. He wished there wasn't so much riding on this job so he could stop feeling guilty about what was going to go down. "Look, I don't need someone analyzing me. Least of all you." He didn't mean to sound like such an asshole, but in his current frame of mind, nothing was going to come out of his mouth like it was covered in sprinkles. "What do you suggest I do? Huh?" He pinned Brandi with a stare that would have most people cowering, but the woman beside him shocked the shit out of him. She simply cocked an eyebrow.

"You either fess up to how you feel, or you walk away."

"What if I don't feel anything?" He knew that was a lie as soon as it spilled out of his mouth.

"Then you must have yourself fooled because even an idiot can see the way you look at her." That's all the spitfire said before getting up and heading back into the house.

Truthfully, Luke didn't know what the hell he was feeling. His best guess was he was in lust with Ava. They had explosive sex and got along good. It couldn't be anything other than that.

After making sure Cole held the ice pack to his face to reduce the swelling on his jaw, Ava ran upstairs to Luke's bedroom and began to throw her clothes back into her bags. She'd shut the door so no one could hear her cry; she knew as soon as she entered his room the tears would fall. And they did. Her vision was blurred as she stuffed her night shirt and shorts into the side of the small tote. As she zipped it up, her head whipped around to see Luke coming through the door and shutting it behind him.

"We need to talk," Luke said softly.

"There's nothing to talk about." She wiped her eyes.

"Yes, there is. I'm not letting you leave like this, Ava." Luke stepped closer and she caught his unique scent once more. Damn him for smelling so enticing.

"Are you going to punch me in the face, too?" she said with venom behind her words.

"I lost my temper. But I can assure you one thing, I would never in my life put my hands on you like that."

"It wasn't the actual hitting that scared me, Luke. It was the look of rage on your face. What did he do that was bad enough to put that look there?" She really needed to know what'd taken Luke to that point. Maybe it was morbid curiosity.

He stepped dangerously close and she backed away until her spine was pressed against the wall. Luke didn't retreat; he only came closer and leaned down to look her in the eyes. "He mentioned something about fucking you," he growled. "So of course, I didn't take that so well. Want to know why?" His head tilted to the side while he waited for her to answer.

"Why?" Ava whispered.

Her breath left her in a *whoosh* as Luke's hand reached down, lifted the hem of her sundress and cupped her between the legs. "Because this," he began to rub her over the top of her panties, "Is mine." Her eyes fluttered shut as he applied more pressure. "It's mine to touch, taste and fuck." Ava groaned as he pushed the scrap of satin to the side and slid his fingers through her moisture. "I'm the only man who does this to you, sweetheart. I'm the only man who gets to come deep inside you while you're writhing underneath me."

Her damn body wasn't supposed to react to him like this while she was pissed at him. But she couldn't help it. Luke turned her inside out with just a look. But he wasn't looking right now, he was touching. And holy hell that was the one thing that unraveled her quicker than anything. "Make me come," she breathed.

"How close are you?" He rested his forehead against hers.

"So close already."

"Good." His fingers delved deep as he thrust them inside her and ground the heel of his hand against her clit. She was swollen and needy, ready to explode at any second. "I want you to tell me this is mine, that it belongs to me," he gruffly said.

"It's yours," she whimpered.

"Come for me. Can you do that?" he cajoled.

Ava nodded furiously as her orgasm ripped through her like a rogue wave shoving a small vessel under its murky depths. She couldn't stop the screams that scratched against her vocal cords and echoed against the antiquated walls of the room. Luke held some sort of power over her; she was convinced of that. No, it wasn't some crazy power trip he'd placed on her, it was deeper. An earth-shattering connection that felt as if it could stop time and douse the earth in shadows. But ignited again, it would burn so brightly that everyone would need to shield their eyes from its beaming rays. She couldn't name it. Maybe in the back of her mind she wanted to, but saying those words could bring this entire thing to a halt and cause him to throw up unbreakable barriers. She'd take what he was giving for now. But eventually, she wanted him to reveal his true feelings. If he didn't feel even an inkling for her what she felt for him, she'd walk away and never look back.

Chapter Sixteen

"**THEY REALLY** want to meet us in Gulfport." Cole drank from his mug at five a.m. trying to convince Luke that this meeting was imperative.

"Why can't you go on your own?"

"Because they want to see both of us. This isn't negotiable, Daughtry." Cole's tone thickened.

"Fuck. I can't just leave her here."

"Then have her friend stay with her. The meeting's at noon." Cole rose from his seat, not bothering to push his chair in. "I'll drive."

"Fine," Luke bit out. He wasn't happy about having to leave Ava for any length of time. He'd bought her some time by telling his boss she was in Savannah, but it was only a matter of time before they learned the truth. At least she'd be safe here at his house while he was gone for a few hours.

"Good morning," Ava's sweet voice called from the doorway.

Luke looked up to see her stunning frame leaned against the doorframe. "Morning."

"You don't look happy." She came over and leaned down to kiss him. It was a quick peck on the lips but it still had the same effect that a deep sensual kiss would have. He felt that shit all the way down to his bone marrow.

"I have to go to a meeting with Cole today."

"Oh. Okay." She shrugged as she poured herself a cup of coffee.

"I want you to stay here, though."

"Luke, I'm perfectly fine going back to my house," she argued.

"Can you please not make this a debate?"

"I'm not debating; I'm telling you that I'll be at my house. See? No debating necessary." She gave a forced smile.

"Damn it, Ava. Why can't you just listen for once?" He stood from his chair so swiftly that it scraped against the tiled floor, making a horrible racket.

"What's gotten into you? Is it that time of the month for you? Do you need a man-pon?" She snickered, lightening his mood just a little.

He had to think of a reason why she should stay here. "What if that ginger fucker is still pissed and comes after you?"

"Who, Chase? Come on, I could poke him in the chest with my pinkie and he'd fall over."

"Please stay here. I'm not asking for much." Luke didn't beg, but he was pretty damn close to falling to his knees and pleading with the sexy blonde only a few feet away.

"If it's that important to you, I'll stay," she finally conceded.

"Thank you," he said as he enveloped her in a warm embrace.

At least *that* was settled. Now he had to worry about what awaited him in Gulfport. Whatever it was, it couldn't be good.

"Hey, Luke and Cole had to run to Gulfport for some kind of meeting today. Do you want to come over and keep me company?" Ava asked Brandi on the phone. She'd wandered around the house for about thirty minutes until she was bored out of her mind. What the hell did people do in these giant houses? Play bridge, smoke cigars and sip fine liquor all day long?

"Yeah, but I can't get off work for another hour," her friend huffed.

"Boss man being a dick again?" Ava felt sorry for her friend. The poor woman hated her job at the local newspaper. Seemed her supervisor liked to toe the line of sexual harassment. But he never went far enough that he could be reported.

"Of course. When is he not being the mayor of Dickville?" Ava knew it was a rhetorical question so she didn't answer. "But I'll be there as soon as I'm released from today's sentence here."

"Okay, see you then."

Well, crap. It looked like she had another hour to kill before her boredom would subside. "What to do, what to do?" She spoke aloud, then chuckled. "And now I've resorted to talking to myself." She cachinnated again at her own absurdity.

A thought came to her and at first she pushed it to the back of her mind. Luke didn't want her in the basement. He made that perfectly clear. But she didn't get a chance to take a good look around, maybe there were still unfound treasures lurking in that damp expanse. She mentally fought with herself over the decision to go down there. The angel on one shoulder shook its finger and told her to mind her own business, while the little horned devil told her that Luke wouldn't find out that she'd been down there. And the red beast was right. He wouldn't know. She'd go down, take a look around and come right back up. Luke wouldn't ever find out because who would tell him? Her? Not happening.

Her thoughts reconciled, Ava found herself in front of the basement door, her hand on the knob. She turned it and headed down the steps. It wasn't as dim as it was the last time she'd been down there. Sunlight managed to beam through the dust-covered windows enough that she didn't need to click on the light. Her eyes adjusted to the change in lighting and soon she was wandering around taking in the items down there. At first she didn't see much of interest, but something shiny caught her eye as she rounded the corner into a small side room off the main area. Squatting down she looked closer.

"Look at you." Her eyes lit up at what she'd found.

She knew there'd be some sort of treasure down here. "With a little cleaning you would be brilliant." She pulled the item out and took stock of it. She wasn't positive but she had a hunch that this was a hand-carved, gilded wall mirror. She was astounded that it was in such good condition; even the glass was still intact. Running her hands over the frame she brushed away some of the dust that'd built up over the years. What it revealed was an intricately carved scene of flower petals and leaves. As she looked closer she could see vines twined in and around the other details. This had to be an antique. Her heart fluttered at finding such a cool thing in a drab basement.

Now to get it upstairs and cleaned a bit. She stood upright and bent forward to carefully grasp the treasure in her hands. When she stood up again a sharp pain hit the base of her skull and the mirror slipped back to the floor. The sounds of shattering glass invaded the tiny room as she was also pulled to the floor. The last thing she heard as her body went limp was the side of her head making a sickening thud as it smacked the filthy concrete.

Luke sat in Cole's truck as they headed toward Gulfport. All he could think about was the fact that he'd left Ava behind and it was eating his guts like some rabid disease. They'd only made it about twenty miles out of town but with each mile marker, the feeling of longing took root even more. Damn it, this wasn't how this whole thing was supposed to go down. He was there to do a job and get the hell out. Now he doubted himself and his actions from the very beginning.

"What's with the broody act?" Cole asked.

Luke looked over at him and winced at the bluish-purple bruise that'd developed from the force of his fist. "Got a lot on my mind." Luke shrugged.

"Wouldn't be a certain blonde would it?" This time Cole wasn't really joking. He'd taken a serious tone and Luke wondered why all of a sudden he was being like that.

He rubbed a hand over his jaw where a two-day beard was starting to cover his face. "I have to tell her."

"You know you can't do that," Cole warned.

"I don't give a shit about my job anymore. They can shove it up their ass."

"Man, I get it. But you have to think of the repercussions of this entire thing. She's the key player in all of this. If you run back and tell her, this entire thing will go to shit. We've worked too long, lost sleep for too many nights and put up with more shit than any two men are supposed to handle. Don't let what you feel for her get in the way of all that."

"Fuck. I don't know what the hell I feel."

"You have to remember, she's lying to you also," Cole reminded him of the harsh reality that he'd been living over the past few weeks.

"I guess that's what bothers me the most. We've gotten so close I wonder why she hasn't said anything."

"She's running scared. I would be too if *Frank the Tank* was after me. He's one bad motherfucker."

"If she told me the whole story, I could protect her."

"Can you really? Can you honestly sit there and tell me that you could stop everything from going down like you know it will?"

"No," Luke bit out.

"Then I think you have your answer. Stay tight-lipped about this and maybe we'll all make it out alive on the other side."

"I fucking hope so."

A few more miles of scenery passed by but it didn't make him feel any better about the situation. Cole was right, they were all lying and covering something up, Ava included. But that didn't change the way he felt about her. He'd bet everything he had that she wasn't pretending to be someone else when she was with him. There was just no way. Other than her name change and the slight appearance shift, Ava was being one hundred percent herself. He didn't doubt that for a second.

"You gonna check that?" Cole pulled him out of his reverie.

His phone was chirping from the dashboard where he'd tossed it upon getting in the truck. Hairs on the back of his neck stood to attention as he heard the distinct notification tone. "Pull over," he demanded.

"Why?" Cole asked.

"Just pull the fucking truck over!"

Cole did as he said and Luke flipped the phone over to see what was going on. One of the first things he'd done when he moved into his grandmother's house for this particular job was to install motion detectors and security cameras in the basement where he kept his supplies. If someone went down there, he'd get an alert on his phone and then be able to see exactly what was going on down there on the screen. That's how he knew Ava was down there the first time. But this time, he was mortified at what he saw. Even though the image in front of him was in grainy black and white, he knew what he was seeing was about the closest thing to his worst nightmare.

"Turn around," he barked.

"We have to get to this meeting," Cole argued.

He shoved the phone in front of Cole's face. "Holy fuck." Cole immediately pulled back onto the road and did a U-turn. He didn't pay any mind to speed limits as he blazed down the road on the way back to Luke's house. "Calm down. She's going to be okay." The other man tried to give him some solace but it wasn't helping the least bit.

Luke kept his eyes plastered to the screen, hoping he'd see her move again. But even after several minutes, Ava's motionless body still lay on the dank concrete of his basement—shards of what looked like mirrored glass scattered all around her. Panic like he'd never experienced before swamped him as he tried to make sense of what he was seeing. They hadn't even been gone long. How could someone have broken in and attacked her in such a short amount of time? It didn't make sense.

"Fuck," Luke cursed and slammed his hand on the dash of the vehicle.

"What?" Cole was genuinely concerned.

"Brandi was supposed to be there with her. Do you have her number?"

"Yeah, here." Cole grabbed his phone and scrolled through his contacts. He hit the call button and handed the device over to Luke.

After a couple rings Brandi answered with, "Couldn't get enough of me could you?" she giggled.

"Brandi, its Luke."

"Oh, hey." She sounded embarrassed.

"Where are you?"

"Just leaving work. I'm heading out to your place to spend the day with Ava."

"Don't go to my house," he ordered.

"Oooookay."

"I don't have time to explain, I just need you to stay away from there."

"Wait. Is Ava okay?" Brandi's voice came out worried but Luke didn't answer. "I'm calling the police."

"No! Whatever you do, keep the cops out of this. Please."

"If you want me to keep law enforcement out of this, you'd better give me a good reason." He had to hand it to her she wasn't one to back down. Something he normally admired but right now, it downright pissed him off.

He did something he was getting to be a pro at. He lied. "Actually, our meeting was cancelled and I wanted to surprise her." Damn, even that sounded lame to his ears.

"For someone who wants to surprise his girlfriend you sure did sound like something was wrong."

"Yeah, I'm sorry about that. I panicked when you said you were heading over there. I apologize." Keeping the worry out of his voice was a chore. On the outside he sounded calm and collected but inside was a rising shit storm that was ready to take down anyone who'd laid their fucking hands on Ava.

"Alright then. I'll just go home. Have a good time tonight. Oh, and will you tell Cole he can call me later?"

"Sure."

"Thanks."

Luke tossed the phone back to Cole and ran a hand through his hair. With the speed they were going, they'd be back to his house in just a few minutes. "Do you have an extra piece in here?" he asked Cole.

"Under your seat."

Luke bent over and swept his hand under the seat until he felt it touch cold metal. It banged against the underneath mechanism of the seat as he pulled it free. "This your spare?" he asked as he released the clip, making sure there were enough rounds inside. The silver casings should've calmed him—they always did—but not this time.

"First one they gave me." Cole sounded somber, like he was readying himself for who or what they might find.

He shoved the clip into the firearm and slid back the hammer just as Cole turned into his long driveway. If he had to put a hole in some crazy fucker today, the entire plan would be ruined. He just hoped that wasn't the case. They'd worked too damn long on this shit for some asshole to come in and blow things to smithereens.

Chapter Seventeen

IT'D SEEMED LIKE she'd been out cold for hours. The blackness swamped her still but Ava was finally coming to. She smelled something strange. It was a metallic smell that had her nose scrunching up in distaste. What the hell was it? Her entire body felt like it'd been run over by a train, the ache mostly in her head though. The room came into blurred view as she blinked rapidly to clear her vision. Basement. She was still in Luke's basement. What'd happened? She didn't want to move just yet. So she laid there on the damp concrete staring at the brick and mortar wall across from her. Something shimmered and caught her eye—the mirror. Which was now in unrecognizable shards, scattered all around her body.

The sunlight was still seeping through the small basement window and causing a glittering effect on the broken glass surface. The pain in her head was a piercing type that made her wince and almost cry out. *What the hell was that smell?* She didn't know but now the sensation of wetness near her head came over her. Was she lying in a puddle of water? Her hand snaked up and over her head to feel where the foreign sensations were coming from. Something was wet. What was it? Pulling her hand back down she focused the best she could on the dark substance streaked against her fingers and palm. Red. A gasp left her lips as she recognized what it was…blood. Panic overtook her as she tried to sit up.

The pain was excruciating but she managed to end up on her butt with her legs extended in front of her. She wiped her hand on her dress to rid herself of the disgusting substance. Trying to keep her breathing under control she got on all fours and stood shakily, using the wall for support. Her stomach roiled and the feeling that she might vomit hit her.

Suddenly though, she heard heavy footsteps on the wooden stairs descending toward the basement. Ava's heart raced as she waited for whoever it was to see her.

"Ava?" Luke's booming voice shouted through the large room.

Her voice cracked as she called back, "Luke."

Through her hazy vision she caught sight of him taking long strides to get to her. "Jesus, what happened? I need you to tell me everything." He grabbed her shoulders and lightly shook her.

She couldn't manage any sort of speech as the pain throbbed insistently.

"She's bleeding." Cole. He was here, too. "We need to get her to the emergency room."

"They'll want a police report," Luke said.

"Yeah, and?"

"You know we can't do that."

"Fuck, man. What if she has brain damage or something?"

Ava's raspy voice finally came out. "I'm fine."

"I'll be the judge of that." Luke swept her into his arms and held her tightly to his chest. He took her upstairs and into the kitchen. Her ass was put in a chair while Luke went about gathering things around her. She felt hands on the back of her head as she sat there trying to think of anything but what was going on. "Cole, I need you to grab my phone and go back over the footage. I want to know who the fuck was in this house," Luke ordered. "Ava, did you see anyone while you were down there?" he asked in a lighter tone.

"No. I was looking at a mirror I'd found and the next thing I know, I felt this sharp pain and fell to the floor," she said almost on a whisper. It even hurt to speak.

"Were the doors to the house unlocked when you went down there?"

"Yes. Brandi was supposed to come over. Oh no. Where is she? Is she okay?" Ava sat up a little straighter.

"Calm down. Brandi's fine, I've already spoken with her."

Something about this whole thing wasn't siting right with Ava. Luke and Cole weren't the laid back guys they'd been before. They almost sounded like they were trying to investigate this whole thing. Like they were some sort of law enforcement. But that wasn't right; they were just good ole country boys. There was no way in hell they could've been with the law.

As she pondered everything, Luke inspected her head. "It's just a minor cut. I don't know what you got hit with but you were lucky." She felt him wiping around the area on the back of her head.

"You okay, Ava?" Cole entered the room once more and patted her on the shoulder.

"Yes. I think I'll be fine." She wasn't entirely sure of it, but she hoped she'd be fine. Once this massive headache subsided she'd be up and running again.

"You need to take a look at this." Concern in his tone and on his face, Cole handed Luke's phone over to him.

Luke studied the screen. "He looks familiar. Not sure where I know him from though."

"Can I see it?" Ava reached her hand out for the device. Luke handed it to her and she gasped when she saw the person. "That's the guy from the grocery store the other day. He was leaning against the lottery machine, staring at me while I waited for you to get back to the cart."

"Do you know him?" Luke inquired.

"No. I was trying to place him but I couldn't. He gave me the creeps, though." Ava shivered, remembering how the man made her feel uncomfortable.

Luke handed the phone back to Cole. "Run it. See who it is."

"Maybe it was just a random break-in. Is there anything missing?" Ava asked.

"No. Cole already swept the place." Yet again he sounded like he was on official business.

Ava needed to point it out. "Why do you sound so official? Like you're some sort of law enforcement?" The room became silent.

"I told you already, I'm ex-military. That's how we talk." He began to bandage up the small cut on the back of her head. "Let's get you upstairs. You need to lie down for a while."

"Luke, I'm fine," she argued.

"No, you're not. You just got smacked over the head with something. You're far from fine." He helped her from the chair and again swept her into his arms.

"Why do you always have to be so bossy?"

"Because I'm an asshole. Does that answer your question well enough?"

"I'd say it does. Thanks," she grumbled.

He climbed the stairs while holding tightly to her, his scent rubbing off on her clothing so she would smell him later. When they reached his bedroom, he put her down on her own two feet and grabbed one of her bags. "Here, change clothes. Your dress has blood on it."

She slowly dug through the bag and pulled out a thin cotton nightgown. Luke watched with a heated gaze as she pulled her dress over her head and stood there in nothing but her panties. She turned to him before she slipped the clean garment over her head. "I need you," she whispered. Something about the tense situation had her desperate for contact.

Luke strode over to her and cupped her face in his hands. "I would love nothing more than to toss you on my bed and bury my cock inside you. But you need to rest."

"Please." She felt tears brewing in her eyes.

"Don't look at me like that."

"You don't want me. I understand." She dropped her head and unfolded the nightgown.

"Hey, we're not going down that road again. I've already established that there's no place I'd rather be than in this sweet body of yours. But this is for your own good." Ava nodded. "Let me help you with this." He pulled the garment from her hands and began to slide it over her head. Once it covered her body he leaned forward and kissed her forehead. "Get some rest, please? I'll come back up and check on you in a little while. If you need anything, just yell for me or Cole."

"Alright, I will." Ava pulled the sheets back and climbed in the bed. Luke stood there with indecision on his face. "The invitation is still open," she teased.

"I can't. If I climb in that bed with you, we'd not be leaving for the foreseeable future."

He left the room and closed the door. Sadness overtook her along with the events of the day. The tears that'd threatened earlier spilled out onto her cheeks. She furiously wiped them away and laid back into one of the plush pillows. She loved Luke's bed but the one thing that would've made it better was Luke.

"I don't think you'll want to see this." Cole brought his laptop to the table and hesitated. The look on his face told Luke there was nothing but bad news on the screen.

"Might as well show it to me." He grabbed the side of the screen and spun the computer so he could see more clearly. "Fuck." He sat back in his seat and scrubbed both hands over his face. The outgrowth of hair was almost a full-fledged beard now and the sound of the course hairs rasping against his palms irritated him. But he didn't have the fucking time to shave.

"We need to hunt this guy down and take care of him," Cole suggested.

"How the hell are we supposed to do that and still fly under the radar?" So many scenarios blasted through Luke's head—none of them were ideal for the situation they were faced with.

"Fuck if I know. But if we don't take care of the problem, the big man will find out and call this thing off."

"Fine." Luke leaned forward and braced his elbows on the table. "I'm putting you in charge of it."

"You know I like to be where the action is." Cole grinned like a kid who'd been abandoned in a toy store. Yeah, Luke knew this was Cole's thing, the more damage he could cause the better.

"But I bet you ten to one this bastard doesn't come out of hiding unless Ava is around."

"So we use her as bait." Luke could see the wheels turning in Cole's brain. But he didn't like the thought of putting Ava out in a situation like that.

"I don't like it," Luke bit out.

"How else do you suppose we get him to show himself? It's not like we can go around town yelling 'here, piggy piggy'."

"I guess you're right."

"How about this, we know he's more than likely not going to show up here again. What if we let her go back to her house and just keep an eye on the place?" Cole suggested.

"I don't see how that's supposed to work. Her house is out on the beach, the only neighbor she has is at least a hundred yards away." Luke tried to think of other alternatives but came up short.

Cole chuckled. "Only a hundred yards, that's child's play to you. Hell, that Columbian in Bogotá was further away than that, you dropped him while he was drinking his Folgers and reading the *Drug Lord Times*."

"Don't remind me. That was a tough one." Luke thought back to that job. It hadn't been easy at all. He'd sweated his ass off in the sub-tropic climate while wearing enough camouflage that even the trees thought he was one of them. "I'll cover the distance but I want you on site somehow."

"I can handle that. Chances are he doesn't know I'm here. If we play this right, I can use the cover as a beach bum for a bit." Cole began to type furiously on his laptop and then stopped. "Just pulled up the property next to hers. It's a vacation rental."

"Is it vacant?" Luke mentally crossed his fingers.

"As of three days ago. Doesn't look like the new vacationers are supposed to come in for another two weeks. That gives us plenty of time."

"We won't need two weeks," Luke said with utter certainty.

"Now the only problem is how do we get Ava back to her house? You insisted she stay here with you, you can't very well be like 'time to go'."

Cole had a point. But if Luke knew anything about Ava, it was that she had a temper. He would have to play on that and hope she would forgive him yet again for being an asshole. "I'll take care of it."

"Good luck. I'll spend the rest of this evening getting everything squared away. If you can get her there by tomorrow before dark, I think we'll have our best shot at taking this guy out."

Luke nodded. This was a throw-together plan, and hopefully it would pan out. If not, they would have to find some other way of tracking this guy down and taking him out of the equation. The one thing he didn't want though was for Ava to catch wind of any of this. If she did, she'd be gone. But on the flip side, if she didn't forgive him for what he was going to do in the morning, he'd lose her anyway.

Chapter Eighteen

AVA ROLLED OVER IN BED and hit a brick wall. Well, it wasn't really a brick wall; it was Luke sitting up in bed beside her. His lamp was on next to him on the nightstand and he was reading something on his phone. He hadn't noticed her awake just yet so she took the chance to admire him. Damn, she couldn't get enough of looking at the gorgeous man in the bed next to her. Even with the firm beginnings of a full beard, he was a sight to behold. How she got so lucky as to have met him was beyond her. She'd vowed to stay single because of her circumstances, but the day she laid eyes on Luke all of that changed. A bit of sadness crept in though as she thought about the future. What if she needed to go on the run again? What would that do to him? Did he even care for her as much as she'd begun to care for him? So many questions stood without solid answers.

"Are you staring at me?" His gravelly voice snapped her attention back to his face.

"Maybe." Her cheeks flamed with embarrassment and she ducked her head.

"And what were you thinking about when you 'might've' been staring at me?" He sat his phone on the table beside him and scooted down under the sheet so he was eye-level with her.

"How handsome you are." She pulled her hand from under the covers and yanked gently on his growing beard. "Even with this you're still gorgeous."

"First of all, men are not gorgeous. And are you telling me you don't like my beard?" One dark eyebrow lifted in amusement.

"It's growing on me." Ava began to run her fingers through the course hair on his face.

"That feels good." She watched as his eyelids shuttered his blue gaze while he reveled in the sensations that her fingers produced.

"I'm sorry you had to cut your meeting short because of me." Ava didn't know why she was apologizing—force of habit maybe. Or maybe it was to have some sort of conversation with him.

"Hey." Luke opened his eyes and began to stroke her face the same way she'd done his. "You needed my help. Don't apologize for that."

For some reason thoughts of the future replayed again. Not necessarily their future together but one where she had to leave suddenly. "Can I ask you something?"

"Anything." His eyes were focused on hers.

"If I had to pack up and leave tomorrow, what would you do?"

"Are you leaving?" His face became serious.

"It's a hypothetical question."

"Then I hypothetically don't have to answer it."

"I'm being serious. Just answer the question."

In mere seconds Luke had her pinned beneath him. He wasn't hurting her but every nerve ending in her body was singing in unison at the way his frame connected with hers. "Well, if I *knew* you were leaving, I'd tie you to my bed and make you stay." He laid his lips on hers and began to kiss her.

Hurt crept in as his words registered. This wasn't about a meaningful relationship like she'd hoped. It was strictly about sex for him. That should've been fine since that's what they started this whole thing out as. But even though every part of her was screaming for him to touch her, another part of her—her heart—was telling her that this entire thing was headed for disaster. She'd finally told herself that Luke wasn't just a fixation or a passing fancy. He meant something. And that something was going to rip her apart if she had to let it go.

"Look at me, Ava," he demanded. She did as he asked. "You're slipping away in that head of yours. I need you here, with me."

"I don't know if I can do this anymore." She felt more tears begin to build and didn't want to let them fall.

"Do what?" He looked confused.

"This. Us. I can't pretend what we have doesn't mean more than it does anymore."

She watched as thoughts flew through his head. What was he going to say? Was he going to beg her to stay and give this thing a shot? Or would he tell her to pack her shit and get out. Either way, if he feigned indifference, she'd be leaving anyway. So it didn't really matter what he had to say at this moment.

"I love you," he said.

Ava shook her head. Did she hear him wrong? He couldn't have said what she thought he said. "What did you say?" she whispered.

"I said I love you, Ava."

It didn't seem real. No, this had to be a dream and she'd wake up any second and be filled with disappointment. It was *too* perfect, *too* surreal. Someone needed to pinch her and make sure she was really hearing this correctly. Ava opened her mouth to respond to Luke's declaration only to be interrupted by his lips on hers once again. He took his time, savoring and licking the seam of her lips while running his hand down her clothed body. She thought for a second he'd be upset that she was wearing her nightgown while in his bed, but thought better of it when she felt his hands glide over the soft cotton of the fabric. She wanted to tell him how she felt, but he wasn't letting her. He was distracting her with his wicked mouth and hands.

Finally he broke the kiss, leaving her breathless and full of need. But still she had to say something. "Luke, I…" He stopped her by placing a finger over her kiss-swollen lips.

"Don't. I don't want you to say anything right now. I just want you to feel." His words were barely a whisper, but she heard him so loud and clear. They were punctuated with the touch of his fingertips moving gracefully down her side, lifting the bottom of her nightgown, until she could feel the cool air of the room on her bare legs and midsection.

Luke's body lifted off hers and he motioned to her gown. He didn't have to say anything; she knew what his request was. Her. Naked. So she grabbed the hem of the garment and pulled it over her head, dropping it off the side of the bed. As she lay back against the plush pillows, Luke hooked his fingers in the band of her panties and slid them down her legs—goosebumps popping up everywhere he touched. She wasn't sure she'd ever wanted him as much as she did right then. There was an urgency building inside that began at her core and felt like molten lava wanting to spew outward. Her eyes connected with his, asking a silent question when he didn't move back up her body.

He shook his head. "I need to taste you." He grabbed her legs and bent them at the knees, his gaze locking on the soaked flesh ready and waiting for his caress. "Fucking amazing." The look of extreme intent was written all over his bearded face as he scooted down the bed and aligned his face with her intimate folds. She'd never been one to enjoy oral sex, but having Luke front and center with her like this was giving her a heady sort of power she couldn't wait to unleash.

"Spread your knees apart for me, sweetheart. I want to see all of you."

She squirmed as she did what he said, his hands running the course of her legs causing her to whimper in anticipation. The lamp was still on beside the bed and the image of his face between her spread thighs had her ready to explode, and he wasn't even really touching her yet.

How pathetic. She was under his spell so much that with just one look she was a heap of need around this man. A man who truly loved her. Ava smiled at that thought. Luke loved her. He didn't just say it in the heat of the moment to make her happy, he meant it. Her thoughts of what that meant were halted by a tickling sensation along the insides of her thighs. She giggled a little when she realized it was Luke's newly grown beard causing her to become jovial all of a sudden. But the humor was cut short as he pressed his mouth to her sex and began giving the most erotic open-mouthed kiss she'd ever felt.

Hands and fingers delved into his hair as he licked her, paying special attention to her now swollen clit. She wouldn't last long if he kept this up. Her hips rose off the mattress as he dipped his tongue lower and fucked her in the same way he would've done with his cock.

"Oh fuck," Ava moaned as he began a sensual figure eight on her clit. His mouth was pure magic wrapped in sin. But she'd burn in hell before she told him to stop.

He concentrated on what he was doing and everything was done with precision. Just when she thought the sensations couldn't get any better, Luke added two fingers to the mix. He slowly entered her and pushed deep as he continued to tongue the outside of her sex.

"Luke, I'm going to come," she hissed. But he didn't speed up, he stopped entirely. "No, don't stop," she scolded.

"I'm not letting you come on my fingers. I want you to come on my tongue." He placed his mouth there once more and thrust his tongue deep inside her achy channel. It didn't fill her up as his cock would have but just knowing his mouth was on her made her lose her mind.

"Yes. Right there." He's managed to find a spot that made her hips buck off the bed and her words to lodge in her throat.

He pulled away for a moment to say, "When I put my mouth back on you, I want you to come all over my tongue." Then he was back at it. His warm tongue plunged back into her and she began to move her hips along with his fucking motions.

The scream that ripped from her throat spurred him on as her release climbed up her body and had her shaking from head to toe. Ava's hands fisted in the rumpled sheets as she felt Luke grab the cheeks of her ass and lift her slightly to get a better angle. If she didn't think his tongue could go any deeper, she was dead wrong. It did. The feeling causing her orgasm to extend past what she thought she could handle. Pulse upon pulse slammed into her until her body felt like a heap of bones on the bed.

Near lifeless she lay there while Luke worked her down from her epic release. Yes, she would certainly take a one way ticket to hell if it meant being able to experience something like that again.

Chapter Nineteen

LUKE WOKE EARLY to prepare for the day. A day he didn't want to have any part in. The plan was simple; the outcome would be anything but. He didn't expect a positive result from what he'd do when Ava woke up, but somewhere deep down, he hoped against hope she would someday see that his intentions were honorable. Even though he knew full well she'd never see it like that. He'd blame it on the way the woman's thought process worked, but he knew damn well that what he was preparing to do would shatter the beautiful soul still sleeping in his bed upstairs. All he could do was stare into his mug of black coffee and hope it would produce some valid answers.

"Morning," Cole clunked into the kitchen with a somber expression on his face. The man was always good for seriousness when the mood called for it. Today was one of those days.

"Yeah." Luke couldn't even bring himself to give a proper greeting.

"Did you figure out how to get things going?" Cole strode to the coffee pot and poured himself a cup. Even the sound of the liquid hitting the ceramic mug gave him a headache.

"I did."

"Wow, you're just full of extended responses today, aren't you?"

"Just do me a favor and play along when I get this rolling. You'll probably need to take her home, too."

"What if our friend is watching?" Cole pulled out a chair and took a seat.

"He won't be. There's no way he's watching this early. Not after his stunt yesterday. He's gonna be smart and lay low for a while today. If he comes out to play, it'll be later this evening or tonight."

"And you're sure about this?" Cole asked, cocking his head to the side.

"I'm not really fucking sure about anything right now. But I don't have another choice."

"Can I ask what the plan is with Ava?"

"No you can't. The more surprised you are the better. I need the effect to make it work."

"Whatever you say. You're the point man on this shit. I'm just the lowly backup dancer." Cole chuckled.

Damn it, Luke wanted to punch the guy in the fucking face again.

They sat at the table in silence drinking their coffee. Luke racked his brain for another way to handle this, but after what'd happened last night, he realized he needed to stick to the plan. The house was silent save for the normal creaking of the antiquated interior. A sound he was starting to get used to since he'd been there. It wasn't until he heard familiar footsteps descending the staircase that his nerves began to go haywire.

"Showtime," he said to Cole as he slapped his game face on.

Ava bounced into the kitchen wearing a pair of cutoff jean shorts and a pink tank top that said 'I'm a beautician, not a magician' scrolled across the front in a calligraphic font. Everything in him wanted to smile at her presence but he couldn't. This wasn't the time or place for that.

"Good morning, you two." Her voice was chipper and upbeat, the polar opposite of his current mood.

"Morning, Ava," Cole greeted and then looked over to Luke.

She went about getting herself a cup of coffee and sitting down at the table with them. Her eyes shot from his to Cole's—he tried to keep from holding her gaze too long. If he did, he'd chicken out of what he was on the verge of doing.

"Are you okay, Luke?" Her sweet voice snapped his attention and broke his concentration for a few seconds. But he quickly recovered.

"Fucking peachy." He shot her a sarcastic grin—by the look on her face she'd picked up on it immediately.

"Am I missing something?" She looked to Cole again.

"Don't ask me, he was a surly bastard when I came in here." Cole played along.

Ava laid her hand on his arm and he jerked it away like her touch had burned him. It did in a way, but there was nothing negative about this type of burn. "Luke, please tell me what's going on. Did I do something wrong."

He abruptly stood, knocking his chair back a couple feet. "We need to talk." He kept his voice steady.

"Okay, then talk. Clearly you have something on your mind." She became defensive. Just what he was hoping she'd do.

"I think I'll step outside while you two hash out what you need to." Cole stood and grabbed his half empty cup, retreating out the back door and away from the line of fire. If Luke knew him well, he'd bet the other man didn't go far.

"Now we're alone. So what's crawled up your ass?" Ava spat. There was the spitfire emerging that he wanted to see.

Luke turned his back, if he looked directly at her while he said what he needed to, he'd cave. "I said some things last night. I'm not a man to take back things I say, but I may've jumped the gun on one thing in particular." He rubbed the back of his neck where an ache was forming.

"Care to explain the *thing* you'd like to take back?"

"I think you know the one." He still didn't turn around.

The room became quiet and then he heard her say, "No. I want to hear you say it. Don't you dare take the coward's way out of this, Luke."

"Don't make me say it, Ava."

"Goddamn it! At least show me the respect of looking at me!" She shouted loud enough to make him jump.

Luke blanked his features and whirled around to face her. A look of hurt peppered her features and it took all the energy he had not to cross the room and wrap her in his arms. This was going to be the final nail in the coffin of this entire conversation but it had to be done. "Look, I was worked up. After everything that'd happened yesterday, I didn't think you'd want me near you unless I said it." He shrugged.

"Are you fucking serious right now?"

"Yes. I didn't know how you'd react if I wanted to go down on you. So I pushed things along a bit to make sure you'd let me." Damn that sounded horrible when he'd said it.

"I cannot believe what I'm hearing. You told me you loved me just to get into my pants?"

"Essentially."

"I don't believe you." He could see Ava was trying to rationalize everything he was telling her. But he wouldn't back down.

"Look, sweetheart, I told you from the beginning, this was only about fucking. It had nothing to do with feelings and shit. Clearly you didn't listen."

"And clearly you're a dick, just like every other man who's fucked me over."

"That very well may be. But you can't stand there and tell me the end of this shit wasn't coming sooner or later." Damn he just wanted this to end. Why did she have to keep coming at him?

"Why did you do this? Why did you act like you cared only to treat me like this?" She wiped furiously at her cheeks—the tears streaming down like ribbons of sorrow. Sorrow he'd put there.

"I think you know why." He gave a smirk and pointed his gaze at the crotch of her shorts.

"Just so you could get laid? Is that what this was about?" All he could do was nod. "Fine. I understand. But when I walk out that door, I won't *ever* be coming back, Luke." she warned.

"I don't expect you to."

She turned to leave the kitchen but pivoted back around. "Do you want to know something, though?"

He kept up the façade of being a dick. "Lay it on me, sweetheart."

"I *did* give a damn about you. You were the first person who made me feel safe. You were the first person who made me see the beauty in myself. But because of you, Luke Daughtry, I will never trust anyone with my heart again."

Her words sliced him to the bone. It felt as though his blood was gushing internally from just four little phrases. He'd done as he'd set out to do, he'd shattered her. But in the process, he'd managed to take his own heart and crush it with the weight of their words combined.

No. This was not happening. What'd started out as a dream the night before had morphed into a nightmare that Ava was now listlessly trudging through. She wasn't sure why but she shook her head to rid the bad thoughts from entering her mind, as if it would help dispatch the bad events from her memory. But they were like sick little demons that wouldn't let her go. She'd woken with such a blissful outlook this morning and now, everything was blank and putrid.

As Ava stuffed her clothes into her bags she couldn't help but flash back to the day she'd began running.

The day her life had been upended and she landed in Mississippi. That was a day filled with zero hope. She'd looked over her shoulder so many times that day, praying she'd escape without them finding her. It wasn't until she ended up in Biloxi that she'd finally thought things were going to turn around. Of course they did…until now. The same scared feelings swamped her as she grabbed what she could from Luke's room and closed her bags—almost breaking the zipper on one with the force of her hands. Every emotion took hold as she fought to rein in each of them. Hurt was the one that kept popping to the forefront. Luke had successfully hurt her worse than any physical damage ever could. He'd reached inside her chest, plucked out her heart and squeezed every last ounce of blood from it. The chill of the sting was such that no amount of warm blankets or thick cable-knit sweaters could erase the frigid loss. What was once a lively beating organ was transformed into a pale, comatose heap that could never be healed. If truth be told, she didn't want healing. She wanted to leave her heart the way it was so in the future, it would remind her what it was like to be beaten so badly from the inside out. If there was a way to see the scars from heartbreak, Ava knew the one covering her insides would be a grotesque lump with the words 'you should've known better' scrolled across its surface.

Each moment she stayed in his house, the more everything became real. Even the scent of Luke while she gathered her things was telling her this was far from over. But why all of a sudden did he change his mind? Why would he so wholeheartedly tell her he loved her and then rip it away? It didn't make sense. What'd happened between last night and this morning to turn him from a caring, sensual man to a cold-hearted asshole? She didn't have the answers she was seeking. The only thing she could do was get the hell out of there before she went down and begged him to reconsider. Ava knew without a doubt that wasn't going to happen. She'd cut off her own tongue before she begged Luke for anything. She *did* have one thing left…pride.

As Ava finished packing her things, she looked around the room to make sure she didn't leave anything out. Having to contact Luke once she was gone wasn't an option. In fact, she hoped she'd never have to look at his face again.

"Hey, Ava." Cole's voice sounded behind her. It wasn't like he had anything to do with this, but it didn't make her want to talk to him either way. "I just wanted to see if you need a ride home."

"I'm fine," she spat.

"Well, I talked to Brandi. She's at work and can't leave."

"Then I guess I'll walk."

"Don't be ridiculous. I can drive you home." Cole stepped further into the room and grabbed one of her bags off the bed, slinging it over his shoulder. "Come on."

Ava didn't argue, she only picked up the rest of her belongings and followed him out of the room. Funny thing was, she didn't bother looking back. It wouldn't have done any good. It was difficult trying to keep the good memories to the forefront as it was. Looking back to see the bed where she and Luke had made love and he'd told her he loved her, no, she didn't need that.

There wasn't any sign of Luke as Cole led her to his truck. It seemed like she was walking to her demise after spending a stint on death row. But even death row inmates were offered a last meal; hell, she hadn't even gotten to drink her coffee before Luke turned into Mr. Hyde. Whatever, just like everything else she'd ever cared for, it was now in the past. One last look around and Ava knew this was it. This was the last time she'd see any of this and truthfully, she'd already made peace with it. She had to. It wasn't like Luke would come running out of the house and beg for her to stay like in some romantic drama film.

Heck, he was probably in the house laughing at her right now. Chuckling about her stupidity in believing he was a decent human being. Well, the joke was on her. She *had* believed that.

"I'm sorry about all this," Cole spoke beside her and sounded remorseful.

"I guess it is what it is." Ava continued to gaze out the window, watching the Mississippi scenery pass her by.

"For what it's worth, I really thought you two had a shot."

"At least that makes two out of three. But apparently the odds were stacked against this deck." Damn she hated being so negative.

"Maybe it'll work out in the end?" Cole said it as a question.

The cynical laugh that bubbled up was something she couldn't help. "Yeah, and pigs will fly and hell will freeze over."

"Did you love him?" Cole asked softly.

"I don't even know." Ava sighed.

"I don't want to take his side here, but maybe he had his reasons."

"Really? There're reasons for telling someone you love them and taking it back? What kinds of reasons could someone possibly have to do something like that?"

"I have no clue."

"Exactly. There aren't any reasons to rip someone's heart out and trample it like it never meant anything to you, Cole."

Cole didn't respond and she couldn't blame him. He was caught between a rock and a hard place. Luke was his cousin and he owed him some sort of loyalty. He was only trying to be nice to her, which in reality, he didn't have to. She had to give him credit though, at least he wasn't acting like a total asshat.

"Can I ask you something?" She turned in her seat and looked at Cole's profile. Something had been bugging her and she thought maybe he could give her some answers now that they were away from Luke.

"Go for it."

"Was Luke in the military?" she blurted out.

Cole answered instantly, "Nope."

"Damn it," she bit out.

"Shit," Cole cursed and smacked the palm of his hand on the top of the steering wheel.

"What?"

"Nothing. I just thought of something I forgot to grab before we left." He turned his head and smiled. But it was one that held secrets. What wasn't he telling her? Just like Luke, Cole was hiding something.

"Um, can you do me a favor? I need to be dropped off at Brandi's work."

A partially panicked expression covered his face briefly before he said, "Luke asked me to take you to your house."

"I don't belong to Luke. And after this morning, I don't give a damn what he says. So take me to her work or I won't hesitate to jump out of this truck and walk there." Her anger was bubbling to the surface.

"Fine." He drove a few more miles and took the turn that led into the heart of town. More silence filled the cab of the truck while he went down Main Street and parked in front of her best friend's work. When he reached for the handle to get out, Ava stopped him.

"Thanks for the lift. I can handle it from here." She hurriedly removed herself from the vehicle and grabbed her bags. She didn't bother waving goodbye or say anything else as she quickly entered Brandi's work.

Once Ava was in the small building that housed the local newspaper's headquarters, she darted back to the office at the end of the hall. The door was closed so she knocked twice until she heard Brandi's voice say "Come in!" on the other side.

Pushing the door open she tossed her bags down in the corner by the fake potted tree and looked at her friend who gazed at her curiously. "This is a nice surprise," Brandi's face raised with a smile but soon fell as she noticed the look of despair on Ava's face.

"I need your help," Ava said, while plopping down in the plastic retro chair across from Brandi's small desk.

"Okay. But aren't you supposed to be at Luke's house? What the hell are you doing here?" Brandi slammed her laptop shut and propped her hands on her fists.

"Luke and I are no more."

"What? How is that possible? You guys were like watching a fucking Nicholas Sparks movie."

"And sort of like those movies, bad shit happened." Ava told her closest confidant about the events from the night before and this morning.

"Jesus Christ. Are you alright?" She jumped from her seat and came around the desk, throwing her arms around Ava in a tight hug.

Ava promised herself she wouldn't cry a river over this thing but the way Brandi was so caring when she wanted to be had Ava about to shed every tear she'd been holding back. "I'll be okay," she squeaked out.

"How are you going to be okay after something like that, Ava? And how the hell could he go from telling you he loved you to telling you he was only with you to get a piece of ass? That doesn't make any sense!" Brandi raised her voice.

"I just don't know. I thought everything was perfect but as usual…the other shoe dropped. Heck, it dropped so hard I think it fell apart." Ava sighed and sat back further in her chair. "Brandi, there's some things I need to tell you. After I tell you them, I need your help."

"Okay."

"You might want to sit down for this," Ava said motioning to the chair behind the desk.

"Wow, this must be some heavy shit. You've never told me to take a seat," she chuckled.

Ava steadied herself for what she was going to reveal.

In the two years she'd been in Biloxi, she'd never breathed a word to anyone. It was how she'd survived all this time. She only hoped her friend would stay tight-lipped once she knew the entire story.

"I've not been entirely truthful about where I used to live. I'm not from California, I'm from Chicago," she began.

"That's not so bad. I thought you were gonna tell me you killed someone."

"I'm not finished." She took another breath and continued her story. "In Chicago I used to date this guy named Frankie. His nickname was Frank the Tank. Frankie, at first, was great. He was what I'd want in a boyfriend. But then things changed. I found out what he really did for a living."

"Okay, you're scaring me." Brandi rose and closed the door to the office to give them more privacy.

"You've heard of the mob, right?" Ava asked.

"Of course."

"Frankie's dad was the head of one of the biggest money laundering organizations on the East Coast. His dad is in New York and Frankie took care of things in Chicago. They'd funnel the money to Chicago to take some of the heat off the operation in New York."

"Jesus," Brandi breathed.

"It wasn't like I agreed with the things they were doing, but in a way, I was scared to leave. I didn't want them to hurt me. They knew full well that I knew everything about what they were doing, so I stayed. It wasn't until the day I left that things changed."

"Ava, I'm not sure you should be telling me this."

"Please, just listen. I need your help."

"I don't know how I can help you."

"Let me finish." Ava waited until Brandi quieted and then continued: "That morning I went to the building where they conducted their business. I was supposed to drop off lunch for Frankie because he couldn't get away. I parked my car behind the building like I always did and took the back door. I went into the office area they had set up and put the food down on the desk. There was a black duffle bag sitting there and I peeked in. It was a shit ton of money. I didn't really think anything of it until I heard shouting coming from the area next to the office. I peeked around the corner and was horrified at what I saw."

Ava could still remember what'd unfolded like it was taking place right now. "They had a guy tied to a chair and Frankie was beating the shit out of him. He and two other guys kept asking where the rest of their money was. But the guy couldn't say anything; he was gagged. I stayed there watching them and when Frankie pulled out a gun I almost screamed but stopped myself. It was like watching a movie, Brandi. He lifted the gun to the man's head and pulled the trigger."

"Holy fuck." Brandi's eyes were wide and filled with fear.

"I didn't know what to do so I darted back inside the office and for some reason, grabbed the duffle bag full of cash. I got the hell out of there as fast as I could."

"But if they didn't see you, how'd they know you were there?"

"They have security cameras on every inch of that place, inside and out. I drove to my apartment and started packing as fast as I could. Frankie left several voicemails saying he knew I was there and knew I had the money. He threatened to kill me when he found me. So I ran. I didn't take my car or my phone, I just left. I took a bus here and have been hiding here for two years."

"Why didn't you go to the police?"

"They had so many cops in their back pockets I knew if I'd accidentally told the wrong one, I'd be at the bottom of Lake Michigan."

"Why are you telling me this now? Why wait until two years later to tell me?" Brandi had a look of hurt on her face.

"Because I think Luke and Cole are somehow involved in this." Ava didn't want to think that, but so many things were causing her suspicion.

"No way. They're just good ole southern boys. There's no way they could be even remotely involved with the mob."

"Luke has a sniper rifle in his basement. Cole had a handgun in his room. Why the hell would they have those things if they weren't involved?"

"I don't know, maybe because they're men and men like guns."

"These aren't normal guns, Brandi. The one Cole had, it looked like some sort of police issue firearm."

"So you think Cole is a dirty cop, and what's Luke? A fucking hitman out to get you?" A laugh bubbled out of Brandi's mouth. "I'm sorry, but that sounds insane."

"I know it does. But what about the person who knocked me in the head in Luke's basement? What about the creepy guy staring at me in the grocery store? There're too many things happening to play it off as coincidence."

"Okay well if Luke *is* some mob-hired hitman, why hasn't he taken you out yet?" Brandi asked.

Ava thought for a second and the only reason she could come up with was, "The money. There's $2 million there. They'd want their money back before taking care of me. Frankie is an idiot but he's not stupid enough to let $2 mil go missing indefinitely."

"You think they have him watching you? To figure out where the money is?"

"I think so. I think as soon as they figure it out…I'm dead." Ava's stomach sank at the thought.

"Where is the money?" Brandi asked.

"I'm not telling you. If they somehow get to you and you tell them, they'll have you taken care of, too. I can't risk you getting hurt over this thing."

"Ava, this sounds like some crazy movie plot. Hitmen, the mob, stolen money, it's all so ridiculous."

"I wouldn't believe it either if I weren't living it."

"Okay, but what do you need me to do?"

Ava reached into her purse and pulled out the item she'd taken and tossed it on the desk. "Luke's wallet was sitting on the nightstand. I took his driver's license. Don't you have a friend at the DMV?"

"Yeah, Eddie Perkins."

"Can you have him run that? I want to know if it's real. If it's not, I have to get the hell out of here."

"So you're going to keep running?"

"I have to. If they've found me, then I'm as good as dead."

"I'll take it to Eddie on my lunch break. *You* need to go home and watch your back, Ava. Lock your doors and don't let anyone in. I'll call you when I hear from Eddie."

Brandi plucked a tissue from a box nearby and carefully wrapped the plastic card in it without touching it with her own fingers. "I also know someone at the sheriff's department. I'll have them run the prints on here; it might tell us who we're dealing with."

"Thank you. Please don't tell anyone why you need this info. I need to keep as few people involved in this as humanly possible." Ava breathed a sigh of relief.

"Go home and be safe." Brandi stood and walked around the desk once more. She hugged Ava.

Ava grabbed her bags from the corner and headed out the door. The next stop was her hair salon so she could pick up her car. After that, she was going home, packing her things and getting ready to run once more. It wasn't what she wanted to do, especially after having her heart freshly crushed. But if Luke was what she'd suspected, it was a good thing things didn't work out with them.

Chapter Twenty

"DID YOU HAVE TO BE so harsh?" Cole asked Luke as they made their way to the basement.

"What other choice did I have?"

"I don't know, maybe you could've told her you needed some space. Telling her that you love her and then saying you used it to get in her pants? Even *I* know better than that, and *I'm* an asshole."

"Look, it was the best I could come up with at the time. Was it the right thing to do? Hell no. I wish I could've come up with something that didn't crush her like that. But what's done is done." Luke started tossing equipment into a backpack.

"What happens when this is all over with?" Cole grabbed the binoculars and tossed them in the bag.

"Fuck if I know. She'll never talk to me again, that's for damn sure." Luke hated *that* fact. If he'd have just thought things through a bit more, he wouldn't have had to see Ava leave with that look on her face. The one that made his heart stop beating.

"Did you mean it, though?"

"Mean what?" Luke pinned Cole with a stare and braced his hands on the workbench.

"Do you love her?" Cole mirrored his stance on the opposite side of the table. Luke stood up straight and folded his muscled arms over his chest. One hand reached up and scrubbed across the beard that was *way* out of control at this point. "Just answer the question, man," Cole prodded.

"Yes, goddamn it! I love her!" His voice rose and had Cole stepping back a foot or so. "And I fucked it up." He hated to admit it aloud; it made it more real when he heard those words come from his own mouth.

"What are your plans? Are you gonna walk away when this is all over?"

"Why the hell are you asking me so many questions?"

"I don't know, maybe because I had to sit in a vehicle with a woman and could hear her damn heart breaking over the road noise." Cole looked pissed.

"What would you know about relationships anyway? You're only good for one night stands and booty calls. You've no right to judge me."

Cole held up his hands in surrender. "You know what, you're right. I know nothing about any of this. But I do know that even though she never got the chance to tell you, that woman loves the hell out of you. So you can finish your job here and walk away, or you can try to make it right. It's up to you."

"How about we shut the hell up about this subject and focus on the task at hand. You need to get your ass down to that beach and start surveillance."

"You're the boss," Cole said as he snatched up the pack with the supplies in it.

Luke watched him tromp up the steps and out of the house. Damn it he felt like total shit for what he'd done to Ava. Why did he have to go and be a complete bastard? He wasn't sure what the hell he was gonna do when this was all over, but for now, the main priority was keeping her safe. If he could pull that off and get his job done, he'd figure the rest out later.

"Are you home now?" Ava didn't even have time to say 'hello' when she picked up Brandi's call.

"Not yet, I'm still at the salon." Ava looked around trying to figure out if there was anything she needed to take with her.

"Ava, you need to get home. I don't think it's a good idea for you to be out gallivanting around," Brandi scolded.

"I'm just grabbing a few things from the shop. I won't be long, I promise."

"Okay. Be sure to call me when you get home safe though."

"I will," Ava assured her friend.

Once they hung up, Ava still stood in the middle of her shop wondering what she needed to take with her. She'd come in here for something but her brain wasn't working properly with all the stress mounting around her. She spun around, hoping something would give her a reminder. When she faced her styling chair, it finally hit her, "My shears," Ava breathed. "Definitely not leaving without these."

She picked up the glittering steel and slipped her ring finger and thumb into the fingerholes. There was zero certainty as to when she'd be able to do her job again, so for old time sake, Ava moved her fingers and listened to the smooth glide of the blades as they opened and closed. What a beautiful sound. The *whooshing* of the steel coming together was like listening to a slight breeze blowing across the ocean's surface. It was in a word…*perfect*. But perfection never lasted long. So Ava tossed the shears into their leather pouch and dropped it into her purse.

She took one last look around the shop that'd been her home for the past two years and said her goodbyes. There would be no coming back to this place once she took that final step out the door. The only thing that was in her future was more running. A life that had no guarantees and no emotion once more. It saddened her to think that it took Luke to make her feel something for life again. He'd brought out the best and worst in her but she loved him all the same for it. As much as it hurt to think about him, she was thankful for the time she'd had with him. He'd showed her that being happy was possible, even if it was only for a brief moment in time.

"Do you see her?" Luke talked in a hushed voice into his walkie-talkie.

"That's a negative," Cole responded instantly.

"Where the hell is she?"

"No clue. Want me to take a closer look?"

"No. Hold back. If she happens to come home, I don't want you discovered."

"Rodger that."

The sun was setting over the ocean and Luke was holed up in the house next to Ava's. Everything was quiet so far, almost *too* quiet. Something seemed off but Luke couldn't quite put his finger on it. He'd been peering out the scope of his rifle for what seemed like hours now and he'd seen nothing but seagulls and a scraggly stray cat. Not to mention, Ava wasn't even home yet. It was going to be tough catching a shark when the chum wasn't even in the water.

Minutes ticked by and finally Luke caught the glow of a set of headlight approaching Ava's house. He made sure his gun was set firmly on its bi-pod and picked up his night-vision binoculars to take a look. It wasn't quite dark yet but the handy tool helped him secure a clear vision of whom or what was coming. Scanning the area, Luke radioed Cole, "She's home," he said through the crackle of the receiver.

"Yup, just got a visual." Cole's voice came out of the speaker with minimal static.

"Don't get too close, she has a watchful eye."

"I can't imagine why," Cole chuckled into the device.

"How about you lay off the smartass comments and keep your eye on the bait," Luke bit out.

"Rodger dodger," Cole laughed again causing Luke to roll his eyes. If Cole wasn't such a good partner, he'd have kicked him to the curb a long time ago. But as fate would have it, they were stuck like glue after Cole managed to save his ass in Bogotá.

"We've got company," his partner relayed. "Get behind your scope, I think this's him." There was an urgency in Cole's voice that Luke recognized immediately.

He tossed the binoculars down and grabbed the butt of the gun, fitting it in the perfect crevice between his shoulder and chest. Once more he scanned the vicinity and then landed on a shadowy figure that seemed to be sneaking around the property. "I've got a bogie near the side of the garage. Do you copy?"

"Copy that. I'm going in for a closer look."

Luke brushed the barrel back and forth until his sites landed on Cole. Sneaking around just as the other guy was, he came up behind the man—and in one fluid motion, reached up and snapped his neck. Cole held onto the body until it softly hit the ground. Suddenly Cole's head jerked up and he took off running.

"Got another one. Can't see him but he's firing on me." Cole's voice came out breathless as he darted around the now dark property.

"Get to cover. I'm trying to find him." Luke searched frantically through his scope and finally spotted a glint of something about fifty yards away. "I got you, you son-of-a-bitch." He adjusted the wind gauge slightly, lined up his shot and squeezed the trigger with maximum precision. The only sound was the slight 'ping' as the bullet left the suppressor on the way to its target. "Bogie number 2 is down," Luke said confidentially through the walkie-talkie.

"I'm hit," Cole bit out.

"Fuck." Luke took one more pass of the area and determined they'd taken out the threat for now. "How bad?" he asked as he quickly broke down his weapon and shoved the pieces into the black carrying case nearby.

"Just my lower leg. No major arteries but it stings like a motherfucker," Cole chortled.

Luke relaxed a bit, but this was far from over. "I think you're the only person on the planet who laughs at getting shot."

"The ladies love scars. The more scars, the more ass you get." Cole cracked up laughing.

"If you say so. Meet me on the beach past Ava's house when you're finished mentally scheduling booty calls for the next five years."

"I think I can milk this injury for at least six years, maybe even six and a half," Cole threw back.

Luke couldn't help but chuckle a little at Cole's positive outlook on the situation. The poor guy had been grazed too many times to count. Getting a hunk of metal slashed through your skin was just another day in paradise for his partner.

Ava hurried around her house packing essentials into a few bags. Just like Chicago, she'd have to leave most of it behind. She wondered for half a second why she'd even attempted to gather things and build any sort of life in Mississippi; it wasn't like it was going to be permanent or anything. There was always a timestamp on this part of her life. She'd come to terms with that fact when she'd boarded the bus in Chicago two years ago. But this was the way things had to be. If she wanted to continue breathing for any length of time, she had to get the hell out of here.

Once a few bags were packed and placed by the front door, Ava hustled into the garage to grab her *other* stash. Just as she did before, she spun the combination until the lock popped free and then she tossed the hunk of metal to the side. There was no putting it back in place *this* time; this was the very last time she'd go into this hiding place.

Sliding back the metal door she took two steps at a time until she was standing in front of the black duffle. The thought of protecting herself crossed her mind as she unzipped the bag and dug around for the gun stashed underneath the stacks of money. The solid chill of the firearm touched her fingers and Ava grasped it while trying to calm her overwrought nerves.

"I can do this," the chant fell from her lips several times while she pulled the gun free. It wasn't like the words could calm her in any way, but being alone while knowing people were after you was one thing that made her want to lock herself in the hiding place and never come out. But she'd gained so much strength over the past couple years. She'd learned to trust people and had some happy memories to get her through the rough times she was headed for. Even the terrible things Luke had said to her didn't dampen the way she felt about him. But knowing there was a good chance he was the one after her didn't sit well at all. It was time to go.

Ava grabbed the handles of the heavy bag and hoisted them over her small shoulder. The weight caused her body to lean to the left a bit but she wanted to keep her right arm free in case she needed to use the gun. She hoped against hope that wouldn't happen, but if it did, she'd be ready. Her body was trembling as she padded through the garage and into the kitchen. Hiking the bag further up on her shoulder she turned the corner and froze. The bag slipped off her arm and landed with a thud on the hardwood floor. Adrenaline racked her body as she raised her other arm and pointed the gun at the person standing in her living room.

"Ava, put the gun down," Luke held a similar weapon in his hand.

"No." Her heart began to beat loud in her ears as it pumped the adrenaline through her veins.

Luke raised his gun and pointed it at her. "Ava, please lower your weapon."

She shook her head and moved her finger closer to the trigger. "I said no!" she shouted, hoping he would hear the seriousness in her voice.

"Fine. I'm putting mine down." Luke began to lower his weapon and then crouched to the floor. He placed the black metal in front of him and stood with both hands raised in front of him.

"Kick it over here," she blurted out. "Now."

"Okay." Luke put his foot over the gun and slid it across the floor. The scraping sound echoing in the room around them.

Ava kept hers trained on his broad chest as she crouched to retrieve the gun he'd slid over. When she stood, she tucked the extra weapon in the waistband of her jeans. "Do you have any other weapons on you?" she asked.

"No." He didn't seem at all phased by having the barrel of a deadly weapon aimed at his chest.

"Good. I'm going to grab my stuff and leave. If you try to follow me, I will fucking shoot you, Luke."

"Ava," Luke's voice held warning.

"Don't try to stop me. I know why you're here."

"Why am I here?" Luke asked, cocking his head to the side.

"You were hired by Frankie to take me out. Well I have news for you, I won't go down without a fight." Ava raised her chin in defiance.

"Jesus. Ava, before you leave, I need to explain a few things."

"I don't want to hear anything from you, Luke. You're full of lies."

"Fine. But at least let me show you something before you go." He began to reach around to his back pocket.

"Hands where I can see them!" she shouted.

"I already told you I don't have another weapon. I have something to show you and I need you to see it."

Ava nodded. "Pull it out slowly and toss it over here."

Luke grabbed ahold of something and brought his arm back around to the front of his body. It looked like he was holding some sort of wallet. With a flick of his wrist, the item was at her feet. Ava held her gun on him while she picked up the black leather item. She turned it over several time in her hands.

"Open it," Luke said.

"I am." With one hand Ava unfolded it and gasped as three bold letters and the unmistakable gold emblem stared back at her. "This isn't real." She tossed it to the floor and gawked at Luke.

"It's as real as they come, Ava." Luke ran a hand over his face, the sound of his beard rasping against his fingers. "And you're holding a weapon on me." He began to step forward.

"Back up," she demanded but he kept taking steps, coming closer and closer.

"I think you know deep down that it's real. So ask yourself what the repercussions are if you shoot me. Do you think they'll go easy on you?"

"Almost $2 million," Ava's voice came out weak. Both men looked at her. "I used some to buy this house."

"That's why they're looking for you." Luke ran a hand through his shaggy hair.

Ava nodded. "Frankie won't stop until he finds his money. And since I took it, he'll want to make sure I won't take anything else. *Ever again.*"

"Get on the horn with the home office. Let them know what we've found. Tell them to get their asses down here," Luke barked orders to Cole.

"What do we do in the meantime?" Cole asked.

"We get her somewhere safe."

Ava glanced over to Cole and sucked in a breath.

"You're bleeding."

Cole looked down to his leg and back to Ava. "Bullet grazed me. You had some company earlier and we took care of them."

Ava stood up so fast her head spun. "They know where I am now?"

"Yes. That's why we need to get you someplace safe." Luke grabbed her shoulders and looked her in the eye.

"No. I'll leave. If I go they won't be able to find me."

"You can't keep running like this, Ava. They'll track you no matter where you go."

"He's right," Cole agreed. "You're best bet is to stick with us. We'll make sure you're safe."

Just then Luke's cell phone rang. Ava watched as he pulled the device from his pocket and stared at the screen. "Fuck," he cursed.

"What's up?" Cole stepped further into the room.

"They never call on my personal number, only the burner phone. They know who I am now."

"Then we'd better get the hell out of here." Cole snatched up the duffle full of money and left the bathroom.

Luke turned to a shaky Ava and grabbed the sides of her face in his rough hands. "Listen, I will explain everything once I have you in a secure location. I need you to trust me. Can you do that?"

Ava didn't want to trust him. She wanted to flee and hope she'd get a running start. But the sincere look in Luke's eyes told her everything she needed to know. She could trust him. He knew how to protect her. "I trust you," she whispered.

Luke leaned forward and brushed his lips across her forehead. Confusion washed over her at the intimacy in the action. "I'm sorry about all of this. The lying and the things I said, Ava."

"I don't know if I can forgive you." She wasn't lying. It was hard to forgive someone when they shredded your heart like it never mattered to them.

"I understand." Luke nodded.

"I need to grab my bags." Ava brushed past his warm body; a shudder wafted over her as the jolt of attraction sparked deep in her core. She shouldn't still be attracted to him. He wasn't who he said he was. But there was nothing that could quell the boiling sensations she felt when close to him. She hated to admit; Luke was it for her. But unfortunately, this wasn't going to have a happily ever after.

Chapter Twenty-One

"THE GUYS ARE COMING from Gulfport. Should be here by morning," Cole informed Luke as he drove toward his house.

It was the safest location he could think of. Ava would be comfortable and he had enough firepower stashed around the property to take down a small country. With his and Cole's talents, they could quite possibly come out of this thing unscathed. He glanced over at Ava in the passenger seat. Her hair was loose around her shoulder and the glow from the dash lights shone on her flawless face, making her appear angelic. Damn it he loved this woman. But now wasn't the time for hearts and flowers. If they made it through this shit, he'd figure out what to do with his feelings. For now, he needed to be in combat mode.

"We'll hunker down and wait it out. I have a feeling Frankie and his boys are on their way. If we can hold them off until the cavalry arrives in the morning, we can get on a plane and get her into Wit-Sec," Luke said, turning his head and looking at Cole in the back seat.

Ava's head popped up. "I'm not going into witness protection. No fucking way."

"You don't have a choice." Luke was all business.

"Yes I do. Pull over!" she shouted in the interior of the truck.

"Ava, calm down." Luke could see she was on the verge of another breakdown.

"How am I supposed to calm down? You want to stash me away in some Amish community, change my name and pretend I don't exist. I can't live like that."

Luke couldn't help but feel saddened by the way the prospect of witness protection affected Ava. Her strong will and determination held steady even though she was in a life-and-death situation. He admired her even more for it. "Okay. Let's get through tonight and then we'll figure out what to do."

Ava visibly relaxed and leaned her head against the window. "I'm so tired," she whispered.

"When we get home you can rest," Luke offered.

"No, I'm tired of running. I've done nothing but look over my shoulder for the last two years. I don't know if I can do this anymore." She sighed.

Luke didn't know what to say to that. He couldn't guarantee she'd never have to run again, although he wanted to. If he could climb a ladder to the moon, he'd hand her that glowing hunk of rock and every damn star in the sky if she wanted. But the only thing she wanted was safety. That was something he'd try to give her until he was taken from this world. The decision was made a long time ago; he'd die for this woman.

"How about you go upstairs and get a shower. Cole and I will secure the house and perimeter."

"Yeah, I'm sure." Luke continued on their path, placing more devices around the grounds.

"I'm sure you have a lot of explaining to do."

"I at least owe her that much. She'll hate me no matter what at this point but I have to clear the air at least."

"You'd better get to it then. I'll finish this up."

"Alright, man." Luke clapped Cole on the back.

"I've got the first watch. I'm pretty much wired so take all the time you need," he offered.

"Thanks, I appreciate it." Luke was honored to have a partner like Cole. He knew that no matter what, the other man had his six. But now it was time to bite the bullet and tell Ava everything. Some things she wasn't going to want to hear, but he knew it was time to tell her.

Making his way through the house, Luke took the stairs two at a time on the way up to his bedroom. When he opened the door the breath was knocked out of him at the sight of Ava sitting in the middle of his bed, her knees pulled to her chest. She looked absolutely beautiful with her hair still damp from her shower and a baggy t-shirt covering her small frame. Instinct screamed for him to go to her, pull her body next to his and never let go. But he couldn't do that. She was like a cornered animal right now. If he spooked her, she'd draw further into herself and shut him out completely.

"Can I come in?" Luke stood in the doorway.

"It's your house." She shrugged. "Or is this your house at all? Was this another elaborate ruse?" She pinned him with a no-nonsense stare.

"Actually, this is my house. The story about my grandmother and family is true. She left it to me when she passed away." He stepped closer to the bed. "I want to explain everything…if you'll let me."

"Seems like we have time. Might as well get to it."

He admired the little bit of sass and fire she was showing. It told him she hadn't yet given up. "I'm not sure where to start exactly, but I guess the beginning will suffice."

"I'd say so."

There was that attitude once more. Luke grinned in response. "When I was first accepted into the academy I was assigned to a case in Chicago. We didn't have a choice back then, you went where they told you." He took a seat on the end of the bed. "The investigation was a homicide."

"Why would the FBI be involved in a murder investigation?" she asked. "That's not really in your jurisdiction."

"Very smart. You're right. But when the suspects have ties to organized crime, we *do* have jurisdiction. This one was one of those cases." Luke watched Ava scoot back and prop herself against the pillows behind her. His mouth automatically went dry at the sight of her bare thighs. He snapped his attention back to her face. "A couple was murdered and all leads pointed to the Bohannan family."

It didn't take long for recognition to dawn on Ava's face. "Bohannan? Wait, that's Frankie's last name."

"Precisely." Luke didn't want to reveal the next part but he had to tie all the pieces together for her. "Ava, the case I was working on was the one involving your parents."

"*What?*" Her eyes narrowed into tiny slits as she tried to process this new information.

"The case had gone cold and myself and a couple colleagues were trying to figure out the connection between the Bohannans and your parents."

"My parents weren't in the fucking mob." Her defenses went up.

"No, they weren't. But their business was secured by Frankie Senior. He owned the building that housed their bookstore."

"So what? He was their landlord. That doesn't mean he killed them."

"Ava, he had a laundering operation in the basement of that building. Your mom and dad discovered it. How do you think Frankie Senior reacted to someone knowing about his little business?" Luke watched the tears begin to roll down Ava's cheeks but he continued. "They were taken care of because they saw too much. The same thing they're trying to do to you."

"Why would Frankie want me as his girlfriend then? Why go to the trouble of having your son date the daughter of the people you killed? It doesn't make sense." Ava shook her head.

"Think about it. If you wanted to take the heat off yourself, wouldn't you want to get as close to the family as possible?"

"Yes."

"Where did you meet Frankie Junior?" Luke asked.

"He was a client when I was in cosmetology school."

"Did he become a client shortly after your parent's deaths?"

"Yes, he did."

"They've been using you to keep us off their trail."

"That still doesn't explain how you ended up here."

"When Frankie Junior needed someone to take care of you, I went undercover. He didn't know me from the investigation with your parents because I only dealt with his father. So I was golden to slip in there and find you."

"You were hired as a hitman?"

"Yes. But they wanted something other than to dispose of you."

"The money," Ava breathed.

"Exactly. But now they know who I am."

"What do we do?" Ava had a worried look in her eyes.

"We wait. Cole and I have everything secure. He's taking the first watch so we can rest."

Ava glanced around the room and back to him. "I'm scared," she said on a whisper.

Luke couldn't help himself. He sat beside her on the bed and pulled her to his chest. The top of her head sat just under his chin and he ran a hand down the damp strands of her hair. "I'm here, sweetheart," he soothed.

Ava pulled back. "Luke, I need you." She looked into his eyes and it was almost like she was pleading with him.

"You have me," he said.

There was no warning when she launched herself at him and fused her lips to his. The force of her actions caused him to lose balance and land on his back on the soft mattress.

"Just one more night, that's all I'm asking for," she said as she lay on top of him.

He thrust his fingers in her hair and tugged. "One more night."

Chapter Twenty-Two

AVA WASN'T REALLY SURE why she was asking to be with Luke again. After all, he'd hurt her beyond repair. If she was a glutton for punishment, this would be Exhibit A. The only explanation she could dredge up was the stress of the entire situation and the information that'd been handed to her. Something like that would cause anyone to seek a moment of bliss. The closest thing Ava could find to achieve her harmony was Luke. Maybe she was using him or maybe she still had feelings for him even though he'd ripped her heart to shreds. Either way, one more night and she'd be through with him and he with her. Now that she knew the truth and knew who he really was, it would never work between them anyway.

As Ava lay on top of Luke's firm body, she could feel his warmth surrounding her like a cozy blanket. His scent that she adored permeated her senses and she found herself closing her eyes and committing it to memory for the last time. Maybe it would get her through the tough times that lay on the road ahead of her.

"Hey, open your eyes for me," Luke's deep voice cut through the silence and Ava did as he said. "Why are you closing them?" he asked.

"I don't know." She didn't want to tell him she was trying to memorize everything about him behind her eyelids. That would interrupt the little bubble they were currently in, and she didn't want their bubble popped.

"You don't know? Or you don't want to tell me?" he questioned.

"Neither?" Her voice sharpened a bit.

"Did you forget what I do for a living? I'm pretty damn good at knowing when someone's lying to me," Luke chuckled.

"I don't want to talk about it." Ava shook her head.

"Then we won't talk about it." He smiled and pressed his lips to hers in a gentle but meaningful kiss.

The kiss began as something soft and sweet but soon morphed into one filled with passion and intensity. It was as if they both knew it was the last time this would happen and they wanted to put everything they had into it. Ava for sure was thinking along those lines.

It wasn't long until Luke took the reins and flipped her over so she was underneath him. His bigger body pressed her into the mattress and she felt the unyielding firmness of his erection prodding her thigh through his jeans. She spread her legs wider to let his hips slip between her legs and he pressed forward, cradling himself against her center. Something about still wearing clothing made the action even more erotic. The rasp of his denim-clad lower half on her body made for one hell of an aphrodisiac, causing her to become wetter with each forward motion he made. Luke's propped himself up on one arm and looked down at her face.

"You look so beautiful like this," he said.

"Like what?" Ava scrunched up her eyebrows in confusion.

"Underneath me. Your cheeks flushed and your body waiting for me. Absolutely breathtaking."

"Please don't say things like that." She looked away.

"Why the hell not?" He sounded like he took offense.

Ava rolled her head back to look him in the eye. "Because we both know this isn't going anywhere beyond tonight. I don't need you telling me a bunch of romantic bullshit. I'm offering myself up on a platter here, so just take it already," she spouted.

"*Wow.*" Luke began to roll off of her.

"Luke, wait." She pulled him back down. "I'm sorry. It's been a crazy day. I shouldn't have taken it out on you by being a bitch." Ava sighed in regret.

Luke, ever the gentleman, brushed her hair away from her face and kissed her forehead. "I understand. And you have every right to be testy. I get it, I really do."

"I don't want you to go. You said one more night and I want that. Please?" Ava felt herself pleading and she wasn't the least bit abashed by it.

"I'm not going anywhere." He swiftly rolled on top of her once more and began an assault of kisses to the sensitive area on her neck.

Ava's eyes rolled back in her head as his lips coasted over her skin and his teeth grazed the area just below her ear. While his mouth was busy with her upper half, one of his hands wandered down and ducked under her top. Again the roughness of his fingers on the smooth expanse of her stomach caused chills to rack her body.

"Are you cold?" Luke asked as he nibbled her ear.

"No, quite the opposite actually." She smiled.

Luke didn't answer. He continued to play havoc on her body with a kiss here and a brush of his fingers there. Soon his exploring hand went higher under her shirt, cupping her breast. The delicate nipple puckered instantly the moment he lightly pinched it. A mewl escaped her lips as he repeated the move and then switched to the other breast. Impatience grew as he went back and forth, toying with her body.

"Luke, I can't wait."

"Thank fuck. Neither can I." Luke jumped from the bed and began to undress in record time. Ava licked her lips at the sight of his cock jutting out when he whipped his underwear down his muscled legs.

"Clothes off. I need to be inside you in the next thirty seconds." Ava hurried with removing her clothing and tossed it all to the floor.

She watched as Luke switched on the bedside lamp and then flipped off the switch to the overhead light. The room was now cast in a sexy glow she could appreciate. Luke's amazing body looked even more perfect in this type of lighting. Ava couldn't help but admire it. When he found his way back to the bed, she was ready and waiting. Her head lay back against the soft pillows, legs bent at the knees, still concealing her arousal and her arms lay by her sides, fingers trembling in anticipation. When he joined her on the bed, she opened to him like a blooming flower, opening its petals to the morning rays of sunlight. The way Luke fit himself perfectly between her legs had her ready to slip over the precipice of something amazing.

Ava's intense gaze followed Luke's as he grabbed his erection in his hand and leaned forward, sweeping the swollen head through her slick folds. "Damn, you already feel good." The pained look on his face told her he was holding back. She didn't want him to. It was time to put up or shut up.

"Now, Luke." The demand came out on a whine.

But he must've been as ready as she was. He let go of himself and unhurriedly pushed inside her depths, the walls of her pussy clamping down on him like it was drawing him in further. When he was completely seated within her, Ava let out a moan at the full sensation. Even though they'd been intimate several times before, every single time felt like their first. It didn't surprise her though, Luke was special. He was the only one in the world who'd stolen her heart. Funny thing was—even after everything that'd taken place—Ava still didn't want it back. Even though he'd thrown it away, a small piece would always belong to him.

"Hey." Luke pulled her from her inner musings. "I don't know where you are right now, but I need you here. With me." His voice was low and genuine.

"I'm here," Ava confirmed.

"Not fully, you're not. Ava, sweetheart, I'm so sorry for everything." Luke began to apologize but she didn't think this was the right time.

To ward off his grand speech, her hands reached around and grabbed ahold of his ass, pulling him farther into her. His hip bones dug into her inner thighs causing a slight pain from the pressure. But it only heightened what she was feeling. He took the hint and began a steady pace, pulling his hardness from her body and thrusting back inward. Each time she could feel the buildup increasing until her body sat on the edge ready to tip over.

"Ask me to make you come," Luke grunted as if he was holding onto his control by a threadbare rope. But she didn't want to ask anything of him. If she was going to fall, she wanted to do it on her own and not owe him and damn thing. "Ask, me Ava." Luke continued to push himself into her, each stroke bumping a spot to send zinging sensations to every nerve ending in her body.

"Please." she wouldn't ask, but she'd beg for some reason.

He slowed, delaying her impending release. Her frustration was evident in the way she crumpled her face. "I need you ask you something," Luke began. "And I want you to tell me the honest truth, Ava." The pace of their lovemaking had slowed but he kept them steady.

"Fine." Ava relented.

After moments passed, Luke finally stopped fighting with his indecision. "Before the other day, did you feel anything for me?" His question shocked her.

"Why are you asking me this now?"

"Because I want to know. Tell me the truth, Ava."

She shook her head furiously. "I can't do this right now." Salty tears began to gather in her eyes.

"Yes, you can. I need to know if you felt anything for me. Anything at all."

"Yes, damn it," her voice raised a bit.

"What did you feel, Ava?" He kept pushing her.

"Don't make me say it."

"Say it."

"I loved you, Luke," Ava blurted out the words he wanted to hear. Oh, how she wanted to not use the word *'love'* in a past tense, because honestly, she *still* loved him.

Luke didn't respond, he only picked up the pace and drove himself deeper inside her body. Her legs fell open to let him go in as far as he possibly could. It seemed like you couldn't even tell where one of them began and the other ended, but it was perfect for this moment.

The coils in her body wound so tight she thought she'd die when they finally snapped. Each plunge of his cock into her body brought more emotion to the forefront and soon Ava felt the warm streaks of her tears begin to trail from the corners of her eyes and onto her cheeks.

"Come for me, sweetheart," Luke commanded.

And soon she did. The dam broke and with it, her heart broke just a little more.

Chapter Twenty-Three

LUKE SAT FOR A FEW MINUTES and peered down at Ava's sleeping form. She lay curled up on her side with a hand tucked under her chin. She was gorgeous in sleep *and* when awake. And the fact that she'd admitted she loved him, well that was what he needed to hear. Sure, she'd said it in past tense, but there was a seed of hope planted that maybe she might still feel that way about him. He didn't know what would happen after this whole situation was over, but he knew for sure he wanted it to include the beautiful woman asleep in his bed.

When he left his bedroom, Luke went downstairs in search of Cole. It was his turn to take watch and let his partner get a few hours of shut-eye. If he knew Cole well enough—and he did—the other man would deny himself sleep because of the dire situation they were all in.

"How're things looking?" Luke asked as he sat at the kitchen table across from Cole.

"All clear for now. One of the motion sensors were tripped but it was a fox."

"Good deal. Why don't you go grab some shut-eye for a bit while I take over?"

"Nah, I won't be able to sleep with all this shit going on. You should know that by now." Cole laughed. Yes, Luke was right in thinking his partner would want to be where the action was.

"Suit yourself." He shrugged and got up to make some coffee. It was only two in the morning and they still had several hours until backup arrived.

"How did things go with Ava? Did you tell her the full story?"

"I did." Luke went about dumping grounds into the coffee maker.

"How'd she take it? Is she alright?" Cole had a concerned look on his face.

"Hey, is everything okay?" Ava answered. She was met with silence on the other end. "Brandi? Are you there?" More silence. She wondered if her friend had a bad connection or lost signal. "Hello?" Ava asked one more time. Chills ran down her spine when a male voice finally answered.

"Hey, baby. Did you miss me?" Bile rose in her throat at the sound of Frankie's voice.

She tamped down her disgust and recognition hit. "What are you doing with Brandi's phone?" Ava asked shakily.

"I borrowed it. Seems your friend can't take a beating very well." Frankie laughed.

"Oh, my God. Please don't hurt her."

"Too late. But if you meet me right now with my money, I promise not to put a bullet in her skull." She heard him take a drag off his cigarette.

"Fine, I'll meet you. Where?"

"Meet me at your beach house in an hour. And don't forget my money, you little bitch. Oh, and if I see you have those Feds with you, I'll ax this chick and you immediately. Am I clear?"

"Yes."

"Good, hurry the fuck up." Frankie disconnected the call.

Ava didn't have a choice. She'd brought danger to her friend and it was up to her to help her. Brandi had been there for her all this time and there was no way in hell she'd let Frankie hurt anyone she cared about. She'd rather take the bullet herself before one was lodged in someone else.

Gathering up some clothes she quickly dressed and slipped on a pair of shoes. She'd go downstairs and ask Luke and Cole what to do and then be on her way. Down the steps she went and followed the only light on in the house. It led to the kitchen where Cole was asleep with his head on the table and Luke was the same but sitting upright. She didn't want to wake them so she did what she thought was best and grabbed a pen and paper from her purse. She jotted down a note and laid it in the middle of the table. Silently she said goodbye to them both and went in search of the duffle full of cash. It wasn't upstairs anywhere, so her instincts led her to the basement. When she turned on the lamp on the workbench, she spotted the black bag but it was empty. "Damn it." Ava bit out. "Where the hell is it?"

She scoured the basement trying to locate the cash but couldn't find it anywhere. When she rounded the corner into a small hallway, her heart sank. There sat a medium-sized safe with a combination lock right in the middle of the heavy door. Panic set in as the thoughts of what she should do ran through her head. She couldn't break into the safe, there wasn't time, and she sure as hell wasn't a safecracker. Looking around, she decided she'd at least take the bag with her. After snatching it up, Ava quietly ascended the stairs and passed by Luke and Cole once more. She slipped Luke's truck keys off the hook by the back door and escaped without waking the men. As her feet crossed the gravel driveway, it seemed like the crunching sound under her feet echoed louder than normal. But so did the nervous thudding of her heart.

Starting the truck she cringed at how loud the engine was when being fired up. *Was it* always *this loud?* she thought. It didn't matter so she threw it into reverse and backed out of the driveway. Once she was away from the house a hundred yards or so, Ava hammered on the gas pedal and shot down the road. She only had forty-five more minutes to get to her house. She prayed that Brandi would be alright and that she wasn't too late already. Frankie would be livid that his money wasn't in the bag, but she'd cross that bridge when she got there. The fact of the matter was, she knew she was a dead woman walking.

Frankie wanted to shut her up and when she saw him again, he'd make sure he accomplished that.

"Damn it." Luke's eyes flew open and he realized he'd passed out.

Cole's head shot up from the table and he looked at Luke with hazy eyes. "What happened?"

"I fell asleep. I can't believe I did that," Luke chastised himself.

"Damn. That sucks."

"What the hell?" Luke spotted a note in the middle of

the table. It was folded in half and had his name scrolled across the front in Ava's handwriting.

Luke,

I know you'll think I'm an idiot for doing this but Brandi was in trouble. I had to go help her. I took your truck. I don't really know if I'll see you again, so I wanted to tell you something. I already told you that at one time I did love you, but I wasn't being entirely truthful. You see, it wouldn't matter how many times you broke my heart, I would always love you. You were it for me, Luke. I hope you find happiness in your life and please think of me every once in a while.

Love,

Avalyn Woods

Luke stuffed the note in his back pocket as he stood. "Time to go," he ordered. "I'm not letting her walk into anything without me."

"Jesus, you really do love her don't you?" Cole

followed as he grabbed up his gear.

"Yes, I do. That's my future that just ran out of here and I'll be damned if I let any*one* or any*thing* take it from me."

"YeeHaw!" Cole snatched up his gear as well and soon both men were in Cole's truck, backing out of the driveway.

Luke was in combat mode now. His only focus was making sure Ava made it through this thing. If that meant he had to run in there with guns blazing so be it. He'd burn down the entire fucking state to find her and make sure she was in his arms where she belonged.

Chapter Twenty-Four

AVA PULLED THE TRUCK in the driveway at her beach house. Brandi's car was there already—*Frankie must've driven it to throw suspicion off himself,* she guessed.

Every nerve in her body was on full alert as she grabbed the empty duffle bag and climbed down from the truck cab. Of course she'd never walk into a situation such as this without protection—and since Luke had confiscated her gun—she *'borrowed'* one of his that she found in the basement. Stuffing it into the back waistband of her jeans, Ava pulled her shirt over the exposed part of the black handgrip. Her hope was that Frankie would think she was too stupid to know how to protect herself.

If that was the case, she had a fighting chance of making it out of this ordeal alive. That small fraction of positivity is what propelled her toward the front door of the house.

Ava said a silent prayer that she wouldn't meet her demise in this home, but either way, she'd never be able to live here again. The thought that Frankie had invaded her personal space caused a sick feeling to settle in her gut. Pushing those feelings down, Ava stood on the stoop outside her front door. She noticed small things while she stood there. How the paint was starting to peel a little on the wooden door; must've been due to the salt from the ocean nearby. The cloudiness of the glass at the very top of the door; she'd never gotten around to cleaning details like that.

"Hey baby," Frankie's voice sounded behind her and she whipped around to face him. "Glad you could make it."

"Where's Brandi?" Ava asked with a bite to her tone.

She was done playing the meek little woman for him. It was time to stand up for herself and go down like a champ—if that was the case.

"Sounds like you've turned into a little bitch. Guess I'll have to break you of that," Frankie said as he pushed her against the door and pinned her arms beside her body.

"Let. Me. Go." Ava enunciated the words.

"Hey, boss." Frankie was interrupted by another man. When the guy rounded the corner she recognized him as Frankie's right hand man, Flynn.

"*What?*" Frankie let her go and turned to the other man.

Ava made a split second decision. She reached behind her, quietly turned the door knob then pushed it open a tiny bit. The men stood there talking but Ava wasn't concentrating on their words, all she could think of was getting inside the house to find her friend. When Frankie stepped forward and pointed a finger in Flynn's face, Ava spun around and shoved the door open. She darted through the opening and slammed it shut—locking the deadbolt and regular locks. Cursing came from the outside along with loud banging on the door. Ava walked backwards as she watched the doorframe shake with the force of the men's actions. The number one priority was finding Brandi, so she hastily began searching the house. The banging outside continued and Ava thanked her lucky stars she'd had strong locks installed when she bought the house. Those locks were the only thing keeping her from seeing the faces of two extremely dangerous men right now.

Fearing there was someone else lurking in the house, Ava refused to call out for Brandi. Being discovered would only complicate things at this point. She didn't really have a plan if she *did* find her best friend beyond running as fast and as far as they could get. She knew in the back of her mind it wasn't a good plan but it was the best she had at this stage in the game.

"You stupid bitch!" Frankie's yell came from outside. Ava began searching more frantically for Brandi. "When I get in there, I'm gonna enjoy splattering your brains all over the walls." He continued to pound on the door.

She darted through the kitchen and heard a muffled whine. *The garage*. Through the door she went that connected the kitchen with the garage. Looking around there was still no sign of her friend. As she began to walk back into the house she heard the sound again. This time it sounded like it was coming from the floor. *Her secret hiding place.* With each step closer to the hole in the floor, Ava heard what sounded like struggling. Frankie hadn't put the lock on the door so she was able to slide it back. A gasp escaped her lips as she saw Brandi sitting in the floor of the area with duct tape over her mouth and her hands bound behind her back. Her ankles were also tied together and Ava watched as she struggled against her bindings.

"Hold still, I've got you." Ava hurried into the hole and began to untie Brandi's ankles and hands.

Once her hands were free Brandi yanked the tape off her mouth and took in a huge gulp of air. "Thanks."

"Are you hurt?" Ava looked her over.

"No. I'd just gotten home and someone put something over my mouth. I passed out."

"Shit. Okay, we need to get out of here."

"Where're they at?" Brandi asked as she stood on shaky legs.

"Outside. But I think we can slip out the back and take off running down the beach. If we can make it a half a mile up the road, there's a 24 hour gas station there."

"Where's your cell phone?"

"In my purse in Luke's truck."

"Luke?" Brandi followed her out of the hiding spot.

"Long story. Come on." She tip-toed with her friend close behind and came to the sliding glass doors at the back of the living room. Both women peered outside to make sure there was no one waiting. They could still hear Frankie's voice toward the front of the house and decided to quietly slide the door open to make a run for it. Stepping outside Ava felt the refreshing hit of salted sea air as she tried to cross the small deck as silently as she could. "When we hit the sand, run. Don't look back, just run as fast as you can," Ava whispered to Brandi.

"Okay." Brandi nodded.

They crossed the deck and landed on the sand. Even though the grainy terrain felt like quicksand, they dug in and put their all into getting the hell away from the house. Brandi was in the lead and Ava watched her clear the end of the house and take off down a flat area of the beach. She wasn't far behind but when she passed the end of the house, something slammed into her and took her to the ground. Her body rolled a few feet as the sand dug into her skin. After she got her wits about her, Ava looked up to see Frankie coming right for her.

"Don't ever think you're fucking smarter than me." He kicked sand at her and reached down to grab a fist full of her hair. Ava wouldn't give him the satisfaction of crying out at his assault so she bit her lip until she tasted blood. "Come on." He yanked her to her feet. "I don't want an audience when I put a bullet in your head." He began to pull her toward the house. "I hope you had a good two years down here, they are fixing to come to an end."

Cole whipped his truck in front of Ava's beach house and Luke was out the door before he'd put the vehicle in park. He yanked his Glock from his shoulder holster and chambered a round.

"You cover the front, I've got the back," Luke barked orders to Cole.

"Got it." Cole was yet again in business mode. His gun was drawn and he was just as ready as Luke was to end this shit.

Luke crept around the side of the house by the garage and listened for voices. He could hear the brush of the water on the sand and the sound of a man's voice coming from the back of the house. This was it. Luke took a deep breath and counted to five as he worked on quelling the adrenaline coursing through his veins. Some people loved the thrill of an adrenaline high but he hated it. It only meant he was in a situation he didn't want to be in. Just like right now.

After the initial energy calmed down a bit, Luke continued around the side of the house and stopped again at the corner. He got down low and took a peek to see what was going on. Terror was the only word to describe how he felt at seeing Ava being dragged up the beach by her hair. Luke's animal instincts took over and he stepped out from the cover of the house and yelled, "FBI! Put your hands where I can see them!" Luke's gun was trained on Frankie Bohannan—son to one of the most notorious crime bosses on the East Coast.

He watched with eagle eyes as Frankie acted shocked to see him standing there. Then as if it were happening in super slow motion, Luke saw him reach around his back and grab for something. It was a decision he had to make when he raised his gun just a little higher and squeezed the trigger. The sound of the gunshot rang out around him and he sucked in a breath as he witnessed the bullet hit Frankie right between the eyes.

Ava fell to the sand when Luke pulled the trigger and he wanted to get to her and make sure she was alright. He took one step and heard another gunshot. The air was sucked from his lungs as pain slammed him in the back and dropped him to his knees. Fire spread out from where the bullet hit and everything began to fade around him.

"Luke!" He heard Ava scream and could see her silhouette running toward him. Right before he fell completely, Luke heard another shot and Cole's voice behind him.

"Got him!" Cole yelled.

"Cole! Luke's been shot!" Ava screamed as she knelt beside him.

Ava watched in horror as Luke's body crumpled to the sand. The only noises she could hear were the grunts and groans from him being in pain and another shot fired. When she looked around Luke's body, she saw Cole take out Flynn. Flynn had shot Luke in the back in a coward move. That didn't surprise her at all; the majority of Frankie's men were ruthless with zero honor. But that didn't matter right now. What mattered was that Luke was dipping in and out of consciousness as she knelt down beside him. Her hand wrapped around his and squeezed as if it would help him stay with her.

"Luke, stay with me, please." Tears formed in her eyes and for the first time in forever, she wasn't afraid to let them fall.

Cole walked up on them and dropped to his knees. "Help me roll him over," Cole said.

"Okay." Ava wiped the tears from her eyes so she could see to help Cole. Luke groaned as they shifted his body to lay on his stomach. "Hold on, Luke." She grabbed his hand again.

Cole used his pocket knife to cut the leather straps of Luke's shoulder holster then yanked it off him and tossed it to the side. Ava watched as Cole made a slit in the bottom of Luke's t-shirt and pulled so that it split down the middle. Her eyes widened and she fell back on her ass in the sand when she saw what was revealed.

"He's gonna be bruised for a while, maybe a broken rib or two, but he'll live." Cole sat back and chuckled.

"A bulletproof vest," Ava whispered.

"He's not stupid enough to go into something like this and not protect himself. Neither am I." Cole thumped his own chest, showing her that he was wearing the Kevlar protection as well.

"Damn it." Luke shifted and tried to roll back over. "A little help please," he groaned.

Ava and Cole helped him onto his back and then into a sitting position. "I thought you were dying." More tears escaped her eyes as she sat there, still in disbelief.

"It sure as hell felt like it for a while. Holy shit that hurt." Luke pulled what was left of his shirt over his head and revealed the vest that'd saved his life. He undid the Velcro and pulled the protection off. He looked around, "You cut my fucking holster?" Luke pinned Cole with a stare.

"Wanted to make sure the bullet hit the vest and not below it. I'll buy you a new one."

"That was my favorite one." Luke looked serious and then started laughing.

"*And* he's back." Cole slapped Luke on the back, Luke flinching.

"Stop laughing," Ava reprimanded.

Both men stopped chuckling and looked at Ava. "Everything's fine," Luke assured her.

"No, it's not. There're two dead guys on the beach and you were shot. That hardly qualifies as *being fine*."

Ava sat there while Luke leaned over and grabbed the sides of her face in his hands. "Look at me. I'm here and I'm alive." Ava nodded.

"I think I'll leave you two be. Gonna go put in a call to the local PD." Cole hopped up and walked up toward the house.

"What happens now?" Ava asked.

"Now I kiss you because you're safe." Luke pulled her to him and pressed his lips to hers. The kiss deepened in no time and she felt herself being pulled under the spell that was Luke once more. She was the one to break the kiss.

"This will never work," she told him, shaking her head.

"Why?"

"Because they'll put me in witness protection to keep Frankie Senior from getting to me. We'll never see each other again."

"They already have him in custody back in New York, Ava. We put in the call and our office there went out to pick him up. They'll need you to testify, but as for Wit-Sec, no, you're not going there."

"Thank you." Ava launched herself forward and landed on top of Luke. Her lips found any surface they could as she pretty much kissed him silly.

"Did you mean what you said in the note you left?" Luke brushed her hair away from her face and gazed into her eyes, his blue irises catching the azure of the ocean waves nearby.

"Yes." She took a deep breath, "I know you don't feel the same and that's okay…"

Luke cut her off. "I love you, Ava."

"But the things you said to me that day."

"I needed you to draw out the man who was watching you. The only way I knew how to get you to go home was to say something like that. I'll never forgive myself for telling you those things." He kissed her forehead. "But I never stopped loving you and I meant it the first time I told you."

"You did?" The tears began to flow once more.

"I sure did. I didn't think I'd ever say that to anyone, but I found it easy with you. You're easy to love, Ava."

"So are you, Luke Daughtry."

Ava and Luke stayed on the beach until the local police department showed up to take their statements. After hours of clearing things up, Luke being checked over by the paramedics and Cole making fun of him for not being a 'bullet virgin' anymore, they were free to go. Only, Ava didn't want to go into her home again. There were too many bad memories living there. She'd tried to build a life in the house that was constructed of nothing but lies. There was no way in hell she was continuing down that road.

"Is everyone okay?" Brandi jumped out of a patrol car and ran over to her and Luke.

"Yes, we're all fine." Ava hugged her friend. "Tired, but fine."

Brandi nodded and smiled. "I guess I have to go make a statement or something, I'll call you later." Then she was off to meet with an officer.

"Listen, I have to fly back to Chicago for a while. I don't know how long I'll be gone," Luke admitted to Ava.

"But you'll be back, right?"

"I plan on it."

"Then I'll be right here, waiting." Ava smiled and pulled him to her for the biggest hug she'd ever given. His warmth gave her strength. And she would wait for him to come back; she'd wait until the end of time if she had to. Luke Daughtry was put in her life for a reason, she now knew it was to show her how it felt to be loved and protected. For those things, she'd wait forever.

Epilogue

AFTER FLYING TO NEW YORK to testify in the trial of Frankie Senior, Ava came right back to Biloxi. She'd never felt more at home than she did there and it was a no-brainer to build her new life in a place where she was comfortable. Her salon stayed busy and she couldn't be happier. The only thing missing was a place to live. For now she'd been crashing on Brandi's sofa but she hoped that would change fairly soon and she'd be able to get her own place.

As she stood in her salon on a Tuesday morning, Ava waited for her next client to arrive. When he breezed through the door she relaxed at the familiarity of having him there. "Good morning, Jack." She smiled at the old man and patted him on the back as he took a seat in her styling chair.

"How ya been, young lady?" Jack tossed his ball cap on the counter and sat back fully in the chair.

"I can't complain. Things are pretty damn good." She spread the cutting cloth across him and grabbed her electric clippers.

"That's good to hear. Now, let's get rid of this hair," Jack laughed.

Ava went about her usual weekly routine of shaving off Jack's extra quarter of an inch of hair. She couldn't help but smile while she did it. To some it might've been a mundane activity but to her, it was who she was. This was where she was meant to be. The only thing that would've made it better was if Luke was here with her. She hadn't seen him in four months and each day apart felt more like ten years instead of twenty-four hours. But she knew he'd come back eventually.

Once she was finished with Jack's hair, she whipped the cape off him and began to hang it on the hook beside her mirror. Jack threw down her money on the counter and smiled.

"Don't hang that up just yet, I'm looking a little shaggy." Ava spun around at the familiar voice behind her.

"Luke!" She took off at full speed and jumped into his muscled arms. Her legs wound around his waist and her arms around his neck.

"Miss me?" he asked.

"More than anything." She buried her face in his neck.

"I'll leave you two be. See ya next week, Ava." Jack slipped out the door and left the two of them alone.

"I'm sorry I had to stay gone for so long. Had some loose ends to tie up in Chicago."

"Do you have to go back again?" Ava felt disappointment coloring her words.

"No, I'm here to stay. Got transferred to the field office here."

"That's wonderful." Ava couldn't stop grinning.

"I'm guessing you want me to stay, huh?" His lips turned up in a goofy smile.

"Of course I do. But just so you know, you still have to pay for your haircuts. I have a business to run," she joked.

"I can think of several types of payment." He let her down and yanked her to him for a kiss that she felt all the way to her toes.

Everything was now right in her world. Luke was back, her life was on track to so much happiness. Every loose end that'd once flown free was tied up with a shiny bow. What more could she ask for?

IF YOU ENJOYED *LOOSE ENDS* PLEASE LEAVE A REVIEW ON YOUR PREFERRED BOOK OUTLET. AUTHORS LOVE REVIEWS MORE THAN WE LOVE COFFEE!

CONTINUE READING FOR A SNEAK PEEK OF *SPLIT ENDS* BOOK TWO IN THE MAGNOLIA SERIES

SPLIT *Ends*

MAGNOLIA SERIES: BOOK TWO
Content for Split Ends is not yet edited and is subject to change

Chapter One

"YOU'VE GOT TO BE shitting me," Cole Matthews gawked at the stark white piece of paper in his right hand. His other hand flailed through the air like he was batting flies away from his face.

"Whoa, you don't look happy." Luke walked by Cole's desk.

"Look at this shit." Cole tossed the letter to the edge of the desk; Luke snatching it up quickly.

This was the last thing he needed. He'd had so many life changes in the past six months—including moving to the FBI field office in Biloxi. That was a leap that he didn't really think about before he found himself knee deep in his decision. His partner Luke Daughtry was transferring to be closer to his girlfriend Ava, so Cole got it in his mind that he should move too. What a numbskull move.

"Am I reading this right?" Luke sat the paper back on the desk.

Cole dragged a hand through his gelled raven hair. "Yup." He blew out a frustrated breath.

"You're *married*?" Luke's face was one of pure shock. Cole couldn't help but think his partner had the same look a cartoon character did when someone handed them a stick of dynamite.

"Apparently so." He huffed.

"Wait, how did you not *know* you're married? That seems like something you'd know about. Were you drugged or something?" Luke chuckled.

"No. Hell, I was nineteen. She thought she was knocked up and I did the honorable thing."

"But I'm not understanding why you're *still* married." Luke's confused expression mirrored Cole's.

"I don't either. I signed the damn divorce papers over ten years ago."

"Maybe they made a mistake." Luke sat on the corner of Cole's desk.

"If there's a mistake *this* big, my faith in the judicial system is fucked."

"Seems like an easy fix though, file again and get rid of her."

"Yeah, I'll get it taken care of. She's gonna be in town for a few weeks. I'm sure we can get it done then."

"Sounds like a plan. Listen, I'm gonna head out. Ava's cooking fried chicken and rhubarb pie." Luke rubbed his stomach.

"You're so whipped." Cole busted out laughing.

"No, I'm in love with the most amazing woman on the planet." Cole didn't envy the googly eyed look Luke wore when he talked about his girlfriend. In fact, Cole had sworn off all emotional attachment to the fairer sex ever since he'd first signed those damn divorce papers.

If there was ever a woman he was head over heels in love with, it was her. *Gracie Callahan*. With her spitfire attitude, her glowing red hair and those emerald eyes; every man in a five block radius turned to look at her when she walked by. Cole hadn't seen her since he was twenty though. He wondered what she'd look like as a completely filled out woman. Would she be the same innocent beauty as she was years ago? Or had she changed over the years like he had? Damn this was going to suck big time. As if he didn't have enough shit on his plate, now he had to entertain Gracie while she was in town. Well fuck a duck.

"Are you sure we have to go?" Gracie looked at her daughter who was whining.

"Yes, for the umpteenth time, we have to go." Gracie continued to toss articles of clothing into her bright red suitcase.

"But I could stay with Aunt Jenna. I'm sure she wouldn't mind." Her daughter pleaded with her while digging through Gracie's jewelry box. Something the almost teenager did quite frequently.

"Cora, I need you to come with me. Please don't make this an argument." She lowered her voice.

Cora tossed a pair of earrings back into the wooden box and turned to look at her mom. "Mom, this is my summer vacation. I don't want to spend it in Mississippi!" The dark haired girl threw her hands in the air and stomped out of the room.

Gracie yelled at her back, "I'm your mother and what I say is the law around here! You're going and that's final!"

She heard her daughter call from the hallway, "Whatever!"

That was Cora's go to response for something she didn't like. When something didn't please her, she just said *'whatever'* and stormed off. The twelve year old was becoming more like her hot headed father with each passing day. The only thing was, Cora had never met her father. And he had no idea he had a daughter. No, it wasn't as if she was trying to be a terrible human being by not telling him about their daughter. It was more for self-preservation. Gracie knew he wasn't in the relationship one hundred percent and she refused to keep him around just because they created offspring. Was it the right thing to do in keeping the information from him? No. But it was the easy thing to do in the circumstances. Cole Matthews wasn't someone who Gracie would consider 'daddy material'. His wild ways and refusal to be tied down was just a couple of the reasons she felt compelled to be tight lipped about Cora. Yeah, they'd dated all through Junior and Senior year in high school and of course, they thought they were destined to be together. They'd even waited until the night of Senior Prom to take their relationship to the next level. In room 265 at the local Super 8 motel they kicked things up a notch and had sex. Actually, just having sex wasn't really the word for it. Cole had blown her mind and body. She'd expected her first time to be rough and possibly painful but Cole made sure he took the time to make her comfortable and cared for. Boy did she feel cared for that night. After the initial nervousness had worn off, he'd taken her to heights she never dared to imagine, even a few days later she could feel the places *on* and *in* her body that he'd been. Even now her cheeks flamed and her panties became damp at just the thought of what he'd done to her. But all good things must come to an end. And their end was when she found out she was pregnant at nineteen. Fresh out of high school Gracie didn't know what she'd do. When she'd gotten up the nerve to finally tell Cole about the baby, he'd proposed and they were married less than a week later. At the time it seemed like a good idea but after being together for only a month, Gracie knew it wasn't going to work out. Cole wasn't there emotionally and there was no way in hell she'd raise a child in that type of environment. So she did the only thing she could think of, she lied. Telling Cole that the pregnancy was a fluke might've been a terrible thing to do but it was better than keeping a man around who clearly didn't want to be there.

Her plan was to fly to Biloxi, get Cole to sign the divorce papers and get out. Even though Cora would be with her, she had her fib ready in case he suspected anything. She'd pass Cora off as a one night stand after they'd broken up all those years ago. He'd believe it, he had to. If Cole caught on to her sham, she'd be knee deep in shit and the consequences of that were life threatening. Getting in and getting the job done quickly was crucial.

Zipping up her bags she began carrying them to the front door.

"Cora, time to go!" Gracie called through the house.

"I'm coming," her daughter popped out of her bedroom dragging her own suitcase behind her. Yeah, Cora had a bit of an attitude. But Gracie blamed it on the fact that her *own* Irish heritage must've bled into Cora's genes a bit too much.

Gracie glanced at the bags by the door and sighed. Time to go. This wasn't a trip she wanted to make, but right now, the safety of her daughter and herself was hanging in the balance. She'd do anything to protect Cora and this was a step she had to take. Gracie would lay down her life for the sassy twelve year old. Time to put that theory to the test.

THANK YOU FOR READING AN EXCERPT FOR SPLIT ENDS!
LOOK FOR IT LATE SPRING 2016!

Author's Note

In 2015 I had the pleasure of attending a book signing in Pennsylvania. As fate would allow, I met the most amazing individual there. Her name is Danielle. Low and behold Danielle is a fellow princess like me. We became great friends over the past months and I couldn't be any more grateful to have her as a part of my life. You're probably wondering why I dedicated Loose Ends to her. Here's why...I found out that Danielle has cancer and is the same age as myself. How devastating to find out that a disease has taken over your body like that? But Danielle doesn't show her weakness. She puts on her tiara and faces each day with bravery and beauty. I don't know that I'll ever be as strong as Danielle. To possess even 1/10 the courage she has would be astounding to me. I know in my heart of hearts she will beat this disease. She has to. If this shining light is taken from this world, there will be a hole that can never be filled with another human being. So Danielle, Loose Ends is for you. It's your book and I hope you love it. And of course I want to say just one more thing…

FUCK CANCER!

Find Taylor Dawn@

Website & Blog: http://www.taylordawn-author.com/

Facebook:
https://www.facebook.com/AuthorTaylorDawn/?fref=ts

Twitter:
@TAYLORDAWNBOOKS

Made in the USA
Columbia, SC
23 July 2017